MW00777487

Magical Midlife
Invasion

ALSO BY K.F. BREENE

LEVELING UP
Magical Midlife Madness
Magical Midlife Dating
Magical Midlife Invasion
Magical Midlife Love (coming soon)

DEMIGODS OF SAN FRANCISCO
Sin & Chocolate
Sin & Magic
Sin & Salvation
Sin & Spirit
Sin & Lightning
Sin & Surrender

DEMON DAYS VAMPIRE NIGHTS WORLD
Born in Fire
Raised in Fire
Fused in Fire
Natural Witch
Natural Mage
Natural Dual-Mage
Warrior Fae Trapped
Warrior Fae Princess

FINDING PARADISE SERIES
Fate of Perfection
Fate of Devotion

Magical Midlife Invasion

By K.F. Breene

Copyright © 2020 by K.F. Breene

All rights reserved. The people, places, situations and craziness contained in this ebook are figments of the author's imagination and in no way reflect real or true events.

Contact info:
www.kfbreene.com
books@kfbreene.com

CHAPTER 1

"THE EARLY SPRING is really helping, Jessie. Yes, I think the grounds will make a full recovery." Edgar hooked his long thumbs, complete with out-of-control nails, into the band of his bright purple sweatpants.

Mr. Tom, the butler/property manager/misguided life coach, had finally gotten tired of buying bleach and changed the color of our house sweats from white to purple, an ode to my gargoyle form, and also a color that didn't show bloodstains as well. Why Edgar needed sweats at all was beyond me. He rarely changed form, and even when he did, he became a swarm of insects and his clothes magically changed with him. But I'd learned the hard way not to question the logic of the original Ivy House team. Their answers were likely to give you brain bubbles.

I surveyed the colorful blooming flowers from my position at the back corner of the yard. They were everywhere—crowding the side of the house, pushing up to the edges of the vivid green grass, lining the hedge maze Edgar kept insisting I wander into for a few hours of "fun," and now popping up between the trees at the edge of the woods. I knew there were just as many flowers on the other side of the house and scores of them swarming the front. Even if he hadn't insisted I take a tour with him to check out the grounds, the sheer volume was hard to miss.

"Yes, they are really coming along." I nodded dutifully, then chose my next words carefully. Edgar didn't take criticism well. A couple of months ago he'd let a dangerous person onto the grounds unwittingly, and now he kept suggesting that I retire him every time he made a tiny misstep. Retirement for a vampire was death. The guy kept trying to get me to kill him. "Did you buy out the flower store, or…"

"Oh no, Jessie, don't be silly. I don't buy flowers—I grow them. I did buy out their seeds, though. I wanted to make sure I had enough."

I nearly made the mistake of mentioning the basajaun, the violent, long-winded, hairy creature who'd helped me escape a group of mages in exchange for access to Edgar's precious flowerbeds. He'd wiped them out, and Edgar had not taken it well. Clearly he worried the situation wouldn't be a one-time deal.

"Ah. I think you do. Have enough, that is," I said.

2

"Yes, that's the other thing I wanted to talk to you about." He pulled his thumbs out from the band of his sweats and clasped them behind his back. "I wanted to work on my preparedness. You know, prevent another goldfish situation." He hung his head a little.

"The goldfish was depressed anyway, Edgar…probably, and no one blames you for accidentally killing it. Granted, yes, when you were changing the water, you probably should've known to take the fish out of the sink before pulling up the drain stopper, but mistakes happen. You didn't need to get me the fish in the first place." Sometimes it wasn't easy to keep from criticizing.

"Well, be that as it may…" He paused, his eyes drifting across the many types and colors of flowers, seemingly planted with no rhyme or reason as to overall yard design. "I'm not one to point fingers, and I am a firm believer in innocent until proven guilty, but I wonder…" He ran a fang across his bottom lip. He'd stopped retracting them altogether. We had no idea why, but I'd had to forbid him from going into town where non-magical people might see him and freak out. If they didn't believe in vampires before seeing him, they'd be forced to change their tune. "I've noticed a few…discrepancies in my flower design."

Ah. So he had been thinking about design, he was

just bad at it.

"What kind of discrepancies?" I asked as I felt a familiar foot step down on the walkway leading to Ivy House's front door.

It was Austin, the enormous, vicious polar bear shifter who'd recently accepted the number one position on the Ivy House council. He'd also finally staked his claim as alpha of our immediate town and two of those surrounding us, a job he'd been doing without the credit for years. He'd only held the new post for a matter of months, and already crime was down by seventy-five percent in the new towns he had a presence in. No one wanted to mess with him, which made me that much happier he was on my side.

"Well…" Edgar bent a little at the waist, clearly uncomfortable.

Austin's path changed; he was now coming around the house, headed for me. Maybe he was beginning to feel people's positions on Ivy House's property, something everyone else with Ivy House magic could do.

Butterflies danced in my stomach a little, the sensation followed by a burst of guilt. Ivy House had given Austin the ability to draw my magic out, something he was excellent at, given his natural talent for coaxing out the best in people, and my magic had been increasing in leaps and bounds. So the little joke I'd pulled on him yesterday—using my new ability for explosions to create a small blast next to him—had launched him over the treetops instead of just making him jump liked I'd hoped. A snap of power had turned into a gush of it, and poor Austin had paid the price.

He hadn't even acted mad. Of course, he'd also changed really quickly into his polar bear and just lain down, waiting for me to heal him. And even if he was mad, polar bears couldn't talk. Probably for the best. The whole situation had been grisly.

"The thing is, it *seems* like someone is…taking the flower tops." Edgar crossed his arms over his chest and tapped his lips with the aggressively long nail on his pointer finger. "It could be a deer, I suppose, because they do like flowers, but normal deer don't tend to like magically treated flowers." Edgar spotted Austin coming toward us and his eyes lit up. "Well, look at that, will you? The town's alpha is coming to visit us. Aren't we lucky?"

"He's part of the Ivy House team, Edgar, you know this."

"Yes, I know, but in the vampire clan I was never promoted high enough to meet important and influential people. I thought I'd die at this job before another heir was chosen. Until you come to your senses and retire me as you ought to, I will continue to bask in my good fortune."

I rolled my eyes, then couldn't help but smile as Austin drew near, his cobalt eyes shimmering with good nature and his movements easy and graceful, somewhat hiding his contained, explosive power.

"Hey," I said, eyeing his white T-shirt, stretched across his shoulders and chest, defining his pecs before draping down his flat stomach. His snug jeans showed off powerful, robust thighs. No burned skin marred his muscular arms, thank God. I mean, I was a good healer at this point (I had to be), but still, that little joke had gone way overboard. "No house sweats today?"

His eyebrows rose in humorous distaste, but he didn't comment, probably since Edgar was currently wearing them. It was no secret that Austin did not love the color change.

He stopped next to me. "I came to ask if you would help me with something this afternoon."

"Yeah, sure, I just need to finish this walk around with Edgar. There's a pressing matter that requires my undivided and urgent attention." I smiled in jest.

"Oh no, Jessie, it isn't that serious. Well...you know...unless it is theft, in which case..." Edgar put out his hands. "I'm no jury, but..."

The humor dripped out of Austin's expression. "Theft?"

"Edgar was speaking to me about the flowers. Don't they look great? In just a couple of months, he has replaced everything the basajaun ate." I lifted my hand like Vanna White might've.

"There are way too many," Austin said, not at all worried about criticizing the vampire. Which was well and good for him—Edgar had never asked Austin to kill him, to my knowledge.

"Yes, well, there *were* a lot of them," Edgar said, bending again.

Austin cocked his head, surveying the property. "It looks like Ivy House is a flower farm for funeral homes..."

I elbowed him. "Or weddings and birthdays. Very cheery."

"It's just..." Edgar paused for a moment. "At the outskirts of the yard, where the flowers tuck into the wood, *something* has been eating the flower heads and tops of the stems."

"Deer?" Austin asked.

Edgar turned a beaming smile Austin's way, replete with multicolored fangs. The whitening strips I'd recommended he use had a hard time counteracting the habitual consumption of blood. "Great minds! I did mention it could be deer. Except deer don't typically enjoy magically treated flowers."

"That's right, you cheat to win your flower festivals," Austin murmured.

I stifled a laugh. Edgar used a magical serum to ensure the flowers grew beautifully regardless of the time of year, which meant he always won the county home and garden festivals against the non-magical competition. He maintained that anyone could use the special serum, but of course Dicks and Janes had no knowledge of the serum. Most of them looked down on Agnes's New Age vibe.

"I haven't had any reports of the basajaun being in town lately," Austin said.

"Ah." I shook my head and grinned. "Duh. I hadn't pieced together he was talking about the basajaun."

"Well, you know, I wouldn't want to call an innocent creature down, so you can understand my hesitation to name names," Edgar said, waving his hands in front of him. "But he *does* love my flowers. That was entirely evident in how thoroughly he ransacked them from the house…"

"I don't think it's the basajaun." I slipped my hands into my jeans pockets. "I didn't give him unlimited access to the grounds, and he has a very firm code of ethics when it comes to trades. He wouldn't encroach on my territory without speaking to me first."

"So you didn't tell the basajaun he could happen by

and have a snack whenever he's in town?" Edgar asked tentatively.

"No. And like Austin said, no one has seen him. He's up on his mountain, probably scaring hikers. It is highly unlikely that he is your flower thief. Besides, he's nine feet tall and super thick—a snack for him is a lot more than a few flowers. It's probably just a deer with deficient taste buds or something."

"Yes, you're right. I just worried..." He sighed in relief. "It would've been fine, of course. This is your house and your yard and, by default, your flowers. I just champion for the grounds. And I did put in that row near the wood to hopefully slow him down so I could try to reserve my future prizewinners, but I wanted to nip the situation in the bud..." He lifted his eyebrows and chuckled. "Get it? Because we're talking about flowers?" Austin turned to look at him with a blank stare. "Anyway, I was hoping to put some parameters on the feeding frenzy. If it *had* been him, of course. I wasn't accusing him, just wondering, that's all."

I stopped myself from laughing. "If I trade for flowers again, Edgar, you'll be in on the negotiations this time."

"Oh, good. Yes, that's comforting." He put his hand out. "I remain your humble servant, of course, merely in charge of growing your flowers, not ruling them."

Austin continued to stare, no expression. It was the look he favored when dealing with Edgar. Laughter slipped out of me.

"If you do strike another bargain, I'll put together a nice little buffet for him," Edgar went on. "I have some real delectable treats. I'd love to plan his courses, even." He steepled his hands against his lips and bowed his head. "If I might be allowed."

Austin shook himself out of the moment. "I'll wait for you out front," he said to me.

I laughed harder and put my hand against his popping bicep. "No, it's fine. We're done. Right, Edgar? There was nothing else?"

"That was it. I just wanted to get my ducks in a row. I'll go ahead and make up a concoction to kill those deer—"

"Wait, what?" I pulled my hand away from Austin. "No, Edgar, you can't kill the deer! Use a spray or something to keep them away."

"Oh no, Jessie, if a rogue deer has developed a taste for my flowers, that's the end of it. They're a real pest. It's like a drug to them. That's why I was a little concerned about that basajaun. I don't want to be immodest, but I *am* the lawn and gardens county winner at the home and garden festival every year. Killing it is the only way."

My mouth dropped open. "No. You cannot... I thought you said deer don't even typically like magical flowers?"

"They usually don't, no, but every once in a while... You've heard of man-eating lions, haven't you?" He tilted his head at me as if to denote there was a very real, very detrimental connection between the two phenomena. Austin was back to staring. "Once they get a taste for human flesh, that's all they want. Same with those deer and my flowers. It's safer to just put them down."

"Don't kill the deer," Austin said, and a whip crack of power infused his words, the alpha in him demanding obedience.

Edgar's jaw snapped shut. He bowed under Austin's hard stare. "Yes, alpha. But please realize that I cannot be held responsible for the creatures constantly loitering around like groupies. I wash my hands of this."

A silent beat followed, in which Austin and I stood staring at each other in the lovely March sunlight. Winter had been cold and sometimes harsh, compared to what I was used to in L.A., but it had rolled away pretty quickly, giving way to sunshine and the sea of flowers around us.

"Okay then." I nodded, turned, and strode for the front of the house. There really wasn't much more to say and do in this situation. Gotta stay away from those brain bubbles.

"I think he has gotten weirder," Austin murmured as he caught up. "Man-eating lions and deer hanging around like groupies? What is he talking about?"

"Best not to question for too long. And it might not even be deer."

Austin shook his head as we made our way to the front yard. Niamh sat on her porch across the way, rocking in her chair next to the pile of rocks she kept on hand in case a tourist happened to wander down the street to look at Ivy House. That poor tourist would quickly learn what an amazing shot Niamh was with those rocks.

"He really has gone overboard with the flower production." Austin glanced at the flowers lining the little walkway that cut close to the house in the front before joining up with the main walkway to the front porch. "The smell is overwhelming."

"Yeah. I need to have Mr. Tom talk Edgar back a bit."

"Why didn't you just mention something back there?"

"Every time he messes up, he asks me to kill him. I don't want to send him into another existential crisis."

"Jesus," Austin murmured, and his tone made giggles dance up through me.

"Anyway, what do you need?"

He stopped on the porch and looked out over the street, the late afternoon sun trickling down through the maple trees and speckling the sidewalk. "Do you have a couple of hours?"

"A couple of hours?" I checked my watch, three o'clock, then looked back at the closed front door. "Well, given I have no job other than learning magic and monitoring the gardening of a partially insane vampire, I do happen to have some free time, yes. Especially since we agreed to take a couple of days off from training so you can heal." I chewed on my lip, guilt worming through me again. "How are you doing, by the way?"

He waved the question away. "There is nothing partial about that vampire's insanity." Austin jerked his head toward the house. "Do you need to tell your entourage?"

"Will we be in town?"

"Yes."

"Then nah, I'm good with just you and whatever shifters of yours pop out of the woodwork. Let's see if they can find me."

"I don't have anyone official yet." He reached out to put his hand on the small of my back, ready to direct me. "But yeah, we'll be good."

The door opened slowly to reveal Mr. Tom, his tuxedo-clad chest puffed out, his pants freshly pressed, and his wings falling down his back like a cape. One hand balanced a silver tray bearing a single white envelope, and the other was fisted by his side.

"Miss. Before you leave without proper protection, putting yourself in potentially grave danger, I have a piece of post for you," he said.

My expression flattened. I felt it. "Were you listening to our conversation at the door, Mr. Tom?"

"From the front room window, actually. It is the easiest way to know what you are up to without having to ask."

Austin was staring again. I had a feeling this was not the way he planned to run his pack.

"I'll grab it when I get back." I motioned Austin down the walkway.

"I think you'll want to read it, miss. It's from your mother. She wants to come visit."

I froze, only one step having been taken. "What do you mean she wants to come visit? How—*Did you read my mail?*"

"What an amazing singing range you must have, miss, with the vocal pitch of that last question." Mr. Tom sniffed. "I merely scanned the contents to ensure it was not a death threat. After that note from Elliot

Graves, I thought it best to start monitoring your mail to ensure none of the messages posed an immediate danger. Magical people can be unhinged…"

"He would know," Austin murmured.

"I also feared a bill or request for money might arrive and go ignored. Sometimes our past lives can come back to haunt us. Since you seem pretty hands-off about monetary matters…"

I dropped my mouth open, about to explode. Hands-off? I always tried to pay for things, but whenever Mr. Tom was around, and he was always around, he would literally push me aside in his haste to take care of the tab. I had no idea what kind of money was available to the estate because he refused to show me any statements or give me access to the bank accounts that were now supposedly mine, simply telling me the estate paid for itself. I wasn't sure what sort of hands-on approach would get me any further.

I swallowed down my annoyance and reached for the envelope. I didn't feel like getting into it with him in front of Austin. "No, Mr. Tom, I don't have any creditors looking to get paid," I said dryly.

"Fantastic, miss. But you do have two parents who wish to see what you are up to. I shall roll out the red carpet."

I'd barely lifted the letter from the tray when he

turned back into the house and closed the door behind him, not responding to my shouted denial that they were coming.

"Oh, and miss…" Mr. Tom stuck his head out of the door again. "They'll be staying a week, or maybe two. Their toilet broke and flooded part of the house. Your mother launched into a rant about the lack of fiber in your father's diet, but you can read that yourself. They are scheduled to get here in three days' time. I'll pick up the essentials. Have fun. I'll alert those on bodyguard detail that you're leaving."

The door closed again with a soft click.

My parents were coming.

My non-magical parents were coming to a magical house.

How the hell was I supposed to keep what I was a secret?

CHAPTER 2

"**D**O YOUR PARENTS usually write letters to communicate instead of calling?" Austin asked as we set out toward town.

I'd skimmed the letter, shaken my head at the detailed fiber assessment, and stuffed it into my back pocket. Mr. Tom had gotten the details correct. They were definitely coming. The letter had been more of a statement of intent than a request.

"Here..." Niamh sat forward in her porch rocking chair as we passed, her thumb and forefinger curled around a rock. "What are ye at?"

"Headed into town," Austin called.

She leaned back and continued rocking. "Let me know when ye head to the bar."

The prospect of my parents' upcoming visit had sent my thoughts into a downward spiral, and when I turned and looked back at Ivy House, I tried to see it as they would. An unnatural, heavy shadow fell over the massive structure, just like always, and light perpetually glowed from the top window in the attic even though that light was never on. Before my parents even got to the house, the judgments would start. I could just hear them now.

"Honey, why did you choose such a gloomy house?" my mother would ask, looking up at it.

"It's fine," my father would say. "The paint is the problem. You need a new coat of paint, Jessie. Maybe an off-white. You should've stained it, but that ship has sailed."

"Paint wouldn't do it, Pete. It's just so…*dark*…" my mom would reply.

That would start them arguing about the best way to fix what wasn't actually broken. As if they didn't live in a house of horrors filled with dozens of unfinished projects, including a partial coat of turd-brown paint near the stairs.

"They do write letters instead of calling, yes," I said, belatedly remembering that Austin had asked a question. "But only when they want to make it impossible for me to turn them down. My mom typically times it so the letter arrives the day before they do. If I try to cancel, she gives me a guilt trip about how she's already planned her whole life around this thing, and if I couldn't do it, why did I wait until the last minute to let her know? The whole situation used to drive Matt nuts.

Matt's the ex."

He nodded, clearly remembering the name. "Not you?"

"Obviously it drives me nuts, yeah. But, I mean…they're my parents. What am I supposed to do? When I need something, I can always count on them."

"Do Matt's parents not have any idiosyncrasies?"

"They do, but he didn't seem too put out by them. I was, absolutely, but not him. They're these really WASP-y socialites, so they had parties and dinners and things where I'd have to bring homemade dishes that were up to their standards, dress a certain way, and when it was our turn to host?" I shivered just thinking about it. "There were a lot of rules. Keeping up with the Joneses type of stuff. It got exhausting."

"Your parents aren't like that?"

I snorted. "Matt's parents could barely tolerate my family. My mom would show up to one of their fancy cocktail parties wearing some sort of Mary Poppins carpet dress. You know, like the material Mary Poppins's bag was made out of? That, but fashioned into a dress. My dad would wear jeans, cowboy boots, and one of those cowboy blazers with patches on the elbows. This in a room full of fancy cocktail dresses and high-powered Armani suits. They did *not* fit in."

Austin chuckled as we reached the end of the street.

"Your parents will fit in around here, at least."

A wave of anxiety washed over me, the familiar urge to run home and clean everything almost overwhelming. I needed to get the beer they liked, the snacks they had to have—

"A TV!" I grabbed Austin's arm and stopped at the corner. Confusion stole over his expression. "I need a TV! And cable! My father cannot live without his TV."

A grin pulled at his lush lips, enhancing his attractiveness. My stomach flipped. The guy was a looker, there were no two ways about it. It got distracting at times.

"I have a TV you can use," he said. "I'll bring it by later."

I started walking again. "I can just have Mr. Tom go out and buy one. He'll bitch, but…"

"This way…" He pointed right, to a street before the main drag.

"Why are they visiting?" I mumbled. "I mean, I know why they are visiting—they have to get out of the house and they have no choice, but why me? Why not Chris?"

"Who's Chris?" Austin asked.

"My brother." I bit my lip. "They probably didn't want to fly. Dang it, I should've chosen another house, much farther away."

"Are they a nightmare, or…"

An older man and woman I'd seen around town walked toward us on the sidewalk, out for a stroll. Austin's arm came around me and his hand touched down on the indent of my waist, right above the swell of my hip. His heat soaked through my shirt and into my skin. A zip of electricity coursed through my body, followed by a rush of adrenaline. I shivered as he applied pressure, directing me in front of him on the sidewalk to let the others pass.

The man and woman both nodded in hello. "Alpha," they said, one after the other. "Jessie." Their smiles were so wide that their eyes crinkled.

"I don't remember meeting them," I whispered as Austin's hand drifted away, taking the heat with it. I shivered again at the sudden chill in its wake.

"Everyone around here knows who you are. The magical people, anyway. Magical people keep their eyes on dangerous things."

My face heated and I wanted to come up with an offhanded remark to deflect being called dangerous, but the news about my parents had put me off my game.

"Have you had to fight anyone to retain your alpha title?" I asked as a distraction, coming up on a dentist's office.

"No one I wouldn't have had to subdue anyway.

Outsiders with too much liquor trying to stir up trouble."

"Well, yeah, that's pretty standard fare for a bar."

"Not my bar." He motioned for me to cross the street, then directed me through a little alley between two businesses run out of converted houses. No dumpsters loitered along the way, and there was no trash blowing across the ground like urban tumbleweeds. This town, small and cute and clean, was nothing like the haunts I'd gotten used to in L.A. The change of pace was nice. I hoped my parents wouldn't bitch that it was boring. You just never knew with them.

Halfway through the alley, the space opened up, showing the rear of a business situated on the main drag. I spied Jasper at the street corner. Gargoyles could blend into their environment, especially if the surfaces contained stone or rock, rendering themselves invisible, but I'd learned how to magically strip away their camouflage. So I could see Jasper's deep gray gargoyle form, threaded through with tan and brown. He was one of three gargoyles who lived in Ivy House—a strong and silent type who'd proven excellent at guarding my back while keeping just enough distance to allow me my privacy.

It was more than I could say for the small collection of gargoyles who'd become long-term guests at a hotel in town. Around a dozen of them had answered my magical summons, but I'd already gotten rid of the guys obviously not cut out for the role, and one guy had left of his own accord. He couldn't handle Niamh picking on him for his lack of hygiene. The remaining six were still auditioning for permanent roles in Ivy House.

Jasper nodded at me in greeting, glanced at Austin, and then turned back to the street. He would guard our front, trusting Austin to guard the rear.

"Jasper found us," I told Austin, slowing with him.

"I know. I smelled him." Austin led the way into what was essentially a small business's backyard. He checked out the dumpster positioned against the fence on the far side, separating this space with the business next door. A pile of empty wine boxes, and a wine barrel standing on end, sat near a set of three steps leading to a back door. Obviously this was the back of a tasting room, this area of the world being big on wine.

"What are you looking for?" I asked, clasping my hands behind my back and watching his movements, my gaze only occasionally snagging on the play of muscle across his back and his tight, well-shaped butt. I was getting better at not staring.

"The actual winemaking for this winery happens at their country estate, about half an hour away. They grow most of the grapes they use."

"All of the wineries in town make the actual wines elsewhere." I tilted my head to read the name on the side of one of the boxes, very familiar with the wineries in town. I grimaced. This one wasn't great.

"There isn't much room back here for a gathering of any kind."

I frowned at the small space, the gravel crunching under my feet and a dark stain near the dumpster making my nose curl. "It isn't a place I'd like to hang out even if there was space."

"What if it were spruced up a little?" He stopped in the center and put out his hands, then squinted up at the sky, getting a full dose of sun on his face. "A few people could hang out back here."

"Next to the dumpster? Are you planning a party or something? Why not just have it in your bar?"

He lowered his face and hands, gave the space another look, and then motioned me toward the front, the busiest strip of businesses in the town. A woman in her twenties caught sight of me emerging from around the corner. When she noticed Austin behind me, her face turned red and delighted surprise flashed in her eyes.

"Hi, alpha," she gushed.

"Alpha." A man behind the woman nodded before stepping into the street around her, avoiding the temporary traffic jam.

"Alpha," someone said across the street, putting up his hand to wave.

Austin ignored them all, staring straight ahead and resting a hand on the small of my back. "Just here, Jess."

He directed me up the stairs before reaching around me to grab the door handle.

"It always weirds me out when you don't acknowledge the people saying hi to you," I murmured, entering the tasting room. "Are we day drinking? Because with the news that my parents are coming, I could definitely get behind that. I'd prefer a different winery, though."

"They're acknowledging me to show respect for my position, and if I reciprocated, I'd do nothing but greet people whenever I went into town."

"What do Janes and Dicks think of people calling you alpha?"

"I don't care. What do you think of this setup?" He gestured around the spacious tasting room, sparse in furniture and plentiful in dead space.

I huffed out a laugh at his response before glancing around. I'd been here before, but I hadn't paid much attention.

"What are they expecting, huge crowds to pack in here?" I whispered, knowing someone would pop out to wait on us at any moment.

He didn't control his volume. "In the busy season, there are enough tourists to fill the place, but I've heard it doesn't typically happen." He didn't move toward the counter.

I didn't wait for him. "Right. So why all the space? Why not add in a few high tables without chairs and maybe a little display area to sell wine paraphernalia? Is this place even open? Where's the pourer?"

"Hmm." Austin finally joined me, leaning against the counter as a woman with a pinched face and an air of smug importance drifted up to the counter. Her smile didn't reach her eyes, and her failure to recognize or acknowledge Austin meant she was probably new to the area. Even non-magical people knew the scary, standoffish bar owner of the Paddy Wagon.

"Welcome." She laid her hand, her pink nails perfectly rounded, on a cream-colored piece of paper to my right. Several similar menus lay across the stretch of counter. "We have two options for tastings. The regular flight, where you can choose five wines, is ten dollars, and the reserve tasting is fifteen dollars. If you buy two bottles or more, the tasting fee is waived. Which would you prefer?"

I glanced at Austin. "What's happening here? Are we doing a wine tour? Because if this is your way of getting me out of meetings with Edgar, then we just became best friends."

He smiled, pulling one of the papers closer. "It's up to you. What do you want, the reserve tasting? One of each?"

I nodded at the woman. "One of each. If we're going to do this thing, we'll do it right."

Her deadpan stare said she didn't appreciate my nonchalant humor. "Would you like to start with white?"

As Austin looked on, I chose a wine from each list. She sniffed and turned to grab the bottles from the coolers at the far right.

"Out of all the winery options, you chose this one, huh?" I asked, tapping my fingers against the counter. "Oh, this town carries Pabst Blue Ribbon, doesn't it? My father likes Pabst. If I don't have it, he'll just send my mom looking for it."

"Of all the tasting rooms on this strip, this one gets the least foot traffic," Austin said as the woman screwed off a cap. The other had a cork, and she set to work. "The tasting room is upscale, though, and the operations at the winery look good."

"You've been to the winery? Are you sizing up your competition or something?"

"No. I'm looking to buy it."

The needle screeched off the spinning record in my

mind. "What's that now?"

Glasses clinked as the woman placed them in front of us. She explained the wines as she poured, but I wasn't listening.

"You're thinking of buying a *winery*?" I whispered as soon as she drifted away.

"Yes." He swirled the contents in his glass and lifted it to sip. I watched his lips press against the glass, my mind struggling to compute the enormity of what he was saying versus the easy, unconcerned quality of his tone.

"How do you have that kind of money? I mean…" I blinked a couple of times and shook my head. "Sorry, that was rude, but… To buy a winery, you're talking millions. Right?"

His face scrunched up. He held out the glass for me. "It's tart."

I took it without comment and sipped, not prepared.

"Oh, man." I lowered the glass to the counter, my right eye shutting of its own volition and my mouth puckering at the sourness. "That wine is intense, and not in a drinkable sort of way."

"I'm from a long line of alphas," he said, as though that explained something.

I lifted my glass and swirled good and proper, running the liquid around the glass to get as much oxygen in there as possible. It would help the flavor, and this place needed all the help it could get. I didn't remember it being this bad. Or maybe it was just the pick I'd made for Austin. I raised the glass and took a cautious sip.

"Ugh." I coughed a bit as my face twisted involuntarily. "It wasn't just the first one. This one is intense, too." I pushed the glass his way. "What does being from a line of alphas have to do with buying a winery?"

"Can we have the next samples, please?" Austin asked the woman, and though the phrase seemed like a polite request, his tone conveyed a command for obedience. He pointed to the ones he wanted, two reds. The woman's previous methodical, unhurried gliding fell away, and she quickly got to work opening the next bottles.

"I'm assuming you don't care what ends up in your glass?" he asked me, his voice back to calm and breezy.

"I do, but in this case I'm not sure it'll really matter." I lowered my voice. "I don't remember the wine being this bad."

"I think that's the root of the problem, right there." He nodded and glanced out the window at the shining day beyond, as though contemplating the meaning of the universe.

"Also, should we be saying 'alpha' in public? I know

you don't care, but…"

He turned back to me. "To properly run a territory, an alpha needs to invest in local businesses, to have a personal say and stake in the local economy. To help sway the decisions that are made for the benefit of the people. If the territory prospers, the alpha typically prospers. If the territory suffers, so does the alpha. Does that make sense? And yes, we can say 'alpha' and 'territory' because those are words that Janes and Dicks know, even if they don't quite understand them in the way we're using them."

"So you're from a long line of *prosperous* alphas?" I surmised, eyeing the glass of red now sitting in front of me. I wasn't so sure about day drinking at this establishment. It might be more painful than pleasurable.

"That'll be all for now," Austin told the woman as she opened her mouth to give her spiel about the wines. Under his steady gaze, her eyes tightened, creasing at the corners.

"Of course." She turned, busying herself with wiping down dustless bottles.

"Maybe lighten up a little," I murmured, swirling the contents of the glass. "You're going to give the woman a complex."

"If it pleases milady."

His tone was light and teasing, his eyes sparkling

and bright. I couldn't look away, my heart speeding up at the raw intensity I saw lurking just beneath the surface. The world around us seemed to slow, and then it dropped away entirely—his focus applied solely to me, and mine to him. Heat blistered through me before pooling down low, pounding. Aching. Manifesting from those suddenly intense, beautiful cobalt-blue eyes.

"I never did take you on that perfect date we talked about," he said softly, his sweet breath dusting my lashes.

Only then did I realize I'd leaned toward him. I found myself remembering the feel of his palm on my side. On my back. I loved the way he always gently steered me into the path of safety when we walked somewhere together. I loved that he was always respectfully aware of me and the world around me. It felt like being pampered for some reason. Like he was freeing me from all of life's little trials.

"Okay, then." I let out a deep breath and tore my gaze away from his. With effort, I turned to face my glass. "Yup." I was just saying words to fill the silence. It wasn't even an uncomfortable silence, which somehow made things worse. This guy needed to come with an emergency brake.

I probably needed to start dating again. Sure, I hadn't sealed the deal with the handsome gargoyle who'd spent a short time at Ivy House, but that didn't mean I should stop trying. I needed to end the dry spell before I embarrassed myself and leaned any closer to Austin.

"Drunk already?" I heard the laughter in his words.

"You're as bad as Niamh. I've had, like, two sips. No, I am not drunk already."

"So you've just taken to voicing your thoughts on the regular now?"

I froze, my eyes wide. "What? Why?" I asked, flustered. "What did I say?"

His dark chuckle brought on a rush of embarrassment that likely showed on my face. I'd clearly voiced the bit about the dry spell. Dang Ivy House for having a personality and seeming like a real person—I constantly talked to her, out loud, and clearly the practice had carried over into the parts of my life where I'd do better to keep my thoughts and feelings bottled up.

Not that I hadn't always had a propensity to think out loud, but I usually had a better grip on myself when in public.

"I am from a long line of prosperous alphas, yes. On my mother's side," he said, then tried his newest pour of wine, wincing with the effort. "I'm a trust fund baby at this point, since I've done very little for myself. So far. The money's been sitting there, collecting interest, waiting for me to rise to my potential."

"What if you never did?"

"My brother's kids will get everything when I die. If I don't use it, they'll be set for life, even if something happens to my brother's territory. If I can create and run a prosperous territory, they'll get even more. Can't lose."

"Oh cra—" I'd taken a sip of the new wine while he was talking, the taste of this one setting off a party of awful in my mouth. I swung the glass his way, not wanting to suffer alone. "So now that you've claimed your title, you're going to buy up some businesses?"

"Yes. It's time for me to invest in the territory. I'll also need to help more of our kind obtain seats of power. I need to build a pack from scratch. It would've been easier to move into a place already structured for our kind." He shrugged. "I wanted a challenge—I got it."

We received our next pours, and I eyed them dubiously. "Can I be in your pack? I promise I won't bring Mr. Tom."

When the silence stretched, I glanced over, only to be caught in his gravity and intensity. Desire moved within his gaze, unfurling a luscious and luxurious and horribly uncomfortable feeling within me. This wasn't good. He was supposed to be off-limits. Permanently friend-zoned. Anything physical would ruin this easiness that we had. It would add strings neither of us wanted. No, a friend was all Austin Steele could ever be, mouth-watering smile and hypnotic stare be damned.

Need that emergency brake!

"I was just kidding," I whispered, my mouth suddenly dry, my stomach flipping.

He reached into his back pocket and pulled out a money clip stuffed with cash. "Let's move on. I've got what I needed. Let's day drink down the way, then we'll go pick out that TV. When are your parents coming again? I want to make sure I'm around to watch the fireworks."

CHAPTER 3

"PLEASE, MISS, STOP obsessing. Everything is going to be just fine."

I laid a blanket across the seat of the comfiest leather chair I could buy. Well…that Mr. Tom could buy. He had wrestled me away from the cashier again so he could pay. He was starting to give me a complex by not letting me buy things for myself.

The chair faced a large TV mounted on the wall, the cords hidden within a little white plastic strip running down to the ground. Eventually I'd get an electrician in here to put a plug in that spot so the cables would be hidden.

The rest of the furniture that had already filled the room, not matching the new leather chair, was resituated so other people could sit in here and watch TV, too.

We hadn't been able to get a quick enough appointment for proper cable, but Niamh's bar connection had outfitted us with a somewhat obscure black box. Given these were desperate times, I hadn't asked questions, just hoped it was magical rather than illegal. I'd go the traditional cable route when there was time.

I'd deliberately chosen a sitting room close to the kitchen so my father wouldn't have far to go for a snack.

"I know, I'm just…" I straightened up to make sure the furniture looked okay and not like a collection of flea market items haphazardly placed around the room.

"It's not cold enough for a blanket anyway." Mr. Tom moved to grab it.

"No, no." I put out my hand to stop him. "It's the fart blanket."

Mr. Tom yanked back his hands. "I beg your pardon?"

"I think he uses a blanket so he doesn't stick to the leather, but it also contains all the farts."

A look of horror crossed Mr. Tom's face. "Who are these people?"

"These people are my parents, and they'll get weirder, don't worry."

I clicked on the TV, nodded when the picture came on, clicked it off again, and laid the remote on the chair arm. I pointed at the empty space to the right of it. "Where's that end table? He needs a place to put his drinks. And the iPad. Put the iPad on the table." At least we had Wi-Fi. It was one less thing to worry about.

I made my way to the kitchen and found Jasper loitering near the wall. He wasn't on duty, but he also didn't have a life other than watching over me. He could be found hanging around most times.

Jasper's brow furrowed when I pointed at him. "We need to come up with a reason you're always just standing around." He watched me silently. "Or maybe you can just stand around outside? Normal homeowners don't have bodyguards loitering around."

"You are not a normal homeowner," Mr. Tom said, catching up to me.

"Yes, Mr. Tom, I know that. Magical people know that. Do you know who doesn't know that? Non-magical people, like my parents. How many times have we been over this?" I sighed. "My parents won't be okay with learning magic exists—if they would even believe it. We have to pretend we're Dicks and Janes, which is going to be incredibly difficult with so many magical people hanging around all the time. Honestly, you should all just join the hotel gargoyles in town for a few weeks. Take a break. I could call for backup whenever I leave the property."

"A break?" Mr. Tom said, clearly affronted. "As if I would need a break. What a thing to say to me! Kicking me out of my home? Turning away all your help and protection? Isolating yourself?" He shook his head. "No, miss, my place is here. Your parents will understand, don't worry."

I opened my mouth to ask if he'd missed what I'd *just* said about my parents, then closed it again. What was the point? We'd just go round and round.

Ulric, another of the live-in gargoyles, sat at the round kitchen table, eating a sandwich and looking at his phone. The midmorning sun highlighted his pink and blue spiked hair, the same colors as his gargoyle form. He looked up when we came in and straightened with a smile.

"Counting down the minutes, huh?" he asked.

"Yeah, they should be here anytime." I pulled open the fridge doors, checking the snack supply. My dad had to have his cheese and salami.

A little thread of excitement wormed through the stressful anticipation of their arrival. Despite their hang-ups, I missed them. I hadn't gone back to Los Angeles for Christmas because Jimmy had decided to stay in New York City with his new girlfriend, probably so he wouldn't have to choose between Matt and me. Another reason I'd stayed was because I'd been told in no uncertain terms that my gargoyle entourage would be going with me if I traveled. (Even people as strange as my parents would have questions if I showed up with an entourage of men.) I didn't call as often as I probably should, so this would be a nice chance to catch up.

I just wished they weren't planning to stay so long.

"What about the salami?" I picked through the drawer in the fridge. "I don't see any."

"It's here." Mr. Tom pointed at the log hanging underneath one of the cabinets. "Please, miss, stop obsessing. I have everything. We are prepared."

"I get it." Ulric went back to his sandwich. "My parents are nuts. My mom has a cleaning complex. If she shows up at my place, she is cleaning within half an hour. Hands and knees, scrubbing the floor, you name it. It's like she is a dirt crusader. You can never rest easy for fear you'll make a mess and send her scurrying for the cleaning supplies. Don't get me wrong, not having to clean for myself is amazing, but still, it's a little much."

"There is nothing to clean around here," Mr. Tom said as he followed me out.

I scanned surfaces and shelves for anything I didn't want the parents to notice. I'd already hidden a bunch of random wooden carvings of magical creatures and artifacts, locked the doll room, and ensured all of the weapons were put away in the attic, up a whole lot of steps I doubted my parents would climb. I hoped they wouldn't, at any rate. The decorative wooden carvings above the archway in the foyer changed as I glanced around, shifting from a lovely scene of a meadow to a gruesome battle with dragons, tigers, and centaurs—swords drawn, heads rolling, and bodies piled high.

"Very funny, Ivy House. Change it back. Come on, you have to help. Try to be normal."

"This is a magical house," Cedric said as he walked down the stairs. One of two gargoyles who'd responded to my first summons for magical help (the other one had been dismembered), he was still here despite having fallen behind the others in flying prowess and protection. Austin hadn't said it outright, but he'd hinted that maybe Cedric shouldn't make the final cut. He wouldn't say it, either. He offered his help and guidance when asked or when something was dire, but he left the major decisions regarding the team up to me, just like Ivy House did.

I kind of hated it. I always felt bad when I had to let people go. No one had lashed out, but somehow their disappointment was worse than anger.

"By definition," Cedric said, "it is not normal."

"Yes, thank you for the lesson on stating the obvious," Mr. Tom said.

He was clearly jumping aboard the send-Cedric-home train, but I didn't know what he was taking issue with—Cedric had just said exactly what Mr. Tom had been repeating for three days.

"I don't feel like you all are giving this the weight you should be," I muttered, entering the front sitting room and giving it a final once-over. "My parents are square. Do you know what square means?" I re-entered the foyer as Ulric joined us from the kitchen, Cedric now waiting at the bottom of the stairs. It felt like I was giving a pre-battle pep talk. "It was a term applied to the young people who followed the rules when the hippie scene was exploding. My parents have never done hallucinogens. They don't watch fantasy-type shows, nor do they read fantasy-type books. They are so firmly entrenched in reality, and have been for so long, that none of this magical stuff will compute. They don't have the imagination for it. They won't understand an alternative lifestyle. We *have* to try to stay mainstream."

"I like all these hot-button words you're using." Ulric laughed. "Alternative lifestyle? Staying mainstream? You got it, daddy-o."

"Respect her, but do not encourage her in this," Mr. Tom said out of the side of his mouth.

I caught movement through the window and then a flash of sun on metal. My heart stutter-started, and I quickly went to look, watching as the rusty red Cadillac pulled up to the curb.

"They're here." I turned to face everyone. "Quick! Hide!"

"What?" Cedric cocked his head in confusion.

"Sorry, no…" I waved the thought away. "Sorry, reflex. But…actually, yes, go to your rooms. Get out of sight. Let's work them in slowly. Quick! Go! If you need anything, use the secret passageways. Ivy House, help them navigate those. They have my temporary permission."

"Don't lock them in for fun," Mr. Tom said.

"I'll just stay in my room, then," Ulric said softly.

I heard voices outside, my parents already bickering as they emerged from the car. I just hoped my dad had pants on.

"You heard her: essential personnel only. Go to your rooms. I will get you when you're needed." Mr. Tom motioned everyone away. Apparently he'd dubbed himself essential personnel.

I opened the door as my parents loitered by the trunk, my mom gesturing toward the house while my dad fiddled with the keys.

"We're not guests, Martha," my dad was saying. "She won't mind if we bring something in with us. We'll have to make fewer trips this way."

"We *are* guests, Pete. We don't live here. Let's go greet her before we all but move in."

"That drip Matt isn't here, so we don't have to tip-toe around anymore. I'll just bring the cooler. I could use a beer after that drive."

"What do you mean, *that drive*?" My mom braced her fists on her hips. "I drove the last half!"

"I know. You frayed my nerves."

I rolled my eyes and started forward, noticing Niamh sitting on her porch, watching the show with a smile. A Jeep Wrangler rolled down the street toward us, Austin behind the wheel, clearly making good on his pledge to watch the fireworks.

Fabulous. Everyone was present.

"Oh, hi!" My mom turned to greet me, only noticing my proximity when I was nearly upon her, her smile large and arms outstretched. I accepted a hug, then groaned with the squeeze.

"Hey ya, squirt." Dad gave me a hug next, much looser, but the following pats on the back nearly beat the breath out of me. "So…" He stepped back and hiked up his pants, looking up at the house. His eyebrows slowly pinched together. He looked at the blue sky, then down the street, then back at the house. "You could do with a brighter paint. That one is too dark."

"Honey!" My mom's eyes were wide as she looked down my body. "Look at you! You look fantastic! Is it Zumba? I just got into a little Zumba myself. It's hard on my knees, but if it worked this well for you, maybe I should try again."

"You don't know if it was Zumba," my father said. "She didn't say it was Zumba. It probably wasn't those diet drinks you keep forcing on me, either."

"I just worked out and ate well," I murmured, forgetting about the transformation when I took the magic.

"And your skin!" My mom ran her hand down her cheek. "Chemical peel? I've heard chemical peels really give a nice glow. I've been meaning to try it."

How did one tell their mother that the great skin was partially a result of having the first layer entirely burned away from a magical spell, and not dying from it because of magical healing?

"Yeah, chemical peel," I murmured. Best just to lie a little.

"Well, you look fantastic. I made deviled eggs." My mom gestured at one of the two coolers in the trunk. "And clam dip. They'll still be good. We put a lot of ice in the coolers. I figured, we never had a party for Christmas, so we might celebrate a little while we're here. Won't that be nice?"

"Mom, why did you bring two coolers' worth of food?" I asked as my dad struggled to lift the first out of the trunk. "I have everything."

"Well, your father needed his beer…"

"I have beer, Dad. Wait, it's stuck…" As I moved in to help my dad, I caught a glimpse of Austin out of the corner of my eye, coming closer. I also noticed a few strangers walking down the street toward Ivy House, their faces tilted up to marvel at the size of the structure. Which meant they'd be commenting on its creepiness next, and then waiting until we were gone and daring each other to sneak onto the property.

Niamh caught sight of them at the same time I did, braced herself, and stood slowly, rock in hand.

"Really? This has to happen right now?" I murmured.

"Blast this thing. Martha, I told you, you put too much stuff in the trunk," my dad said.

"It's not the stuff, it's your muscles, Pete. They've atrophied. You should be exercising in retirement. Lifting a beer to your mouth is not exercising."

"Depends on how many times you do it," my dad responded.

"Here. Let me help." Austin lightly jogged around the car, winking at me as he did so. "Let me help you, sir."

Dad started, his eyes widening a little when he caught sight of Austin.

"Well, my goodness." A smile slowly spread across my mom's face. "Jacinta, who is this?"

"Oh, this is Austin. He's a friend of mine."

Niamh cocked back her hand and then let fly, a rock

sailing through the air in a lazy arc before slamming against the arm of the teenage boy whose mouth had dropped open while looking at Ivy House. He jumped and grabbed the spot, the skin clearly smarting. When he looked around, he caught sight of Niamh straightening, having just picked up another rock.

"What the hell?" the kid hollered.

"We don't want Peeping Toms around here," Niamh yelled at them.

"It's lookie-loos, not Peeping Toms," I mumbled as the second projectile struck home, clunking the boy's friend on the noggin.

"Ow!" The kid rubbed the offending spot.

"Is that old woman throwing rocks at those boys?" my mother said, aghast.

"Yeah, um…" I racked my brain for a way to put a positive spin on this. Niamh would surely be hanging out at Ivy House, and I didn't want them to hate her. "We get some vandalism down this way, so Niamh tries to head them off. Ivy House is the oldest house in the town—it draws a lot of unwanted attention."

"Ivy House? Is that—"

One of the boys rattled out a string of foul language as Niamh threw another rock.

"Did you hear that? Disgraceful, that language. Serves them right. Clearly they are up to no good." My dad looked around his feet, but the only rocks in the vicinity were some decorative pea gravel. "I better help."

"Dad, no. Leave it." I patted his shoulder. "One crazy person on the block is enough. You don't need to help her."

"As if he could—he has terrible aim." My mom clucked her tongue as the boys took off running. "I should make him clean around the toilet," she said. "It's more than a little sprinkle with those tinkles."

Austin's grin broadened.

"I could hit those kids from here," my dad grumbled. "I've got good aim! My softball team won second place."

"That was twenty years ago, Pete," my mom said.

Austin reached into the trunk and pulled out one of the coolers, his biceps popping but showing no strain. "Should I take this to the house?"

"Oh, yeah, thanks." My dad worked the other cooler out, heaving it from the car.

I reached for it. "I got it, Dad—Niamh, would you stop throwing rocks!" I yelled. She was still trying to hit the fleeing boys.

"Grab a bag." My dad jerked his head at the duffel that had fallen from the corner of the trunk when the coolers were taken away. I grabbed it and hurried after them.

"It's very gloomy, Jacinta," my mother said, pulling a suitcase out of the back seat while looking up at Ivy House. "It looks like some sort of...black cloud is hanging over it, doesn't it? It reminds me of Halloween."

"Your mother is going blind, Jacinta," my dad said over his shoulder. "She keeps losing her glasses."

"Those are reading glasses, Pete. I don't need them to see a big house. Look! It's not even nighttime, but the window up there is glowing."

"Listen to that, will ya, Austin? She fancies herself Stephen King now." My dad shook his head as he made it to the porch. "Next she'll say she sees a bat."

Mr. Tom waited by the front door, his tuxedo as freshly pressed as ever and his posture straight and tall.

"Where do you want these?" Austin asked him.

"What...are those?" Mr. Tom asked. "They are visiting...with coolers? Like some sort of tailgaters?"

"Who's this?" My dad half turned to me. "What's he wearing, a tux with a cape? Is this one of those superhero convention things where everyone dresses up like a superhero? Is he some sort of James Bond with a Superman fetish or something? I didn't bring a cape. I don't even own a cape."

"He's the butler, Dad. He came with the house. Head to the kitchen, Austin." I jerked my head to get him going. "Yes, Mr. Tom, they came with coolers. They get worried I won't have the things they want, so they bring them. I thought maybe they'd trust me now, since I am no longer twenty, but here we are."

"That's your mother. I try to tell her, but she just won't listen." My dad set the cooler down just inside the door, opened the lid with a loud creaking noise, pushed aside a head of lettuce, and grabbed a can of beer. He held it out to me. "Wanna beer?"

Apparently we would not be waiting to get everything sorted in the kitchen.

"I would." Niamh lifted her hand as she came up the walk, leaving my mother behind to continue rooting through the car. Lord knew what she was looking for, or why she didn't just take everything out so the rest of us could help carry it in. "I'll take one of them, if ye please." Niamh stopped in front of my dad. "How're ya? How's it goin'? I'm Niamh from across the street."

He passed over the can of beer before reaching down to grab another. He squinted at her. "Are you Irish?"

"Guilty. Leave that there," she said as Dad started to mess with the cooler. "Come inside and sit down. Earl can handle all that." She said it with the authority of one who lived there, an authority she deserved given she sat on the Ivy House council, but my parents didn't know

49

that. Still, my dad went with her willingly enough, muttering about her excellent aim and "punk kids." Thank God she knew where I'd set up his TV lounge.

"A butler?" My mother finally caught up, rolling one suitcase and carrying another. "The house came with a butler? What sort of house comes with a butler?"

"It's just…he had the job of caretaker, and when I bought the house, I didn't want to turn him out." I took the suitcase she held.

"Kinda weird with the cape, though," she murmured as we finally crossed the threshold. "Does he always wear that, or is he trying to impress us somehow? Though I don't know who would be impressed with a cape…"

"It's…a long story. Go and sit down. Do you want—"

"Oh no, no, I'll just see to the things I brought. I made deviled eggs. And clam dip. I figured that since you couldn't make it down for Christmas—"

"I know, yeah. You said. Seriously, Mom, relax for a minute. It was a long drive. Do you want a beer? I'll help Mr. Tom get things organized."

She paused, looking up at the bloody scene Ivy House had left on the wood carving area in the foyer. While only I could see the carvings move, anyone could gawk at the still images.

Great. I'd hoped the house would change the scene

before they came in.

"My goodness, that is horrific. Just what sort of place is this, Jacinta?" my mom asked.

She had no idea.

"Just…here." I went back to the other cooler and grabbed out a beer. "Here. Go check on Dad. Niamh can be colorful."

"Well, we need a tour, don't we?"

"We…will," I said, leading the way to the lounge. "We'll get to that. Go check on Dad. The TV and cable box are new—I'm not sure if he'll be happy with the setup."

"Oh, he's fine." But she went in anyway.

I met Mr. Tom in the kitchen, standing over the cooler Austin had taken in, staring down at it like it was a dangerous bug with too many eyes. Austin had the same look.

"It's just a cooler, you guys," I said.

"It's simply that…I have not heard of grown adults showing up to stay at a house with their own food and drinks, as though suspicious of the food and drinks they are liable to be given. Do they assume I will poison them?"

"There's just certain stuff they prefer. My mom didn't know I have a butler who shops and makes food."

Austin bent to pull out a plastic bag of dried cranberries. He arched an eyebrow at me.

"It's for salads. Seriously, you guys, this isn't that weird. I mean…it's a little weird that they would bring a cooler instead of just getting here and going shopping as needed, but…" I shrugged.

Austin put the cranberries on the island. "What is…clam dip?"

I couldn't help but laugh. "It sounds gross, but it's actually good."

"That cannot possibly be true," Mr. Tom said, removing items from the cooler as if they might explode at any moment.

"It's cream cheese and, yes, canned clams, and other stuff. It's good, seriously. Anything with cream cheese is good."

"Cream cheese and seafood. Hmm, can't wait." Austin laughed, heading for the door. "I'll grab the other cooler."

"Yes. Because they brought two," Mr. Tom murmured, lifting a roast and looking at me. "An entire roast? She is planning to cook dinner for everyone, I presume, since my cooking is so lacking?"

"Oh my God, Mr. Tom, stop making this about you, would you? I thought you were happy to meet the people who made me."

"That was before they attempted to replace me."

I stared at him for a solid beat. It hadn't occurred to me that my mother might try to wrest the control of the kitchen, cleaning, and laundry away from Mr. Tom. Nor had it dawned on me that Mr. Tom would be affronted by this very standard behavior of hers. I tended to like when she did dinners and cleaned for me. That meant I had less to do. But the inevitable friction between Mr. Tom and my mom added a whole new layer of tension to my parents' visit.

When Austin came in with the second cooler, I grabbed his arm in desperation. "Can I borrow your cabin for a couple weeks? Please?"

He laughed softly. "This is going to be a lot more fun for me than it will be for you."

CHAPTER 4

I AWOKE, AS I always did, to Mr. Tom's face looming over me, his hands up to ward off an attack should I startle and react. I hadn't in months, but he still hadn't forgotten those early magical days when I'd accidentally flung him across the room. Using his hands as a shield hadn't helped then, either, but you couldn't fault the guy for trying.

"What are you going to do if I ever bring someone home?" I asked, the smell of bacon wafting through the air. My stomach growled.

"One can only hope I will eventually be faced with that conundrum, miss." He straightened up to give me more space now that I was awake. A steaming cup of coffee waited on my nightstand.

I picked it up and took a sip. "What are the parents doing?"

I struggled to sitting and glanced at the clock. Nine in the morning, early for him to be in here. Magical people tended to move around more at night and sleep in late. It was a schedule I'd grown used to, although my parents adhered to a very different norm. Case in point—after their travels, a few beers, and a large snack that Mr. Tom had made before my mother could get into the kitchen, my dad had fallen asleep in his new chair, seemingly oblivious to all the other people in the room. My mom had insisted on ushering him to bed in embarrassment. I'd helped get them situated in their room, and that had been the end of it. They hadn't come back down, opting instead for an early bedtime.

"*The* parents are currently filling downstairs with either smell or noise, that is what *the* parents are doing." He sniffed. "Your mother commandeered the kitchen. She had the gall to try to rip my wings off so she could give them a fresh wash!"

I couldn't help chuckling. "She doesn't know they're wings, Mr. Tom. She probably thinks you never wash your cape."

"I took a shower this morning, I'll have you know."

"Right but…" I let it go. "She's making breakfast?"

"Yes. We'll need to let the others wander freely to-day. You'll have to make those introductions." He moved toward the door. "And your father needs a hearing aid. The TV volume is up so loud I worry it'll crack the windows. When one of his racecars go by the screen, it sounds like thunder. There are a lot of racecars!"

I sighed. "He's hard of hearing. It's only for a week or so. We can tolerate it for that length of time."

"And your mother clangs and smashes the pots and pans off each other. I had to take over and set them out for her so she wouldn't deafen me. I can only imagine all the chips and scrapes we'll have on the dishes."

"It's only a week or so," I repeated. "It'll be fine."

Rigid, he left the room, leaving me to get ready.

After a shower, I checked my phone and noticed a missed FaceTime from Austin. My hair was still wrapped in a towel, my body encased in a robe, but I shrugged and took the phone over to the window. Looking down at the beautiful gardens, more flowers popping up every day, I hit the button and waited for it to connect.

The picture clicked on, showing a bare chest ripped with muscle before the image swung dizzily, giving me a peep of Austin's nude package, what had to be his bedroom, the ceiling, and then his ear. "Hey," he answered.

I froze. I'd seen Austin naked a good few times—bouts of semi-public nakedness were inevitable for anyone who changed form—and it stopped me short every single time. His perfect body was hard to look away from, rendered even more pleasing by his confident grace, and the sudden heat dripping through parts of my body was equally as hard to ignore.

"It's FaceTime," I said to his ear, a little rougher than I'd intended. "You FaceTimed me. I FaceTimed you back."

After a beat, the phone pulled away from his head and his confused face filled the screen. "Oh. Sorry, I must've hit that by accident. I didn't notice."

"Clearly, yes. You gave me a peep show."

He glanced down, and a sly smile tweaked his lips. He shook his head and looked away.

"You're trying not to make a dirty joke, aren't you?" I asked.

"Busted." He laughed, thick and deep and pleasing. "How are your parents settling in?"

I pulled the towel off my head and headed toward the bathroom, where I grabbed a brush. "They went to bed shortly after you left for the bar."

"Wow. That early, huh?"

I sat at the little vanity desk I never used so I could prop the phone up on the shelf that was probably intended for skin care products or something. Thank you, Ivy House, for making sure I didn't need any. Not that I'd use stuff like that, anyway. Beauty was such a hassle. I'd rather not bother.

"Yeah, I'll probably have to keep different hours for

training for the week," I said.

"Assuming it is just a week."

"Don't remind me. My mother had very little to say about the time frame, and my dad just grumbled about the new toilet. They're playing it off like this is our substitute Christmas celebration, since I didn't get down to them this year. Don't worry, the clam dip and deviled eggs weren't touched. You can try them when you come for dinner tonight."

He laughed again, sounding more buoyant and carefree than usual. "Yeah, your mom cornered me yesterday with the invite. It was like she didn't hear me when I said I'd probably have to work. She just kept telling me what time it would be."

"She didn't hear you. She doesn't often listen to the answers to her questions. Then she delightedly asks the questions two or three more times because of it."

"What are we having?"

I put the brush down and used my fingers to shake my hair out. "I don't know. It depends on who wins the fight between her and Mr. Tom. Of course, she won't know it is a fight, and that will enrage him. There was already a scuffle regarding breakfast." I told him about my mom trying to get Mr. Tom's cape so she could wash it. By the end, Austin was bent over laughing.

"Classic." He wiped his eyes. "I might be around

more this week. This is some good entertainment."

I laughed and shook my head, picking up the brush again. "You only say that because you won't have to be the referee."

"Yes, exactly. Hey, listen…" His voice drifted away as he watched the brush glide through my hair.

"What?"

His eyes fluttered. "What?"

I stopped brushing for a moment, leaning toward the phone. "What's with you this morning? Has the idea of buying a winery gotten you all squirrelly or something?"

His smile faltered and an uncomfortable expression crossed his face. Apparently not.

"I was just wondering…" He scratched his temple before moving through his room, the camera showing the light brown stubble on his chin. The image bounced as he set down the phone, and when it settled, I found myself staring at his chest. The urge to take a screenshot was strong. "Edgar is working on translating a part of the book that should allow you to set magical snares." To everyone's surprise, Edgar had been chosen to translate a book that acted as instruction for my magic. He had to but (laboriously) read a passage and the knowledge for that spell blossomed in me as though I'd known it all along. "He's not exactly sure what those snares might do when triggered—blow someone up, rip off a leg, sound an alarm, discreetly let you know someone has tracked through them... Can you squeeze some training in to go over it? By the way, what's the status with his flowers? I forgot to ask when I spoke to him earlier."

I stopped working the brush through my hair for a moment. His muscles lengthened and contracted as he pulled a beige shirt down over his abs.

"I can get a training in, yeah, but are you serious?" I finally asked. "You suddenly have an interest in Edgar's flowers?"

He bent until his face took up my view once again, his smile infectious. "Think I've gone native?"

"I don't think I'd be able to handle it if you turned as weird as that vampire."

He laughed. "I want to know if he's found out what's eating them. I haven't smelled anything suspicious around the property, but I want to make sure the flower prowler poses no threat." He bent until I saw the top of his head.

"You put your shirt on before your pants?" I asked, unable to help it. Watching his morning routine fascinated me.

"Yeah, don't you?"

"No, pants before shirt. Though I usually start with

panties, then a bra, then pants. Since you don't have a bra, I suppose it makes sense to go from underwear to a shirt, then on to pants... I can see that. If you put your underwear on before the shirt, that is."

His eyes found mine from beneath thick black lashes. He didn't speak for a moment, but then he straightened up, his shirt bunching as he brought his hands up to secure his pants. "I'll be shifting today, probably a few times. I'm free-balling it. One less thing to keep track of."

My face heated and I looked away, back to brushing my hair. "No purple sweats?"

"No. In case you change."

"Why should that determine your choice of pants?"

"I'm tired of the purple sweats making it seem like I've looked when I haven't."

My face flamed a little hotter. Every time I stripped before shifting, he turned completely around so he couldn't accidentally look, a courtesy I never afforded him. Even still, his sweats were always tented by the time he turned back. If Niamh was there, she'd inevitably accuse him of using a mirror to look over his shoulder. She liked to make an awkward situation worse. It was part of her charm.

"How are jeans going to help with that? I assume you're wearing jeans?"

"Jeans are uncomfortable as hell when you have a hard-on and no briefs."

"Ah. So that's the real reason you're free-balling it—trying to force self-control."

His lopsided smile was adorable. "That purple sucks, anyway. It in no way matches your other form. It's much too drab."

I laughed and stood with the phone, dropping the towel into the laundry. It would be interesting to see who came in to grab it—Mr. Tom, as usual, or my mother, whom I'd banned from doing my laundry in my teens because she shrank everything but wouldn't give me money to buy more. The ban hadn't worked. She hated seeing clothes in the laundry basket. The woman was a machine.

"When did you want to train?" I asked, flicking on the light in my spacious closet and propping up the phone on my dresser, against my jewelry box.

Austin was on the move again, walking through his house, a place I'd never been. I had only been to his cabin on the lake, a place he usually didn't tell people about.

"I have to hit the bar and put in a couple orders," he said, "but I can run and do that now. Early afternoon? Lunchtime?"

When I was sure only my face showed in the picture, my robe hit the floor and I pulled out some knickers. "Yeah, whenever. I'll probably need a break from the parents by then."

"Great. I'll just swing… What are you doing?" His tone had changed, almost aggressive.

Panties on, I paused with bra in hand. "Changing, why? You did it."

The movement behind him stopped, and a pained expression took over his face. He swore, looking to the side. "Wish you would've waited on that."

I couldn't help a smile even as heat unfurled within me. A wave of shivers coated my body from the contrasting chilled air kissing my skin. I did my best to ignore the sensation, putting on my bra. "You need to get laid, son. This is becoming a problem."

He shook his head and breathed out through his mouth. "You're a pretty lady. Can't be helped. Talk to you later. Wear a muumuu."

I laughed as the call ended, the screen going black before morphing back into his contact image. For a moment I just let myself be still, owning the confusing emotions and feelings rolling through me: heat from our exchange, pleasurable aching down low, the strange contentment of having shared our morning routines, the comfort and joy of our deepening intimacy as friends, and the worry regarding the budding longing I felt to be near him. To call him again and keep talking. To speed up time so he could get here a little faster.

"Keep it steady, Jacinta," I murmured to myself, pulling on a pair of pants and a shirt, smiling a little as I noted the order. "He's the only normal man in your life. You're clearly reacting to that as much as him as a person."

The bedroom door opened for me as I reached it.

"Thank you." I stepped through it.

"What?" Ulric walked toward me in the hall. "Me?" He grinned.

"No, sorry. The house. She hears." I made a circle in the air with my finger.

A pained expression crossed his face. "Don't tell me those things. This house is a lot to get used to. Not to shift the topic or anything, but can I come out now? It smells like bacon. Or can I at least fly out the window and hit a diner in town? If I smell bacon, I need to eat bacon. I don't think I'm alone in that."

"Give me fifteen minutes. I'll go try to explain you all to my parents first. Then yes, I'm sure there is bacon, though we'll have to make more, since my mom didn't know to cook for the house."

"It's not Mr. Tom? Damn. I was hoping he'd come around on his stance regarding bacon. Did he make a special allowance because of your parents?"

For some reason no one could understand, Mr. Tom would not allow bacon in the house. He claimed it was bad for us, which wasn't untrue, but then why were chocolate and cookies allowed? We'd all just kind of gotten over it, because we didn't want to make it ourselves.

"He conveniently forgot about it at the store, but my mom brought some in her cooler."

Ulric blinked a few times as we stopped at the top of the stairs before drawing out his words. "She…brought some…in her…cooler?"

I laughed. "Yeah, I'll explain later."

The blaring TV assaulted my eardrums before I even hit the ground floor. I made my way to the make-shift lounge and found my dad in his designated chair, his arm on the armrest, the remote in his hand. The man on the screen was casting a fishing lure into a calm lake while expounding on the best lures for big-mouth bass.

"Hey, Dad, everything good?" I asked.

"Heh?" He turned in his chair to look over his shoulder, and then turned down the TV. "Oh. Hi. Late one last night, huh?"

I moved so it was a little easier for him to see me. "Yeah, kinda. You good?"

He grunted and turned back to the TV. "Quite a

setup you've got here. Lots of sitting rooms. How many sitting rooms does one house need? Although, if the house is this big, what else are you going to put in it, I suppose. There was an orange rug in my room. Did you decorate this place?"

"No. It came furnished. Mostly."

He grunted again. "Well, I don't know about the orange. That was a big thing in the seventies, that rusted orange color."

"Yeah. You guys should've brought the color palette from your house. I could've closed my eyes and picked at random. What do you bet I'd land on brown?"

He scratched his stomach. "Nice, big house, though. Lots of room. I had to turn the TV up so I could hear it, it's so far away. Least I can see it. I should get a new TV. What's this picture? A bunch of pixels, right?"

I lifted my eyebrows. "Yes. Lots of pixels, you've got it."

"Yeah. We still got that old one you gave us. It's not as clear as this one."

"Put it on your Christmas list. Do you need any-thing in here? We've got a big garden if you want to check that out. There's even a hedge maze."

"A what?" He muted the TV. "A hedge maze? What is that?"

"A big maze made out of...hedges. They're like

thick bushes but really tall, and they're used to form the walls of a maze." His blank stare said he still wasn't getting it. "A corn maze, like in pumpkin patches, but made out of bushes and in my backyard."

"You have a nice garden, huh?"

Clearly he wasn't interested in discussing backyard mazes. It was probably a little too weird for his taste.

"Yes. Nice, big garden," I said, just trying to go with the flow.

"That bed is awfully soft, the one in the guest room? I'm not used to soft beds. I kept waking up. Or maybe it was the thumping above me. Probably a rat. Old houses like this have lots of vermin. Our house had a mouse problem a while back. I'll set some traps, don't you worry. If there is one thing I know how to do, it's how to get rid of vermin."

"Oh no, no, that's okay, Dad. Thanks. We don't have rats. That might've been Mr. Tom, the butler. He was probably—"

His finger hovered over the remote, about to un-mute the TV. "Is it Tom or Edgar?"

"Mr. Tom is the butler, and Edgar is the gardener. Remember the guy with the dentures?" Given Edgar's issue with retracting his fangs, we'd called them out as malfunctioning dentures when he'd come in yesterday afternoon to meet the folks. Thankfully he hadn't said much, keeping those chompers mostly under wraps.

"Oh yeah, the balding guy with dandruff. I use Head & Shoulders. Got rid of that problem. I told him so." He snapped. "Earl. Irish lady called your butler Earl."

"Yeah, Mr. Tom is kind of a nickname. He'd like it if you used that."

My dad's brows knitted together. He unmuted the TV and turned back to the fishing program. Apparently that didn't make much sense to him, and now he planned to ignore it and the hedge maze both. Hopefully he did that for all the weird stuff he was bound to run into.

"Okay, well, let me know if you need anything," I said.

My mother was in the kitchen, her half-moon glasses perched on the edge of her nose as she looked up at the top oven, the house having two stacked on top of each other.

"Hey, Mom."

She glanced over, smiled, and then returned to studying the buttons. "You had a late one, huh? I'm just trying to figure out how to do the warm setting. Do you want some breakfast? I made enough for your butler and gardener and the Irish rock thrower, too, but the butler hasn't come in since I started making breakfast, and none of the others have stopped by. How about your friend from last night? The big, burly man. He's certainly handsome. Are you two dating?"

"Austin? No. It's right here, Mom, the one that says 'warm' on it." I pushed the button for her.

"Oh yeah. Warm. That's a good hint." She pulled open the oven and extracted the plates covered in grease-coated napkins. Why she was looking for the button to warm when about to take out the food was beyond me. "I couldn't find any paper plates. I'll get some at the store today."

"No, it's fine. We have real plates. Mr. Tom prefers—"

"And paper towels. You could use more paper towels. You don't care what kind I get, do you?"

"No, honestly, Mom, it's fine. Mr. Tom—"

Ulric popped into the doorway with a smile.

"Honey, look out!" My mother shoved me, grabbed a potato off the counter, and chucked it, all in a fast collection of somewhat rickety movements. Despite the way it was launched, that sucker flew true, directly for Ulric's head.

"Holy—" Ulric bent to the side, batting the flying spud away. "I'm friendly! I'm friendly!"

"Martha, what's going on in there?" my dad hollered from the other room.

"Mom, oh my God, he lives here!" Half shocked and

half trying not to laugh, I put up my hands and danced between them. "That's Ulric. He's staying here for the moment. *At* the moment."

"What?" She incrementally lowered the second potato, having reloaded in a hurry.

"I live here, ma'am." Ulric stayed put, not attempting to step any farther into the kitchen.

The laughter finally bubbled over. "Really, Mom? A potato? You wouldn't pick up a knife or something heavy…"

"Good aim, though." Ulric beamed. "Now we know where Jessie gets her fierce streak. You should take up rock slinging with Niamh."

My glare shut him up.

"Who is he?" my mom asked, finally lowering her weapon.

Jasper stepped in beside Ulric, his expression one of deep interest. "I smell bacon."

I widened my eyes. It clearly took bacon to get him to say full sentences.

"Mom, meet Ulric and Jasper. Cedric—a youngish guy named Cedric—is also living here. At the moment."

"Oh." My mom dropped the potato onto the counter. "Well, it is a big house. And you didn't get *that* much in the divorce settlement, did you? I guess it makes sense to take on a few roommates. But Jessie, why not just buy a smaller house? I'm sure there must be something you can afford in this area—"

"Oh no, ma'am, you have it all wrong." Ulric took a seat at the island. "You see, we're doing a sort of work exchange program. Jessie here has a large property—with extensive woods—and we're all in the same doctorate program studying the global effect woods have on our ecosystem. Well, Jessie was nice enough to put us up for a few months so we can study her trees for the experience portion of our program." He spread his arms with a smile. "Just a bunch of tree-hugging fellas, that's us."

Wow. Ulric was really good at making up stories on the fly.

"Austin recommended them," I said, going with it. It probably should've occurred to me before now to have something worked out. "He looked into their backgrounds and everything."

"Oh, Austin did?" She pondered that for a moment. "He seemed to have a good head on his shoulders." Her gaze snagged on Ulric's hair. "Well, I have some breakfast ready if you want some."

"Yes, ma'am."

"Yes, please." Jasper joined Ulric at the island.

"Speaking of…" I leveled a pointer finger at them. "Austin wanted to check out some things later today.

Trees. The woods, I mean." I wasn't great at lying. "He asked if I'd help. You guys should probably join."

"Yeah, sure." Ulric tracked my mom's movements. "After breakfast."

I just hoped I didn't blow anyone else up. How would I explain a charred gargoyle to my parents?

CHAPTER 5

AUSTIN STEPPED OUT of the Jeep, fatigue dragging at him. The bar was a lot busier now that he'd taken on the alpha role, people rolling in from all over, wanting to congregate in what they deemed the new magical epicenter of the area. Austin had had no idea the people around here were craving a larger magical presence. There wasn't a strictly magical town for hundreds of miles, and no other alphas anywhere close. Or maybe they wanted a more organized magical presence. Whatever the reason, they'd been coming to the bar in droves, their presence signaling to Austin that he should extend his territory. So far, it was three towns, but given the growing patronage, soon it would probably be five.

He needed to establish a pack. Usually a territory didn't grow this fast. People tended to balk from accepting a new authority figure. Of course, he wasn't exactly new, and his situation was far from normal. He should've thought of that before making the switch.

"Can I be in your pack? I promise I won't bring Mr. Tom."

Goosebumps rolled across his skin, and he stopped just before stepping over Ivy House's territory line.

"Give me a minute," he murmured, hoping the house would hear him. It knew he was there because of his magical connection to it, but Jess wouldn't. Not until he stepped over that invisible line. Out of habit, or maybe a respect for his privacy, she only tapped in to their magical connection if she was worried about him, or worried about herself and counting on him.

He hadn't been so respectful of her privacy. He had his side of that magical connection open twenty-four seven, mostly out of fear for her safety. Without an established pack to watch the borders of the territory, she was open for attack. He'd gotten that wake-up call a few months ago when a few teams of mages had waltzed in, watched the town, and made off with its prize. Jess. He would not close the connection until she was ten times more secure.

The other reason? He didn't really like thinking about that.

He hooked his thumbs through his belt loops and turned toward the street, taking in the nice day and noticing the trunk on Jessie's parents' car wasn't latched properly. As he walked over to inspect it, he saw the handmade bumper sticker—a piece of computer paper cut into a strip and taped on. It read:

I leave the trunk open
so the wife can breathe.

Surprised laughter bubbled up through him. Those two were a trip, *so* much different than the serious household he'd grown up in.

"Hey." Niamh stepped out onto her porch, an empty sack in hand for carrying their clothes once they shifted. "What're ye at?" She closed her door behind her. "Ye look like ye just got stabbed with a pitchfork, so ye do."

He ambled toward her, in no hurry, soaking in the sun and the quiet street. "I'm good. Need to work with Jess on the new spell Edgar pulled from the book. Did he mention it?"

"Yes." She paused next to her chair and checked her rocks. Seeing they were accounted for, she walked down her porch steps and across a little patch of cultivated grass Edgar must manage, because no way would Niamh be bothered. "He wouldn't stop going on about it. He's delighted the alpha of the town called him directly. He kept saying that—the *alpha of the town*—as though ye aren't also a part of Ivy House. He thinks of ye as royalty, the muppet. The hemming and hawing out of him would drive a person mad." She rolled her eyes. "Did ye hear?" Niamh commenced a slow pace across the street toward Ivy House.

"About what?"

"Jessie's mom. Got startled by the pink-haired one and threw a potato at his head."

Niamh knew Ulric's name, but since he wasn't officially on the team, she treated him like an intern. It was actually quite hilarious.

"She tried to hit Ulric with a potato..." There were at least five follow-up questions Austin needed to ask, but his mind split in too many directions to grab one of them.

"Yeah. He startled her, and she grabbed the closest thing at hand." Niamh huffed out a laugh. "Would've hit him in the face, too. Slow, though. He saw it coming."

"She's an older Jane."

"Yeah. Who hasn't battled. Good aim, though. And did ye hear the el' lad the other day? Gettin' ready to grab a rock himself and help me with those tourists?" She nodded slowly. "Jessie comes from fire."

"We could've guessed."

"It's funnier to see it in action."

He had to concede that.

"Edgar told you what the spell was?" he asked her, getting them back on track.

"Yeah, the tripwire. He's thinking the base spell is a simple tattletale situation. Anyone crosses the line, and the spell weaver—Jessie, obviously—will be alerted. The trespasser won't be the wiser."

"The base spell. So she could alter it, then?"

"He thinks so, yeah." She paused at the threshold to Ivy House's property line, turning back to look over the street like he'd just done. He wasn't sure why she was dragging her feet.

He wasn't sure why he was, either.

"The text will draw out her ability to create the spell, but she'll need to alter it on her own," Niamh said.

"That's for the best. Start with something non-dangerous, and then work at changing it through study and practice."

She made a dismissive gesture. "All this learning magic is bollocks. It would be easier if she came already knowing everything so she could start throwing her weight around."

"Weren't you the one talking about retiring?"

"That was before I got the energy of youth—"

"Martha!" Pete's voice rang out across the front yard, originating from an open window on the second floor. "Martha, your glasses are in here!"

"Oh, how'd you get that window open?" Martha's face appeared behind the screen. "I tried earlier and it wouldn't budge."

"I didn't open it. It was open when I got up here. You must've gotten it open and forgot. Do you know how to work that shower?"

"Yes. Turn it toward H. For hot." Her voice drifted away as she probably moved into the bathroom to show him, clearly not having seen Austin and Niamh standing on the sidewalk.

"Or Ivy House opened it for them when they weren't paying attention," Niamh murmured, head tilted up, watching the newly empty window. "I don't trust that house not to cause a little mischief."

"You think Ivy House is going to out Jess?" Austin asked.

Niamh's gaze roamed the large expanse of the building. "Maybe not *out* her, but it's already messing with them. The images in the wooden carvings changed at least twice yesterday evening, and I only noticed because her el' lad was staring. He thought something was off, I could surely tell. Didn't pass any remarks, though. Noticed, then looked away. If I had to bet on it, I'll say that Ivy House will aim for something a little more obvious just to see what happens. This is the same house that likes to send people sprinting out of it in horror."

Austin had to concede that point. Despite technically being an inanimate object, the house had a mind of its own.

He took a deep breath and eyed the front door. Time to get the show on the road.

"Dreading going in there, huh?" Niamh said.

Yes. Because, if he was being really honest with himself, he knew that once he went in, he wouldn't want to leave. Heading home alone lately had seemed like a punishment. His solo lifestyle wasn't a comfort to him anymore. He kept reaching for the phone, wanting to talk to Jess or invite her to the bar, even on his nights off. Maybe especially on his nights off, when he could devote more time to her. He'd never had a friend like her, even when he was younger. He'd never thought about anyone this much.

He'd never been so wary of someone changing his life so completely since walking away from Destiny, the woman who had nearly ruined him.

"Dreading trying out Jess's spell and potentially getting blown up again," he deflected.

A motor started up from somewhere behind Ivy House.

"Ah, here. C'mere. This'll take your mind off things." Niamh plucked at his shirt.

He glanced at the front door, feeling Jess moving around inside, somewhat annoyed, probably from dealing with Mr. Tom or maybe her parents. He felt the pull of her, the need to be with her, to train her. Coaxing the magic out of her and watching her shape it into something magnificent... He was probably the luckiest man on earth. Every time they trained, he could see envy in the faces of the gathered gargoyles, wishing they'd been granted the rare privilege. Probably envious of Jess's smiles when she mastered a particularly complex spell, or the way she fawned over him when she hit him with something nasty. The pain was worth her apologies, worth her touch as she inspected the damage, worth the pleasing feel of her magic as she healed his ailments.

He blew out a breath and rubbed the back of his neck.

"Yeah, okay." He started after Niamh, who surprised him by heading for the side of the house. "Where are we going?"

"Edgar is going to mow the yard." Niamh picked up the pace.

He didn't bother asking why he should care. Why *she* did. The people of this house were strange. Jessie had told him it was easier to roll with it, and he'd found that to be true.

At the property line, he paused for a brief moment before finally stepping over it. Almost immediately, he felt a surge of recognition from Jess, followed by…dare he say pleasure? She was happy he had come.

He hated how good that felt.

At the back corner of the house, Niamh crouched beside a large bush with blooming red and white flowers. About fifty feet away, on what looked like his second trip across the lush green grass, Edgar pushed an older-style lawn mower, green flying up in its wake, coating his purple sweats. Pollen tickled Austin's nose, and the overwhelming floral scent slapped around his senses. The vampire had gone way overboard with the flowers. *Way* overboard. The basajaun eating up the garden had addled the vampire's brain. *Further* addled it, he should say.

"Why doesn't Edgar get a mower that has a bag to catch the grass?" he asked. "Or hell, get a ride-on mower. Mowing all this grass and the lawn up front must take him forever."

"If there is anything that vampire has, it is time. He likes to fill up his days. He mows, then he rakes up the fresh-cut grass, then he prunes, then he fancies around with the flowers…"

"He should probably spend more time learning to make doilies if he ever hopes to get one halfway decent."

She huffed out a laugh. "Seen those, did ye? Yeah, he's hopeless. I burn 'em in the winter just so he has a reason to give me more. It keeps him busy."

Something metallic clattered within the mower. Edgar paused and stared down at the machine for a moment before looking behind him.

"Keep moving, ye gobshite. A little farther. Don't get suspicious," Niamh murmured, riveted to Edgar.

"What are you hoping for?" Austin whispered.

"Just wait," she said.

Another object clattered through the mower, followed by a third, pinging and clacking around the parts before rattling out the back and flying up at Edgar's body. More followed, sounding like metal popcorn popping. The vampire yelped and then jumped before pushing the handle forward again, staring at the grass in front of the mower.

Niamh began to chuckle. "Janey Mack. Only he would keep going."

A flurry of pings and pops now, more foreign objects rolling through the cutters and gears of the lawn mower. The sun caught their exit, glittering on metal, before what looked like a host of little spikes stabbed into Edgar's legs.

He screamed and jumped, dancing in place like someone was shooting at his feet. He pushed the lawn mower forward again, sending another score of metal projectiles through the machine and at him. He shrank back from the onslaught but didn't move to the side to get out of the way, opening himself up for some body shots, the small slices of metal stabbing into his stomach and upper arms.

"Nooo!" he howled, his face pointed toward the sky, but he persisted in pushing forward, doing nothing to stopper the flow.

The absurdity of the scene, and Niamh's helpless laugher, brought forth chuckles from Austin.

In the house, he felt Jess run toward the back door, anxiety pooling within her. Someone (or several someones) was on her heels, though he couldn't feel who. While he did have a magical connection of sorts to the other protectors, he barely felt them when he tried and not at all when he didn't, and he didn't have much of the ability to sense who moved around Ivy House. He wondered if that trait was only granted to people who actually lived on or near the property. He was fine doing without.

Finally stopped for a moment, Edgar plucked one of the items from his person and studied it for a moment. He slipped it into his pocket and looked down at his legs, the lawn mower idling, the rotors surely still turning in that older machine. In a feat of perseverance or stupidity or both, Edgar slowly grabbed the handle and bent to push it forward.

"He's going ta keep going, the donkey." Niamh leaned forward, shaking with laughter. "What is he at? He's a fair queer one, all right."

"What's in the grass?"

"Nails." She guffawed into her cupped hand. "I half hammered a bunch of nails into the ground."

"Why?" he asked Niamh, utterly bewildered. Or maybe he was asking the question of the cosmos.

"Just to keep him on his toes, sure. 'Tis good to have some wee danger in our everyday lives."

More spikes rolled through the machine. The vampire yelled, dancing again, but continued to push the mower, crying out with each new onslaught. Austin couldn't look away.

Jess ran out from the back door and into the grass, headed for Edgar.

Austin was moving before he'd consciously thought of it, exploding out of the bushes and running to cut her off.

"No, no, Jessie." Edgar put out his hand, still pushing the mower, amazingly enough. He looked like he was tap-dancing. "This is a dangerous job. Don't approach."

Austin caught Jess when she was within feet of Edgar, ripping her up off the ground and holding her against his chest to stop her from going any farther. She twisted within his grasp, trying to see Edgar. Ulric and Jasper flanked Austin, faces hard as they scanned Edgar's shimmering body, specks of shining metal amid seeping black blood.

"Oh, gross, vampires bleed black?" Jess said, clearly unable to help herself. A beautiful blush seeped into her cheeks. "I mean…"

"What is the meaning of this?" Earl jogged out next. "Edgar, what is happening? Has the lawn mower attacked you? Why are you screaming?"

"It's…" Edgar finally shut off the mower and then looked down at his legs, one hand still on the handle. "I'm not sure. It seems there is something in the grass. Have no fear, Jessie. I will root them all up and throw them away so no one will step on them. I'd hate for someone to be enjoying the lovely day and get one of these stuck in their feet."

"There has to be an easier way to root up whatever they are," Ulric said, a smile spreading across his face.

"They're nails," Niamh said, catching up. She point-ed at the ground in front of the mower. "Look like 'em, anyway. I wonder how those got there…"

Austin glanced at her. She put her finger to the side of her neck and pulled it across her throat. "Snitches get stitches," she mouthed. She clearly did not care about his higher status within the Ivy House council.

"Oh. Nails?" Edgar moved out from behind the mower.

Jess pointed at his legs, his sweats tacked to his thighs and shins. Her mouth opened, but no words came out.

Edgar put his hands on his hips and bent, surveying the ground. He reached down, gripped one of the offending spikes with his fingernails, and pulled it out. "So they are. Yes, how strange. I wonder if whatever has been eating my flowers has also taken to nailing the grass down."

Jess wiggled in Austin's arms, asking to be put down. He released her, feeling her slide down his body until she was standing on her own. Uncomfortable, parts of him aching but thankfully not showing it, he stepped away and clasped his hands behind his back.

"Something is still eating your flowers?" Jess asked, looking at the ground below her feet. "Would anything that ate flowers also hammer nails into the grass? That doesn't sound plausible."

"Stranger things have happened around here." Edgar looked toward his cottage, and it was anyone's guess what he was talking about, but if it had been initiated by a person, Austin suspected that person was probably

Niamh.

"Show me the newest flowers that have been eaten," Austin said, ignoring the nails.

Jess glanced from Edgar to Austin. "Can you handle the flower situation while I go show my dad where the towels and everything are, and then we can chat about it?"

"Sure."

She pointed at Edgar. "Are you okay? You've still got…nails stuck in you."

Niamh put a fist in front of her mouth, shaking with suppressed laughter. Jess finally noticed, and a knowing gleam lit her eyes. She shook her head.

"One thing at a time," she murmured as she turned. "I'll be back."

"Miss," Mr. Tom said, hurrying after her as if seeing his window of opportunity narrow. "This is a good chance to talk to you without that woman always underfoot."

"That's my mom, Mr. Tom, be nice."

"Yes, miss, I know, and she is a lovely woman…except when she is stealing the laundry out from under me. Why, she even took *my* laundry! She shrank my favorite pair of purple sweats." They reached the back door, and Mr. Tom grabbed the handle and pulled it open for Jess. "Have you seen the refrigerator?

Condiments everywhere! No rhyme or reason—"

The door shut behind them.

"Sounds like it's going well," Niamh said, her eyes teary from laughter. "That Earl could do with a little razzing, too."

"When did you become a practical joker?" Austin asked, motioning for Edgar to lead the way. He seemed completely oblivious of the implications of what they were saying.

"Do ye need to ask? I got the promise of an action-filled life, and instead find myself looking at half-eaten flowers in the biggest swamp of daisies I've ever seen in my godforsaken life." Niamh tagged along with them.

"There aren't that many daisies. Besides, they add a nice pop of white," Edgar said, leading them to a patch of tulips cut through with lilies and speckled with the aforementioned daisies. The garden was starting to look like his doilies.

The last row of crowded flowers *did* have a noticeable bare spot, the green stems ending abruptly, the buds or petals stripped away entirely. The rough breaks in flora bespoke teeth, the cuts not even and the ends smashed. The missing flowers were clustered together, as though an animal had been grazing.

"The basajaun made a much bigger mess," Austin said, bending to sniff. The flowers were so plentiful that they overwhelmed his senses, any other scents completely washed out. He coughed with the onslaught, then sneezed three times in quick succession, his eyes watering.

Edgar put a hand on his heart and bowed his head. "I do, of course, believe Jessie when she says it is not likely that basajaun. I do not doubt her for a moment. She is not the type of person to lie…"

"But?" Austin asked.

"Well." Edgar grasped his hands in front of him. "It's just that the basajaun did only eat the flowers, not the stems. He made an awful mess when he was *permitted* to eat the flowers, but at the moment he does not have permission, so maybe he is showing restraint. I can't think of anyone else that could sneak onto these lands without anyone knowing. Ivy House would alert us if it were anyone dangerous, though her lax treatment of flower theft is a dereliction of duty, in my opinion, even if it *was* deer. Which it still could be, even though deer poop gets all over. I haven't seen any poop."

"All animals poop," Austin said, trying to step lightly through the flowers. A calla lily crunched under his boot. Edgar drew in a sharp breath. "I don't see any tracks."

"Correct. No hooves. Deer leave hoofprints—"

"We get it," Niamh said. "You don't think it's a deer."

"The basajaun didn't leave any tracks when he ransacked my flowers the first time," Edgar said. "Their magic keeps them from being detected in that way. No poop, and no tracks."

Austin turned as Jess reemerged from the house in a flowing tent of a dress that blew against her side and outlined a shapely hip. He meant to turn away, his body tightening, but instead followed the outline to the swell of her full breast, unencumbered by a bra. A familiar ache overcame him as he watched her legs churn the fabric, sucking it into creases he'd dreamt of exploring. With his tongue.

He ripped his gaze away and scrubbed his fingers through his hair. "I'll speak to Jess. Maybe it's time to head up the mountain. That basajaun has a soft spot for her. I doubt it'll lie."

"Speak to me about what?" she said as she reached them.

"Visiting your hairy friend on his mountain. Maybe you can finally try your hand at scaring hikers."

He earned a smile. "I'd be up for it. But we have to be back by dinner or my mother will pitch a fit."

Austin looked back at the house, seeing Cedric jogging toward them, often late to the party, Earl not in tow. "No Earl?"

She rolled her eyes, resting her hand on his arm and nudging him toward the trees.

"No," she said dryly, steering him deeper into the wood with the rest falling in behind them, Ulric and Jasper flanking the group. "He's staying behind to, quote, make the parents more comfortable, unquote. What he's really doing is protecting his interests. He doesn't like that my mom is cooking and cleaning. It's stressing him out. I think he is determined to wait on her whether she likes it or not. Unfortunately, she has the same end game with him. She's about to go to the grocery store and Mr. Tom is trying to head her off. It's warfare in there."

"It's funny," Ulric said. "They are out-helping each other. Jessie's mom doesn't seem to notice the tiff, but Mr. Tom is getting more wound up by the second."

"It's only funny because it isn't your mom and butler," Jess said.

"This is true."

She curled her hand around Austin's arm. "This close enough?" She looked up at him as they walked, using her other hand to pull out the deep brown fabric covering her athletic frame. "You said to wear a muumuu, right?" She laughed, clearly delighted. "It's actually a great idea for when we change. One piece of clothing, no stress."

"That is a good idea," Niamh said. "Have Earl order me one or two. Something other than brown, though. You look like a stack of turd."

"No undies? For shame," Ulric cried. "What has happened to your modesty?"

"You've all ruined me," Jess replied, laughing.

Austin gritted his teeth, trying not to think about what was under that drab brown fabric.

He stopped, ripped off his shirt, and tossed it at Niamh to put in the sack. "Let's get to it. We don't want to be late for dinner."

CHAPTER 6

P ETE SAT ON an overly hot blanket that unfortunately made his begonias sweat in the pretty comfortable, though a little stiff, armchair, watching a huge TV with crystal-clear clarity that hinted at the finer things in life. Amazing how a few more pixels meant all the difference at halftime.

He glanced at the wooden fireplace mantel, a pretty neat old-school carving that really lent some class to the place. Real craftsmanship had gone into that mantel; he could tell by the quality work and attention to detail. Unfortunately, that attention to detail was starting to wear on his grasp of reality.

He'd first checked it out last night, after sitting in this same chair. At the time, he'd thought the scene was of a mountain meadow with a sun, some trees, and a lone man carrying a spear, or maybe a woman with small tits. It had reminded him of those cave drawings in *National Geographic*. Obviously the carving had been a little more fleshed out—no stick figures—but the spear had definitely hearkened to more primitive times.

This morning, though, the scene was completely different. It showed a log cabin in a prairie-like setting with some kids sitting around the fire. There was no way he would've thought a log cabin in a prairie was like a cave painting—that just didn't make sense. Why would cavemen envision a house when they lived in a cave? Either he'd had too much hooch last night, or he'd seen some other carving in the house and thought it was in this room.

The last was highly likely. They were everywhere, the carvings, in almost every downstairs room.

Except the same thing had happened in that front-facing sitting room last night, the one he'd sat in before moving to the TV room. He could have sworn the images had changed. It had started out as a grisly scene someone should've gotten fired over, and the next moment it was a high mountain tableau with a couple of blackbirds. Later…something else. He couldn't remember what. It hadn't been blackbirds, at any rate. He would've noticed. Blackbirds were a nuisance. He hated seeing them, even in wooden carvings.

Maybe he was just overtired. That car ride had been long, made longer by Martha getting them lost. She did not understand these new high-tech phones with the built-in navigation. Either she'd pick the wrong address in an entirely different city, or she'd forget to tell him when to turn (she hated using the voice option but constantly missed the cues).

Another glance reassured him the prairie scene was still there, so that was a good sign. He couldn't afford to crack up. He was nearly positive Martha would check him into a home if he lost his faculties.

Think of the devil…

She walked into the room, wringing her hands with an anxious look on her face.

"He just will not let me help." She huffed and sat down in the chair next to his, separated by a small end table, and looked absently at the TV. "He made us lunch, he got us drinks, he cleaned up—he is really going out of his way for us. The least I can do is clean up the kitchen for him. But no, he hustled me right out. It is bad enough he fought me to pay for the groceries. It really is too much. Entirely too much."

"He's the butler. That's what he does."

Martha clucked her tongue. "Butler." She shook her head. "Who do we know that has a butler?"

"Jessie, apparently. He's as old as the hills. He'll probably drop dead before we leave the place."

"Oh, Pete, that's terrible." She would've swatted him if she'd been closer.

He slid a glance at the carving, careful not to be noticed. Still a prairie. He issued a soft sigh.

"How can she afford a butler?" Martha said, straightening the already straightened coasters.

"I'll bet he works for cheap. He's probably worried that if he retires now he'll die—"

"Pete, would you stop?"

"She didn't want to kill him off by putting him out of a job."

"I swear, you're terrible. He's not that much older than us. The gardener is…somewhat…up in his years, though."

"He is *much* older than us, and that gardener looks like a walking corpse. They were probably a two-for-one deal. It's a real motley crew Jessie has hanging around this place."

"Yes, but how can she afford them *and* this big old house?"

"Cheap area—cheaper than we're used to, at any rate—and you said it yourself: it's old. She probably got it for a steal. That Peggy woman probably gave it away. It's going to need all sorts of repairs."

"She does have those nice gentleman for roommates at the moment. That's something. She certainly has the space for them. Though what is this house's love of capes, I'll never know." She clucked her tongue again. "A butler. No, that's just absurd. Our Jessie isn't the type to have a butler. Can you imagine?" She sucked in a breath. "Oh, Pete, what if they are dating? What if—"

"He'd die if anything got physical. I don't think you need to worry about that."

A pop caught his attention on the opposite side of the wooden mantelpiece, which, mercifully, still showed the carving of the prairie. He glanced over, finding a new crack running up from the ground to about door height, where it zipped to the side in another straight line. If he hadn't been in full possession of his mental faculties, he would have said it looked an awful lot like a door. A secret door, into some sort of bluish glowing area inside the wall.

"Do you see? The house is old. It's falling apart." He pulled his gaze away lest it open a little more. A crack he could handle. A door opening by itself he could not.

A pitter-patter thumped across the ceiling, like a toddler running on the floor above.

He and Martha both looked up.

"I sure hope that's not a rat," Martha said.

"That would be an awfully big rat."

"Remember that movie with those large rats? This house might have something like that, only those rats existed in swamps."

Sometimes he had no idea what his wife was talking about, but he'd learned early on in their marriage that it was best just to agree.

"Uh-huh," he said, directing his gaze back to the TV.

She stood as the thumping sounded a second time, the pitter-patter moving back the other way.

"I hope she's not hiding a child somewhere in this house," Martha said, walking to the newly formed crack in the wall and shoving at it. It clicked shut, like a door latching.

There shouldn't be a door in the wall that randomly opened by itself. Especially not one that glowed an eerie blue. There had to be another explanation.

He snuck a glance at the fireplace. Prairie. Clearly he'd imagined the different scene or noticed it elsewhere in the house—that was the only explanation.

"If this place is falling apart, it'll be expensive to fix." Martha looked up and down the wall. The crack was completely gone, the wall flush. If Martha hadn't seen it as well, he would've thought he was seeing things. She couldn't put him in a home if she was seeing the same things. Still, he'd best ignore it, just in case.

"She's a grown woman, Martha. She knows what she's doing," he said, turning up the volume.

"Well." Out of the corner of his eye, he could see her put her hands on her hips. She was getting stubborn. "I'm going to do some dusting. Surely a butler up in his years takes ages to get around to everything. Since he won't let me braise the roast, at least I can find another way to be of help."

"'Don't call me Shirley,'" he said out of reflex, quoting the movie *Airplane!*

The pitter-patter sounded for the third time.

"And I will check out whatever that is. God, I hope she isn't hiding some sort of love child," she muttered, heading out. "We haven't seen her for a while. Maybe she adopted. Lord only knows what she's gotten up to. Starting a new life might've addled her brain, poor dear…"

Her voice trailed off, so Pete didn't hear where her train of thought led her, but he suspected it would somehow end where it always did—with Martha wondering if all his marbles were still rolling around in his head.

He chanced a glance at that mantel, just for grins.

An utterly flat piece of wood waited for him, no carvings or designs or anything, except for a woman in the center, staring at him.

"O-kay." He flicked off the TV, placed the remote on the little table next to his chair, and stood. Time to get some air. He'd check out the garden first, and deal with the rat infestation later. There would be no re-homing him, thank you very much. He just had to get a grip on reality and then he'd be all set. No better place than a garden to clear his head and regroup. There was very little in a garden that had ever been able to shock him.

CHAPTER 7

I TOUCHED DOWN, out of breath, having flown to and from the mountain where the basajaun lived. Unfortunately, it was a large mountain, and we hadn't been able to find him quickly enough. With dinner fast approaching, we'd decided to head home and look for him later.

Changing from my gargoyle form to my human form was a breeze now. It was slightly more difficult to pretend it was natural and comfortable to walk around nude within a group.

I tried to keep from covering myself as Ulric changed into his human form and reached into the sack of clothes he'd carried for the group, making it so Niamh didn't have to wear it around her neck.

"Jessie, here." He tossed my shapeless brown dress to me.

I shrugged it on as the others changed. Edgar was the only one who didn't have to change, but I could tell he was grateful for the chance to take some deep breaths to calm down after being dangled above the ground by one of the gargoyles. He wasn't very keen on heights.

"Where's Austin?" Niamh asked, not at all worried that she was still partway through changing. I was the only one who seemed to care about the whole naked thing.

As if on cue, the enormous snow-white polar bear cut through the trees ahead, nearing the patch of flowers that had been munched on. For such a large creature, he was eerily silent, but he was venturing a little too close to the edge of the wood for my liking. I doubted my parents would be staring out the windows at the back of the house, and even if they were, the long shadows should mask Austin's movements, but just in case...

I started forward to meet him, wanting to look at his wounds again anyway. We'd practiced the tripwire spell before heading out, and it hadn't gone well—or rather it had gone too well. Austin had insisted he was fine before we left for the mountain, but I knew for a fact that the guy could handle a great deal of pain. I'd attempted to heal him from the air, but I'd sensed it wasn't working properly from that height, especially with my level of fatigue. If he was still in pain, I wanted to do whatever I could to help.

"It bears repeating that the basajaun might not have

been on his mountain because he's been here, robbing the flowers," Edgar mumbled.

"If he's been here so recently, Austin will smell him," Niamh replied, "and so ye can shut it."

"Amen," Cedric said. "I still don't understand why you are so worried about those flowers. You have a million of them. Only a small portion are being eaten in a place they shouldn't even be planted. Why not just forget about it?"

"Why don't I just…" Edgar scoffed indignantly, and I tuned him out. If Cedric didn't know not to question Edgar's idiosyncrasies, there was no help for him.

The flare of light from Austin's shift back into human made me squint, and the searing heat coated my front. It only lasted a moment, and then he stood facing me, his chest rising and falling with fatigue. I'd made everyone fly slowly, and thanks to Ivy House magic, he had the stamina of a twenty-year-old. He shouldn't be this winded, which meant…

I tore down my block on our magical connection, allowing me to check in with his emotions and, most importantly, his pain level. A swell of agony made me stagger. The speed and distance had clearly made Austin exponentially worse than when we'd set out, but he hadn't cried uncle or slowed down.

Jasper was by my side in an instant, his hand on my

arm, steadying me.

"You good?" Jasper asked, crowding my side, peering down into my face.

"Was the flight too long?" Ulric hurried over.

"I'm fine. It isn't me. It's Austin." I shrugged Jasper off, reaching Austin a moment later. "You idiot. What were you doing? I could've stopped and healed—"

The words died on my lips. My dad stood twenty paces away, a daisy in one hand and his other hanging limp at his side. He stared at Austin, frozen, his face slack and his eyes wide. He'd seen him shift. He'd seen a polar bear where no polar bear should be, then watched as it changed into a man.

"Dad?" I said, stepping forward quickly, almost positive the blood was draining from my face.

He blinked rapidly a few times as I marched through the rows of clustered flowers, wondering how the hell I was going to talk my way out of this one. Someone else followed me, and a glance confirmed it was Ulric, who was great at spinning a tale out of thin air.

"Hey, Dad, whatcha doin'?" I stopped in front of him.

He cocked his head before swinging his face to me slowly. He cleared his throat. "I was just checking out the gardens. Why do you let him plant so many flowers?

I can barely breathe through the smell back here. Up near the house, though, he has some really good-looking rosebushes. I'd like to get his secret on those. I can't keep the deer from eating mine."

"Yeah, totally. He loves talking about flowers. Say, listen, you looked a little shaken up a moment ago. You okay?" I reached back and touched Ulric's arm, a silent cue to get ready.

"Well, I'll tell you what." Dad huffed. "You were all over me about airing out my begonias, but you don't say boo to your friend there, doing the exact same thing. You see? I know what I'm about. If a young, fit man like that needs a little air on his nether regions, don't you think I do, too?"

It was my turn to stare and then blink rapidly, my mouth hanging open and my eyebrows at my hairline. "His...begonias?"

"Yes. Look at him there, letting it all hang out. Sometimes a man just needs to air out the bells and tackle."

"This is true, sir," Ulric said, and I could've kicked him. My father didn't need a green light to walk around naked.

"Anything...else on your mind?" I asked tentatively.

"Yeah, that butler is in charge of dinner, and I think it'll actually be ready when your mother said it would.

It's a Christmas miracle."

"Christmas miracle?" Ulric said.

"You kids better wash up." My dad nodded, turned, and strode for the house as though nothing too crazy had gone on.

"Maybe he didn't see," I said, watching him go, the daisy still in his hand.

"Maybe..." Ulric said. "But he could see Austin standing in the trees, and a naked man is a lot less conspicuous than a polar bear."

"But...wouldn't he say something?"

"Jessie, we could use your help over here," Niamh called.

"I'm good." Not one ounce of pain made it into Austin's words, and yet I could feel that he was nearly crippled with it. I'd really gotten him good with way more power than I'd known I possessed. Ivy House must've increased my access again, apparently under the impression I could handle it. And maybe I could, but Austin was another story. Thank God he'd been in his bear form when he tripped that magical wire.

"Hand me my clothes," he said.

"*Jessie*," Niamh said.

Forgetting about my dad for the time being, I jogged back to Austin, standing tall and proud, acting the part of the tough guy who didn't feel pain. Even though I knew better.

"I got this." I took Austin's clothes from Niamh, who'd picked up the sack Ulric had dropped a moment ago. "Everyone else hit the showers. Oh…" I snapped and pointed at each of them in turn. "You can try the clam dip, but don't eat much of it. It's a hot commodity in my family. She didn't make enough for this many people."

"No, thanks." Ulric made a face and started walking toward the house. Jasper and Cedric followed, with Niamh close behind.

"Jessie, did I hear correctly that your father wanted to speak with me?" I nodded, and Edgar edged closer. "I hadn't intended to go in for dinner. Maybe I'll just pop in afterward?"

"That's fine, Edgar. Or chat with him tomorrow."

"Oh." Edgar smiled, his fangs tucked away, for once, and his teeth whiter than I remembered. He must've asked Agnes for an elixir that would help. He'd really been putting in an effort to pass for normal with the parents staying. "That's a much better idea, yes. I think I'll just grab a spot in the woods somewhere and watch what comes by."

"You'll want to mask your smell," Austin said. He'd barely moved since he'd changed, each action probably radiating aguish through him.

K . F .   B R E E N E

"Yes. Great idea. A good old-fashioned mud bath ought to do the trick." Edgar put up his thumb before hurrying away.

Austin's eyes flicked to me. He didn't say anything.

"You don't have to play tough with me, Austin. I peeked. You're—"

"Did you like what you saw?" His voice was low and thick, sending shivers across my body.

My face heated. "You're in incredible pain," I said, ignoring the sexual innuendo. He tended to relax when he was dealing with pain. His focus slipped, and his grip loosened on his usually iron-clad self-control. "Why didn't you slow down or opt to find the basajaun another day?"

He shook his head, his eyes roaming my face. "I'm good."

I laid my hands on his chest just above his pecs, his skin too hot. Heavy bruises marred his ribs. A gouge bled from the left side of his stomach and another gash dribbled blood down his thigh. Moving around him, I found scrapes and scores down one side of his back, the skin already black and blue around them.

"Okay," I whispered, guilt tearing at me, thinking about how best to heal him. Thanks to Edgar's diligent work with the book he'd found in the garden, I didn't have to guess when it came to healing anymore. I had a few options at my disposal.

The fastest healing method would work quickly, but Austin would be in excruciating pain until the end. That one was best with large or near-fatal wounds. The second type masked the pain a little, like a localized numbing effect, making the patient more comfortable. The third and slowest method allowed me to make the patient feel however I wanted, completely cutting out the pain. This was dangerous in battle because the body would still be hindered by the slow-healing wound. The person would feel capable of moving like they normally did, without actually being in a condition to do so. But all he had to do was hang out and eat dinner. He'd be fine.

"I'm so sorry," I said, erasing his pain while grazing my fingertips down his broad back. "I really thought I toned the magic way down. I shouldn't have let you test the tripwire."

"I offered to test it knowing this was a possibility. It's fine, Jess. This is my job."

A discolored area was just above his left butt cheek, and I curled my fingers around his hip before running my thumb over it. Dirt, not a bruise. My other palm flat on his spine, I closed my eyes and magically felt down into his body, sussing out the hurts and aches, of which there were plenty. If he'd been non-magical, or even in human form at the time of the incident, I probably would've killed him.

Fear welled up inside of me. I *had* to be more careful. I had to try harder. To learn faster. I couldn't subject my people to this. I couldn't ask them to wander into harm's way, potentially being swatted down hard enough not to get back up.

I tried to move back around to his front, intending to delve down into the ribs and see if anything was broken—my magic could essentially act as an X-ray, which was pretty freaking amazing—but he tensed.

"Probably best if you stay back there," he said softly. "Things are looking up on this side."

I chuckled and kept moving, but I stood farther away as I circled around him so I didn't touch his erection. The thing had a long reach.

"It's nothing I haven't seen a few times before." I placed my palm against his ribs and closed my eyes. Deep muscle bruising. The magical razors hadn't just slashed through his skin and muscle; they'd clearly packed a punch as well. No broken bones.

"You'll heal. Is the pain gone—" My breath hitched as I felt one of his hands low on my hip, sliding around. The fingertips on his other hand dusted my jaw line. Fire erupted in my core, suddenly pounding. He wasn't the only one with a loose leash on his control.

He spread his hand across my lower back, his ring and pinky fingers technically on my butt, his other hand curving around the back of my neck. Soft pressure urged me to step forward, closer to him. Against him.

I fluttered my eyes open, meeting his cobalt eyes, deep and soft but also burning with desire. They settled on my lips, almost like a physical presence. His hand on my back slipped lower, his pinky and ring finger on a cheek now, the rest of his hand sure to follow. Heat coursed through my blood, and it was hard to breathe. Hard to think.

"You are absolutely amazing," he whispered, his breath feathering me with the scent of honey and cinnamon. Electricity crackled between us, heat soaking into me through his touch. "Your power is awe-inspiring. It is an honor to train with you, Jacinta. It is worth the pain."

I shook my head, wanting to tell him that nothing could be worth that pain, but the words wouldn't come.

I wet my bottom lip, prompting a low groan deep in his chest. His insistent pressure still urged me forward until I couldn't help but give in, feeling his hard length throbbing against my stomach, his solid muscle scorching my palms.

His face inched down, his eyes on my lips, his proximity delicious, the feel of him winding me up until I could barely tolerate the tightness in my core. I slid my hands up over his stellar chest, winding one of them around his shoulders while reaching the other up to cup his jaw, wanting this so badly. Wanting a kiss, wanting the hand on my butt to squeeze and grind me against him. To lift up my dress and touch what was underneath. Unlike with Damarion a few months ago, I didn't want to back off. I didn't want to push away. This time, I was all systems *go*.

CHAPTER 8

"W<small>E SHOULD GO</small> in," I managed, my voice husky and words slightly slurred. It was like I was drunk on his proximity.

"Are you sure?" He skimmed his full lips across my jaw line and down my neck, sucking a little skin into his hot mouth. I moaned. I couldn't help it.

"We work together, Austin. We shouldn't do this." Control precarious and fleeting, I pulled back just a little, but only so I could tug at his neck, wanting to taste him. To feel those lips on mine. We'd kissed once, after a winetasting that had gotten surprisingly intense, and he'd been a master at it. Sensual and passionate. I wanted to see what else he was a master at. And I was afraid of what it might do to me. "We're friends. We need to stay friends."

He kissed the other side of my neck, giving me chills, sending a shock of pure heat straight down to my core. My moan rode an exhale, and my eyes fluttered shut.

"You're right," he said softly, before tracing his tongue down the shell of my ear. He sucked in my earlobe, and I melted in his arms. He kissed across my jaw and then leaned his forehead against mine, tensing. His arms constricted around me, squeezing me tightly to him, surrounding me with his strength and power. "You're right," he repeated, so soft that I barely heard. "I wouldn't be able to fight my way out of this one. You'd ruin me forever."

He released me, and as his words filtered into my consciousness, he stooped to grab the clothes he'd dropped, his movements stiff. He walked off into the trees, leaving me standing there, shivering from the cold that replaced his warmth.

Ruin him?

What was he talking about? I'd probably engineer a horribly awkward situation, but I definitely wouldn't ruin anything, not even with my magic or building status. If one of us had the upper hand, it was surely him. The townsfolk trusted him, listened to him, and he led the guys who reported to me. He owned the local watering hole I hung out in, for criminy's sake. He was the town alpha, and I was just an upstart with magic I barely knew how to work. If something got going between us and ended in flames, it would be my setup that got torched. Which, let's face it, would almost certainly happen, because I wasn't even looking for a longtime thing and I also had zero experience with loving 'em and leaving 'em and still staying friends. He had this all wrong, laughably so.

Then again, his head wasn't in the right place. He'd been battling incredible pain and fatigue for a few hours, and suddenly his mood had been magically lifted. His situation was the equivalent of someone on serious pain meds saying cockamamie stuff. I needed to give the guy a break.

I also needed to get into the house and check on my dad, who *had* to have seen Austin shift, and make sure Mr. Tom hadn't sent my mom packing for trying to help. There were a lot of fires to put out just now— Austin would have to handle his own.

"Should I meet you in there?" I called.

He walked out a moment later, clothes in place, no shoes or socks, head held high and control firmly back in hand. He glanced at the eaten flowers before pausing at my side. "I'm good. Let's go try some dip."

The guy could bounce back on a dime, another thing that gave him an advantage. I was still nervous after a couple of awkward dates and a failure to launch with a handsy suitor.

We started walking together, quietly at first, then I gestured back to the edge of the woods. "At first I thought Edgar was a little… Well." I scratched my nose. "You know how he can be about the flowers."

"Hysterical?"

"When they're eaten, yeah. But honestly, he does have a point. Most animals would leave signs."

"The animals in this area most likely to eat flowers like that are deer and rabbits, and they would absolutely leave prints or droppings. The fact that they haven't does make me suspicious. This is Ivy House property, though. Because of Edgar's faux pas, the house has stopped letting anyone hike through or roam around without my say-so."

"Regardless, humans don't eat flowers."

"It might still be the basajaun. That's the only thing that makes sense."

I nodded. "I'll ask Ivy House to wake me up if he comes onto the property. I can't ask to be alerted when every deer or rabbit shows up, though. They're all through the woods."

"I'm sure you know this, but you can have her alert you for anything that's not a standard animal."

"I did know that, yes. I can also set a magical snare that *won't* razor-punch someone." I grinned as we reached the back door. "Too soon?"

Something occurred to me, and I stopped and turned toward him, my head much clearer after the brief walk and cool air.

His eyes still smoldered, and looking into them nearly undid my newly level head.

I swallowed, keeping myself in check. "Do you know if my dad saw you shift? Because if so, what the hell, right?"

A small crease worked between his brows. He dug his hands into his pockets and nonchalantly took a step back. "He must've. I wasn't thinking clearly when I came in. I'd forgotten your parents were here. Sorry about that."

I waved it away. Given the state he was in, that was entirely understandable. "What's with the lack of reaction? How the hell could he ignore something like that?" I bit my lip. "Maybe he was studying the flowers and didn't notice…"

"Maybe. It would be hard not to notice the light or feel the heat, though. Maybe he only looked up after I'd finished changing?"

I shrugged. That had to be it. There was no other explanation.

"It's only day one." I reached for the door.

He moved around me and got there first, pulling it open, but he didn't rest his hand on the small of my back like he usually did. "Milady."

I huffed out a laugh. For some reason, I liked when

he called me that. It was stupid and silly, reminding me of the time of knights and ladies-in-waiting, but…well, there it was.

"Also, it's day one-point-five," he said, and waited for me to go through before following. "Don't begrudge yourself that point five. You've earned it."

Instead of turning right and heading into the kitchen, I hung a left, aiming for the closest entrance to the secret passageways.

"I'm going to get changed really quickly. Want to…" I paused, pointing at the door, not sure why I'd asked him up to my room after what had just happened.

He shrugged. "Sure."

I continued to pause.

He grinned. "I'll keep my hands to myself if you do."

The breath gushed out of me and I laughed. He always made everything so easy. He had a talent for deflating or deescalating situations that might end badly, including what had happened between us outside. I had been very slow in hitting those brakes. If he hadn't backed off at the end, I wasn't even sure I would've.

"Sounds good." Within the secret passageway, I said, "Oh, did you want to shower?"

He didn't answer for a moment, making me look

back as I got to the door of my closet.

"Yeah, sure. I don't have any fresh clothes, though. Or boxers."

"If you lay your clothes down somewhere, Mr. Tom or my mom will bustle through and knock that out for you."

"And we already know your dad's views on going around naked. I wouldn't even need to wait for them to be dry. I could just free-ball it through dinner."

"Please don't encourage him." A wave of exhaustion hit me when I stepped into my room, and I found myself gravitating to the little table by the window. I sank down into one of the chairs, looking out the window at the dwindling day.

Austin took the other seat and crossed an ankle over a knee, looking out with me. "This is what you do at the end of a day, huh?"

"Yes. Often Mr. Tom will wander in with some snacks or something to drink, and then leave me to just sit here and gaze out. It's a nice view."

"It is. Peaceful. I have a view of woods from my bedroom. No hedge maze, though. My view is lacking for it."

"I'm sure Edgar would build you one if you asked. Maybe plant you a ridiculous amount of flowers, too. I'd loan him out."

"No, thank you." The silence lengthened for a moment. Then he said, "One day, when your parents aren't here and there's nothing going on, we should come back here and enjoy the view, stress-free. Maybe with a glass of wine."

Butterflies fluttered through my stomach. "That would be nice."

✧   ✧   ✧

AFTER OUR RESPECTIVE showers, Austin using one in a spare bedroom and opting to wear his somewhat dirty clothes instead of the purple house sweats, we landed back downstairs. Niamh sat in the TV room with my dad, her feet up and a beer in her hand. Neither of them spoke, just stared at the blaring TV.

I noticed one of the dolls sitting on a chair in the corner, the baby face turned down, its eyes much too lifelike for my taste, given the dolls in this house actually *did* come to life.

"What is that thing doing there?" I pointed.

My dad struggled to swivel in his chair, trying to see what I was talking about. Niamh, who now had the flexibility of a much younger woman, easily turned and glanced at the offending doll.

"Your mammy brought it down." Niamh took a sip of her beer, unperturbed.

"Why? What was she doing in the doll room?" I demanded.

"She thought you had a love child and went to check it out," my dad said, equally as unperturbed.

"A…what?" I stared in disbelief.

"You might have a real rat problem, Jessie," my dad said, grabbing the remote and putting the TV on mute. "There was some awfully big thumps from above. That's the second floor—you shouldn't have that kind of noise coming from the second floor."

"Woulda been better off with that love child instead of rats, eh, Jessie?" Niamh asked, laughter infusing her eyes.

"Ah well, I don't know. Rats are easier to get rid of. Though…" My dad swiveled again, this time to look at me. "We haven't gotten one call from Jimmy, did your mom tell you? She's called him a few times, sure enough, but that kid just does not want to pick up the phone. He's worse than you. Have you heard from him?"

"He's away from home for the first time and he has a new girlfriend. He's busy." I also knew that if he had a hard enough time picking up the phone to call his mother, he wouldn't spend much time thinking about his grandparents. Eighteen-year-old boys didn't seem to think about family until they needed it, or at least mine didn't. I missed him something awful, but I also didn't want to cramp his style. Not yet. Not until I couldn't stand it anymore. I'd also need to figure out how to explain my new life. Given how it was going with the parents, I'd need to think a little harder about explanations when he finally came here. "He's hoping to come out for Mother's Day."

My dad grunted and reached for the remote. Our talk was apparently done.

In the kitchen, Ulric and Cedric sat at the island in front of a plate loaded with cheese, salami, and crackers. Each had a drink—Ulric with a beer and Cedric with orange juice. My mother stood at the sink, her hands submerged in the suds foaming up out of the basin. An empty dish rack sat in front of Jasper, who was wiping a plate with a towel before moving to put it away.

The oven door lay open with Mr. Tom peering into it. "Honestly, Martha, you don't need to do that. You can just sit down. I'll take care of them in a minute."

"Don't be silly. I just wish you'd let me help more. You have your hands full catering to all these people!"

"I assure you, it is nothing I can't handle."

"Hey." I stopped by the island, Austin beside me. Ulric lifted his drink in salute.

"Oh hey, honey." My mom turned with a smile, pulling a yellow rubber glove from the glistening foam.

"I hear the woods expedition went well. Your father says there are a lot of flowers out back. I think I'll check those out tomorrow. Maybe get some pointers from Edgar."

My mother was the worst gardener in history, or maybe second only to me. Edgar would likely make it sound easy, especially given he had a magical elixir that actually *did* make it easy, and if he encouraged her, she'd probably end up mass-murdering a bunch of innocent flowers. It would be a travesty.

"Did Dad mention anything else, other than the flowers?"

She thought for a moment. "No. He said the weather's nice, but I knew that."

I chewed on my lip. "Nothing about...seeing anything weird?"

She tilted her head. "Like what?"

"Like...animals...in the woods?"

"No. Why?"

"We have a problem with something eating the flowers," Ulric said, peeling the label on his beer.

"Oh yes." She scoffed loudly. "They are constantly after my roses! I had to put wire fencing around them."

I let it go. Clearly my dad hadn't said anything, and there were other extreme matters to attend to. "Why'd you bring down a doll, Mom?"

"The dolls! You didn't tell me you had so many dolls! I didn't remember you having that many dolls when you were married to"—she put a gloved hand to the side of her mouth—"*you know who.*"

"We all know who, Mom. I haven't been secretive about the divorce—"

"Oh, here." My mom quickly took off her gloves and laid them beside the sink. "Do you want a beer? Austin?" Her smile spanned her whole face for Austin, it seemed like. "You'll have a beer, won't you?"

"Yes, please. Thank you," he replied.

"So polite. I'd worried about the younger generation and their manners, but all of you boys are so polite." She dug into the fridge.

Mr. Tom jerked upright, hitting his head on the edge of the oven. He winced and rubbed his head. "I am perfectly capable of…" But the beers had already been pulled free of the packed space.

Austin grabbed a couple of brown bottles—my mother favored Coors Light over my father's Pabst—and twisted off the caps. He handed one to me and then stepped back, giving me space.

"You are a true entertainer, Mrs. McMillian," Ulric said with a sly grin. "An amazing host. You know what people want before they know it themselves."

"Oh now…" My mom batted her hand at him,

pleased by the flattery. "Call me Martha."

Mr. Tom glowered and then shut the oven. "It has another half-hour. We held off a little in case you ran late, miss."

"Niamh was right," Ulric muttered to Cedric. "He's often late with dinner."

"Don't mind them," my mom told Mr. Tom. "I'm always late, aren't I, Jessie? Time just gets away from me." She took a long sip of her beer.

"She's trying to make you feel better, Mr. Tom. Is it working?" Ulric said.

Mr. Tom met Ulric's mocking grin with anger. "I will just check on the others."

"Jessie, how about some clam dip? I brought some up since you didn't come for Christmas. I figure we can have a sort of mock Christmas dinner. I made some deviled eggs, too."

I didn't bother telling her that she'd informed me of this twice already. "Awesome. Sounds great."

My mom pulled the plug on the sink before heading back to the fridge.

"This is such a lovely, big kitchen," she said. "We can all gather right here. I hardly have to move at all. And with Tom helping with the cooking, it's almost like a vacation."

"If you let him do all the work, like he wants to, it'll

completely be like a vacation," I said. "You can even go winetasting in town."

"Don't be silly, I couldn't let him do everything." She eyed me. "But winetasting. That's an idea. It's such a cute little town. We only drove through. I'd love to visit some of the shops and things."

"And wineries," Ulric said.

My mom grinned sheepishly, resting the Tupperware of clam dip on the island and grabbing the chips. "Do you have a chip-and-dip party set, Jessie?"

"I've told the others they can only have a taste so you and Dad can get enough," I said, putting down my beer and rooting through the cabinets. "I think we do."

"Don't be silly. They can have as much as they'd like."

"I do not think you should be worried about that, Mrs. McMillian," Ulric said dryly. Cedric shook his head.

"Call me Martha, please! You make me feel old." My mom watched me dig through the various crystal bowls and platters.

"What…" Mr. Tom bustled in with two empty cans. They clinked down onto the counter. "Miss, what are you looking for? Here, let me help you. I swear, the whole place is in complete disarray. Does no one respect my role in this household?"

I got out of the way after telling him what I needed and, on impulse, ducked into to the fridge to pull out two deviled eggs. I handed one to Austin and bit into the other.

"Really? Can't pass one to me?" Ulric put up his hands.

"You're giving Mr. Tom a hard time. You don't deserve one," I replied, laughing.

"I am not worried about what a disco-haired upstart has to say regarding my affairs," Mr. Tom grumbled. "I was storming the gates when his parents were in diapers."

I nudged him with my foot, hoping my mom hadn't noticed.

"I am hurrying, miss. Please, have patience," he responded, clearly misreading that nudge. "There are fine things in this house."

"How about you, Austin?" my mother said, sounding like she was continuing a conversation no one had started.

"How's that, ma'am?" Austin asked, stepping up to the corner of the island, his arm brushing mine.

"You're a handsome young man. Do you have a woman nailed down yet?" she asked.

"Mom," I said through my teeth. I knew where this was going.

"Not yet, ma'am," he answered.

She clucked her tongue. "Well, isn't that a shame. Such a well-mannered, handsome man with no attachments." She shook her head. "Yes, such a shame. Does your mother have as hard of a time setting you up as I do with Jessie? I swear, everyone I mention isn't good enough."

"I live five hours away from all of them, Mom," I said, staring daggers at her. "I'm just taking a little me time after the divorce."

"I'll never understand this new emphasis on *me* time. Back in my day, if you had a bump in the road, you just got on with things, right, Tom?"

Mr. Tom finally pulled out a crystal set. "Yes, madam, on that we can agree. I have repeatedly told the miss that she must get back out there. She has had a few failed dates, not strictly her fault, but that is no reason to give up."

"Yes. Exactly. My, isn't this beautiful? Jacinta McMillian, when did you get such beautiful dishware?"

I didn't bother correcting her on the last name. She'd never acknowledged the name change before; it seemed less than likely she'd start now, which was actually preferable. I didn't really feel a connection to it anymore, anyway.

"It was left over from the last owners," I said. "Most

of this stuff came with the house."

"Such a steal." She finished transferring the items into the new bowls and pushed them into the center of the island. "Though I did see a couple cracks forming in the TV room." She waved her hand at the far wall. "Must be the plaster or something. The plaster is coming off. I just pushed on it, and it seemed to click back into place, so that's good."

I widened my eyes, looking at Mr. Tom. His brow furrowed. Could she be talking about the secret doors? They were innocuous enough to look like cracks in the wall when they were popped open. What else could it be? But why was Ivy House opening the secret doors for them?

"I better get a bowl for your father," she muttered into the suddenly still room. "He won't want to come all the way in here to get it, and I doubt all these young people with good hearing want to go into that room with the blaring TV. They'll be deaf in an hour!"

"Let me, madam." Mr. Tom reached for the Tupperware of clam dip, prepared to scoop some into the smaller dish he already had at the ready.

"No, no, I have it, don't worry." She shifted, throwing her shoulder against his arm, knocking him out of the way. I'd never seen her so pushy. "Anyway, Jessie, you have a handsome young man right there. He looks about your age. You two should go out. What are you waiting for?"

"We can't, Mom. We work together."

"What, on the woods stuff? That's not really work. You don't have a boss. I don't think it's a problem." My mom took the bowl from an increasingly hostile Mr. Tom and spooned some of the thick white dip into it.

"I do owe you that date," Austin said, watching me pull the chip bowl closer and grab a ruffled chip.

"You going to try that stuff, alph—Austin?" Ulric asked. Jasper leaned over the island, watching.

"When in Rome…" Austin reached for a chip.

"There, see? A date is a great idea. You two seem like you get along." My mom beamed.

"It's just as friends," I said, my voice tinged with warning, hoping my mother would just drop it. I wasn't so sure a date, even as friends, was a great idea. Not after that episode outside. When it came to Austin, my brakes weren't holding up as well as I would like. "Anyway, Mom, what about the dolls?" I said. "You can't leave those things lying around the house. Wait…did you leave the door to the doll room open?"

Austin paused with a chip barely dabbed with dip nearly to his mouth. Ulric's eyes widened. Everyone knew what those dolls were capable of. Giving them free run of the house was a nightmare. A literal nightmare.

I closed my eyes, mentally pinpointing the door to their room. Thankfully, it was shut. I'd have to keep checking it vigilantly, just in case. My mother could not be trusted. Neither, it seemed, could Ivy House.

Having apparently ignored my question, my mom fussed with rinsing out the empty Tupperware. While she was otherwise occupied, Mr. Tom recognized his opportunity and grabbed the smaller bowl meant for my dad, then the bag of chips, and hurried out of the room.

"Drat that man." My mom fumed after him. "He just will not take a break. He's doing too much, Jessie, he really is. He doesn't need to wait on us!"

"Mom. Listen to me, those dolls need to stay in that room. That's their room."

"Tell that to the rodents you have running through it. Your father and I heard a big one up there. I'd hate for those lovely little dolls to get chewed up. I made sure to move them around the house so they can be enjoyed and stay safe. Your father is going to tackle that rodent problem tomorrow. It's the least we can do."

"We do *not* have rats, madam," Mr. Tom said on re-entry.

Ulric, Jasper, Austin, Cedric, and I all exchanged anxious glances. None of us wanted those dolls running around the house willy-nilly, able to terrorize us at will.

I connected eyes with Jasper. "Go," I mouthed. "Put them away."

"Make sure you shut the door behind you," Ulric whispered urgently.

Ivy House had better stop animating those dolls for my parents to hear. I didn't know how I'd retaliate, but I'd think of something.

"Hmm. This is actually really good. Seafood dip is good, who knew," Austin murmured, reaching for another chip.

"I have very thoroughly checked every inch of this house for rodents and applied the correct defensive measures," Mr. Tom said, missing the exchange about the dolls. He'd never considered them a problem.

"Well, something up there is knocking around." My mom patted Mr. Tom on the arm when he was within range. "It's a big old house—it can be hard to get to every inch, especially with all those stairs. Don't worry; Pete is an excellent mouser. He'll help you out. Now." She glanced around. "Where are the table settings? I'll just go set the table, will I?"

Mr. Tom hung his head.

"I guess I need to make good on that date finally, huh?" Austin said quietly, still by my side, grabbing his third dip-laden chip. "Your mother said so."

CHAPTER 9

A VIBRATING SCREAM filled my head and tore through my body, jolting me upright in bed. The darkness crowded in around me and pushed against the windows. My heart thudded, but no other sound reached me, the night still. Whatever had awoken me wasn't auditory—it was magical.

My phone clattered on my nightstand, and I jumped. Austin's name blinked onto the screen. I'd left the connection between us open to monitor his healing—he must've felt me startle awake.

"Hey," I said when I put it to my ear, breathing heavily. "What's up?"

"What's going on? Are you okay?"

Another blast pounded through me, shaking every bone in my body.

The alert! I'd set the tripwire before I'd gone to bed. Someone was out there.

"Something must've tripped my magical wire," I whispered, slinking out of bed and onto the floor.

"Can you see what it is from your window?"

"*I don't feel a presence,*" Ivy House said through our magical communication. "*It's not the basajaun. I do not feel whatever is out there. My defenses are blind to it. There is a spell out there, that I do not know, that can have this effect. I thought it would've been lost with time...*"

Fear trickled through me. That was a huge blind spot. Ivy House had always been able to feel someone stepping onto the property. If she couldn't feel the danger, neither could I.

I crawled on my hands and knees across the floor, the phone in my hand, Austin saying something that was lost to the distance. Crouching below the window, I put the phone back to my ear. "I'm about to find out."

I rose oh-so-slowly, conscious that my head would interrupt the plane of the window and hoping the darkness would mask it.

"You can't feel anything through Ivy House?" I could hear his voice shaking with movement. He was probably jumping out of bed.

I double-checked what Ivy House had said; the wood sparked to life in my mind's eye, various dots flaring where animals roamed, lighting up my internal map. Edgar in the trees, the disturbance surely within his line of sight. I ripped away the barrier to our magical connection. His emotions roared to life—confused, incredulous, and a little let down. The affected area was a blank space on my Ivy House map. Whatever it was, Edgar could clearly see it, but Ivy House definitely couldn't feel it.

"Magic," I said softly, my heart picking up the pace, probably pounding at a dangerous pace now. "It must be magic."

"What's magic?" Austin asked.

I quickly described the situation as I lifted up enough to see outside. The backyard spanned in front of me, the moon but a sliver, shedding next to no light. Which was exactly what drew my attention to the animal across the way. I sucked in a startled breath.

"I see it," I whispered hoarsely. "I see it!"

"What is it?"

I shook my head, then blinked a couple of times. "A deer. A great big buck. A seven-pointer. No, six? One side of his antlers has seven points; one has six. He's the biggest deer I've ever seen in my…"

My words faded away. My breath caught in my chest.

"He's a shifter, isn't he?" I asked. "A deer this big has to be a shifter."

"Likely." Austin's voice turned fierce. "I'm coming. Don't move. I'll be there soon."

"Wait, but…" Dead air. I hadn't gotten to tell him the unnerving issue with this animal.

It glowed.

Its body looked like it was shrouded in a sheen of pale blue against the black backdrop.

I grabbed both edges of the windowsill, my phone on the ground, wondering what to do next. Ivy House couldn't take care of the problem for me, not when she didn't know there was one. This was up to me and my team.

I could use the defenses, but I hadn't practiced with them as I should've. I'd probably kill instead of trap or maim, and I didn't feel comfortable doing that. Not until I was sure the creature posed more of a threat than eating Edgar's flowers. The right thing to do would be to trap it with my magic so I could question it. For that, I'd need to get closer. I wasn't totally set on magical nets.

What if I spooked it before I could do a magical net, though? Deer could hear crazy well, regardless of whether they were shifters, and I was the world's worst sneak. If I spooked it, it would know the jig was up. If its intent was dangerous, that would mean it would change its plan of attack. Knowing about the intrusion meant we had the upper hand right now—if it knew we were onto it, it would regain the advantage. I couldn't risk it.

Flight!

I could head up to the third floor, jump off the roof on the other side of the house, get high into the sky, and follow it when it inevitably moved on. I could find out where it went, and if it changed into its human form, I'd know who we were looking for.

But I had smaller wings than a male gargoyle, and I had to beat them more often, which could be loud, especially if I thought I was falling out of the sky and panicked. It would be smarter to recruit Ulric, small and swift, or Jasper, a great glider.

I chewed my lip, feeling Austin on the move, but he was still too far away. That deer didn't eat much at a time. It wouldn't be here for long. I had to get a flyer in the sky right now, or I needed to attack the intruder, hopefully stunning it so I had a chance to get a net or magical binding around it.

I turned around with purpose and immediately screamed. Mr. Tom was standing just a few feet behind me in his house sweats, staring out the window. I hadn't felt or heard him enter the room. I ignored him so often that it had become commonplace.

"Edgar was wrong—clearly it *is* a deer eating his flowers," he said, sneaking toward the window.

"Damn it, Mr. Tom, announce yourself, will you?"

"Sorry, miss. I felt your distress. Is it my eyes, or is

that creature glowing?"

"It is. It's almost certainly a shifter, and it must have a thick layer of magic on it to shield it from Ivy House."

Mr. Tom knelt next to me. "These are bad tidings. Someone has figured out how to make themselves invisible while on this property."

"Yeah, and we need to find out who that someone is, not to mention how to prevent it from happening again. If magic can get them in here, there has to be some kind of reverse spell to strip it away."

"Now you're thinking like a sorceress."

"Too bad I can't do magic like a sorceress."

"Yet."

I backed away from the window. "Let's get Ulric. He can follow it—"

"No time. Look!" Mr. Tom pointed.

The deer, still munching, lifted its head, looking over the gardens. It paused as if in contemplation before walking a few steps, every bit as graceful as a natural deer. It didn't bow back to the flowers, though its hesitation said it was thinking about it.

"It's not eating as much as it wants to," I whispered, watching in fascination, not sure if I was studying it or I was just too torn to act. Go get Ulric, or go down there and try to blast it with magic?

"It's holding back. Why, I wonder?" I paused for

another moment, considering, then forced myself into action. I wouldn't get any answers sitting here. "I'll get Jasper, actually. If anyone is good at silence, it's that guy. Keep watching it, Mr. Tom. Try to figure out what it's after."

Jasper opened the door after the second soft rap, his room two doors down from my parents'. Even though I was in a hurry, I didn't want them coming out and asking questions. They'd just slow everything down.

The door swung open, Jasper's eyes puffy with sleep and his unruly light brown hair in a halo around his head. He didn't respond, just waited for me to speak.

"I need your help. Hurry!" I waved him down the hall after me, breaking into a jog. Back at my room, easing in beside Mr. Tom, still crouched at the window, I pointed to the deer. It was working away from Edgar's position, staring at the house all the while. "Can you get into the air and follow it without being detected?" I whispered.

He bent beside me and then leaned forward, bracing his large hand against the windowsill. Both of us were far enough back and low enough that the darkness of the room would mask what little of us might be visible from the deer's vantage point. "Is it glowing?"

"Yeah. Looks like a shifter, too. Ivy House can't feel it. That's what's been eating Mr. Tom's flowers."

"Edgar's," Mr. Tom said.

"Sorry, yeah. Edgar's. Can you follow it, Jasper? Without being noticed?"

"For how long?" Jasper asked.

"I don't know, until...you have something to report, I guess. But it can't know you're there."

He stripped off his shirt and jogged out of the room. I felt him heading for the stairs. He'd use one of the third-floor openings in the floor or wall and take to the sky.

"Now what, miss?" Mr. Tom asked, a buzz sounding from his pocket.

I shook my head, needing to do something more. This creature was on my property, and Ivy House couldn't defend herself. It was on me to pick up the slack. Everything in me wanted to run out there and teach the shifter a lesson. Teach it—mostly likely a him—to invade my space and mess with Edgar's flowers. Logic had to reign supreme, though. That deer would be back. Haste without planning caused mistakes. Right now we had the upper hand—we needed to keep it.

Mr. Tom swore under his breath. The light from his phone screen highlighted his cheekbones and eyes. "It's Niamh. The house across from hers has a prowler. She just caught a glimpse before the figure slipped behind the bushes. She's wondering if she should engage."

"What is it? Is it a shifter?"

Mr. Tom bent to his phone, typing out a message. I wondered why he didn't just call, but was thankful for it. Text was quieter and there was less room to insult each other. It would be quicker.

I clutched the windowsill, my mind whirling. I couldn't be sure the entity at the front was a danger to me, not yet. Could just be a burglar. I had to get ready to move, though, just in case.

"Not a shifter," Mr. Tom said as his phone vibrated with a new message. "A human form. She doesn't know what magic it is."

I paused. "Tell her to keep watching, but not engage. If it is a powerful mage, she'll be on the losing end of that battle. We need information before we combat this. If it comes on Ivy House's property, have her text, just in case it has the same spell as the shifter out back." I pushed away from the window and crouch-crawled to the center of the room. "Come on, let's get ready to fly in case something kicks off."

I stood and made my way downstairs, pausing again at the bottom of the stairs. Did we head to the front, or back? Austin would likely approach from the rear through the woods, and if he caught sight of that shifter, he'd give chase. If the entity at the front joined in the battle, we'd need to intercept. If not, and we went to the back to help Austin, we'd leave the front vulnerable.

"Mr. Tom, go get Ulric and Cedric. Have them watch the front in case that prowler heads this way."

With him dispatched, I made it to the back of the house. Once there, I stripped off my clothes and changed form. Mr. Tom joined me not long after and followed suit.

Minutes ticked by. I felt Jasper invade the airspace, high overhead. The fact that I could sense him in the air made it that much stranger that I couldn't feel the deer whose hooves were in Ivy House dirt.

"Wee 'aft oo fiiiin du schpell—" I sighed and stopped trying to talk. I was getting better at working around the enlarged teeth and prominent canines in this form, but it was an ongoing struggle. I'd wait to tell Mr. Tom that we needed to find the spell that might allow a creature to walk past magical surveillance undetected.

Although...he had set off my magical tripwire, so there *was* substance to him. It actually didn't get past magical surveillance. It was just Ivy House that was blind to it. But why?

"Ook." Mr. Tom pointed, his long claw tapping the window.

The deer worked around the side of the house as if

tracking the flowers. We followed its progress from within the house, moving from window to window, staying well back or within the shadows.

Mr. Tom glanced at his phone, the screen somewhat obscured by his long nails, not lit up. No text message from Niamh. The prowler at the front wasn't an issue. Not yet.

The deer shifter didn't eat any more flowers or do much of anything but look. It moved its head like a person might, checking each window, pausing for a long time with its snout slightly raised, looking at the second or third floors. Given my room spanned the back corner of the house, I had a sinking suspicion that it had a special interest in my room.

Edgar's movements registered. He was creeping along at a snail's pace, the vampire who'd once been great at stalking prey having lost his edge many, *many* decades ago. Adrenaline coursed through me. If he wasn't careful, he'd be the piece that upset this whole night.

Jasper circled the house, far overhead, his eyesight clearly amazing. I hoped that deer's wasn't so good, though even if it was, spotting a dark-skinned gargoyle within the dark sky would be a feat. Jasper wouldn't blow it.

The deer jerked and my heart stopped. Its head

swung toward the front of the house. Its body tensed, and then it exploded into movement, bounding away through the trees. Jasper soared in that direction a moment later.

"Oh 'rap," I said, the breath leaking out of me, my swear muddled.

The deer shifter must've seen the prowler at the front. It would have had a clear vantage point from its last location. Given it had run, they probably weren't on the same team. One threat was bad enough, but two opposing threats? At the same time?

Or maybe it was just a shifter that had lost its way, with a rare magic that hid it from Ivy House, and a burglar that got unlucky with timing? Totally unrelated. Maybe the shifter spooked because it saw someone, not because it saw an enemy that might not know it wasn't just a deer.

My gut pinched and then swam. Not even wishful thinking helped me swallow that one down. Danger was coming this way, and it was happening when my parents were here.

I jogged to the front of the house, where Ulric and Cedric waited in the sitting room near the window, wanting a look at that prowler, only belatedly registering my dad coming down the stairs. Having emerged from the seldom-used sitting room attached to the dining room, I slid to a stop just before the entryway. My wings snapped out, not in control, punching a vase on a stand. It flew across the room and smashed into the wall, the pieces tinkling as they rained down onto the floor.

My dad startled, pausing with one foot on the ground floor and the other still on the step, holding the banister for support.

"Ennnd innn…" Mr. Tom prompted.

Blend in.

It should have been in my wheelhouse, but other facets of my magic had taken precedence in my training. I was now seeing the flaw in that thinking.

"Heeeey, Daad," I said, super nonchalant, my wings still stretched out behind me, my body covered in tough, light purple, luminescent skin that shed streaks of light whenever I moved. Although I had smaller teeth and a more reasonable jaw than the creature form of the male of the species, I still did not look in any way human. Hiding my long fingers ending in claws behind my back would do nothing to detract from the effect. Even hiding in shadows would not make this in any way normal. Not even remotely. The only thing that could be worse, I figured, was changing back right in front of him and standing around in human form while naked. Not sure if that would be worse for him or for me, but I was definitely not going to do it.

I hope he doesn't have a heart attack, I thought without meaning to. Reducing the stress of this moment for my dad was a lot more important than seeing the prowler with my own eyes. Niamh and hopefully the guys could tell me what they saw. No one would be able to help my dad cope with this situation if it went off the rails.

Further off the rails.

He stared at me for a very long moment, the only sound the ticking of the grandfather clock behind me. Austin surged onto the property at the edge of the wood—not the rear, like I'd thought he might—still a distance away but coming fast. He'd made incredible time. He was still too late for the deer, although not too late to give my dad another polar bear peep show that hopefully wouldn't drive him over the edge.

"Dooooin' 'ood?" I tried the last again. "Guh-ood?"

"Jacinta, how many times have I told you to enunciate when you speak to someone." My dad's foot slowly left the step and joined the other on the ground floor. He didn't remove his hand from the banister. "Your mother has me taking something called melatonin. She claims it's to help me sleep, but I don't know. I'm starting to see things." He shook his head, turning down the hallway. "Doesn't cure my midnight hunger, either.

Is there any clam dip left?"

He didn't wait for me to catch up. Austin was nearly at the house.

I darted into the sitting room and to the guys hiding behind the curtains.

"Sheee anneee'tang?" I would've grimaced, if my face could contort that way, and then I changed form.

"See anything?" I asked, slipping to the side of the window and quickly looking out. I had precious little time with Austin coming closer and my dad in the middle of the whole thing. It was clear my dad would not handle the idea of magic well, I needed to keep it away from him.

"Shhom une." Ulric pointed.

Someone.

Shadows draped and pooled across the front and side yards of the house across the street from Niamh's, still and quiet. No movement caught my eye. No glowing form.

"Gooone," Cedric grunted out.

"Mr. Tom, see if Niamh saw it leave," I said, getting one last look, squinting into the darkness. "If not, we'll need to check it out. Cedric and Ulric, stay here until we call you. Don't let my dad see you. I need clothes."

So as not to dart past my father in the kitchen while naked, I ran upstairs, threw on some house sweats and a t-shirt, and tore back down and out the back door.

"No running in the house," my father called after me, clearly on autopilot. Or else not caring that this was my house and he technically didn't have the right to enforce rules.

Austin stopped at the edge of the flowers to shift before beelining for the back door. I hurried to meet him.

"Hey." Austin grabbed my arms and raked his gaze down my body, clearly assessing me for damage. "You okay?"

Jasper flew directly overhead. He must've lost the trail.

"Yeah. I didn't leave the house." I nudged Austin to turn toward the munched flowers, but my dad's voice stopped me short.

"Young lady, you'll catch the death of cold out here at night with just a T-shirt." He stood in the back door, a bag of bread dangling from one hand, a half-eaten cookie in the other, and his cheek puffed out like a chipmunk's. His eyes narrowed at Austin. "Son, now…I understand the need to let the begonias air out—it is very good for circulation, no matter what doctors or my wife will tell you—but that is my daughter there, and calling on her at this time of the night without a stitch of clothing on is pushing it."

"Yes, sir. I apologize. I keep late hours." Austin turned, providing an opening for me to pass him. Jasper touched down somewhere within the trees, something I only felt, thankfully. None of us could see him.

"Here we go." Mr. Tom scooted past my father in his house sweats. He carried more in his hands. "I was just bringing some sweats now."

"So the cape isn't just for suits, you wear it with leisurewear too, huh?" My dad shook his head at Mr. Tom. "We all like the idea of superheroes, but even Superman took his off once in a while…"

"Superman is just a—"

"Never mind," I said, stopping Mr. Tom. We didn't need to get into it.

Tight-lipped, Mr. Tom held out sweatpants for Austin. "Here, Mr. Steele. And miss, you can wear the sweatshirt so you don't look cold."

My dad nodded once. "That's more like it." Mr. Tom's word choice, thankfully, hadn't registered. "Don't stay out too late." He headed back to the kitchen.

"Thank God it wasn't your dad that I had to convince about magic," Austin murmured. "I don't know if it could be done." He ushered me toward Jasper. Edgar darted out from the bushes.

"Your tripwire worked, Jessie, congratulations," Edgar said, smiling at me. "Job well done." He turned somber. "I owe you an apology, though. It was not the basajaun after all. I have egg on my face."

I waved that away. "What'd you see?"

"A larger deer, probably a shifter, snapped me out of a doze," Edgar said. I glanced back at the house, really hoping my dad wasn't looking out. Thankfully, I didn't see a face in the lit kitchen windows. "It approached like any deer might, wandering through the wood and looking for food. After that—"

"I was watching. What about the magic? Did you notice anything about that strange glow around it?"

Austin slipped on the sweats before stalking across the grass, his stride long and purposeful. I followed, trailed by everyone else.

"Just the color, density, and reach of the glow," Edgar said. "I was a bit too far away to get a more detailed look."

"How good of a mage is the woman in town?" I asked as Austin tramped through the flowers. Edgar issued a soft squeal. "The one who makes the flower elixir. Would she know much about different spells?"

"No," Mr. Tom said as Austin bent to the munched section, studying the ground. "She's low level, which is why she's in a small town making magical Miracle-Gro for a vampire so he can cheat at local gardening shows."

"For the last time, it is not cheating," Edgar said.

"That sneak, Marg, could use the same elixir—"

"Grab me a light, Edgar," Austin said.

Edgar let out a breath, like a tire losing air, before puffing into a swarm of insects and buzzing away.

"Miss," Mr. Tom said softly. "Your father is back. He's apparently as nosy as your mother…"

My dad stuck his head out of the back doorway. "What are you all up to out here? It's a bit late for a garden party."

"He needs double the dose of melatonin," Mr. Tom murmured. "Or maybe a sleeping draft. That is something Agnes *can* help with."

"Nothing, Dad," I called. "It's fine. Just head to bed."

My dad stepped farther out. "Well, it can't be nothing, what with all you gathering around in the middle of the night. You having some animal problems? I noticed something was getting at your flowers over there. First rats, now critters—this house is overrun!" He took a few more steps, clearly intending to join our huddle.

Jasper finished the transition into his human form, thankfully in the shadows of the trees. Likely my dad wouldn't have noticed him from such a distance; not that it would've really mattered at this point. The cat had gotten out of the bag a few times over. It was amazing that he wasn't giving in to it.

"Just saw an animal prowling and trying to figure out what it was," I said. "It's nothing. Probably a deer."

"I followed it through the woods," Jasper said quietly, talking quickly, clearly trying to get this out before my dad got within hearing range. "About halfway to the property line, the illumination wore off. I dropped in altitude enough to continue tracking it, the low light making things difficult. It stopped for a moment, and then vanished. I saw the image of the deer wink out."

"It isn't a mage, so it must've taken a magical elixir of some kind," Austin said. "How close did it get to me?"

Jasper shook his head. "I didn't see you running in, so it couldn't have been very close. Then again, my focus was acute."

"And you're sure the witch in town wouldn't know about that kind of elixir?" I whispered to Mr. Tom.

He shrugged. "She might know, but she wouldn't be able to make it. Illumination and invisibility are master-craft potions. Tricking this house would take the very best."

My stomach churned, and Austin looked up at me, the weak moonlight falling across his face. His eyes smoldered with determination. I knew what he was thinking. Only the very best could make a potion powerful enough to trick Ivy House, and there was one mage who'd continually shown interest in me.

Elliot Graves.

I'd never officially met him, but everyone who had agreed he was the biggest, baddest mob-boss mage in the world. He'd been trying to take me by force, thwarted at every turn by Ivy House. If this was his doing, he'd just found a way around my best defense.

"We need to move you," Austin said, his voice low and rough. "You're not safe here."

"She's as safe here as she is anywhere," Mr. Tom said. "More so, because elixirs don't last forever, and the second the mask is peeled back, Ivy House will spring."

Austin's jaw clenched, but you couldn't argue with that logic.

"It's fine. Right now, that deer is just checking things out," I said. "It doesn't suspect we're onto it, so we still have the upper hand."

"Even if it did, it would come back anyway," my dad said, reaching us. "When it comes to eating flowers, they have a short-term memory. I chased one with a tire iron early one morning. I sure scared it something good. You should've seen it take off. Came back the very next night." He put a hand to his hip, the other holding up a half-eaten sandwich, and looked at the ground. "Well, no wonder it's a great mystery," he said. "A bunch of geniuses, standing around tracking in the dark. Go grab a light, Jacinta, and we'll see what we've got."

"I've got it." Edgar loped back into the area, a camping lantern in each hand.

My dad watched him. "That man sure runs funny. Though for his age, it's a blessing he runs at all."

"You have deer in L.A.?" Mr. Tom asked.

"They live in the burbs on the edges of a nature preserve," I said as Austin flicked on the light and studied the ground.

He traced a small indent with this finger. "I don't get a scent. All I get is the smell of flowers."

"Yeah, the stink of the flowers will nearly blow your hair back," my dad said. "That's hard-packed dirt. If that deer was just walking around, you aren't going to see much. Get it wet tomorrow night. You'll see a track, all right."

Austin stood. To me he said, "I'm going to have Jasper show me the trail. I'll report back when I'm done. It sounds like…" His eyes flicked to my dad and back. "It sounds like we've been down this road before"—he was talking about Elliot Graves sending someone for me— "though this time, I'm not sure what the end goal is."

My father's face scrunched up. "Well…they don't have any end goals. They just forage. That's what they do. The flowers are tasty, and they come to eat them."

I ignored my dad. "I'm going with you. It's not out of the realm of possibility that the deer is a lure in the eventuality someone—usually you—checks it out. He's already figured out how to circumvent Ivy House's defenses. It would make sense if he tried to take out my next strongest defense."

"Or maybe he knows we'll all check it out together, since it's on Ivy House property, and is waiting to ambush us. If I go alone, I'll be the only one who gets—"

"No." I grabbed his arm, an uncomfortable feeling coiling tightly in my stomach. "We go together. I'll…go high, so we'll be separated, but we'll check it out together."

Austin stared at me for a long moment, clearly not wanting me in danger, but probably recognizing a hopeless cause when he saw one.

"Well. You crazy kids have fun. I think I'll retire now." My dad about-faced and headed for the house.

Mr. Tom watched him go. "That man is the prime example of a Dick ignoring anything that doesn't fit into his world view. I've never seen anything like it. I mean, I've heard about it, but never actually witnessed it."

"Oh yes, it's quite extraordinary," Edgar said. "I've seen it a lot."

Austin shook his head. "Fine, but you will stay with

me, not in the air. Call Ulric and Cedric down here. What about the few you have in the hotel?"

"Leave them there. I don't want to bring any more people into my world who don't expressly belong. Those guys aren't great anyway."

"If they aren't great, why haven't you turned them loose?" Austin asked, stripping out of his pants.

"I know, I know, don't push me." I glanced at Mr. Tom. "Anything from Niamh?"

"Yes. She saw him or her leave, someone clad in leather. They were not glowing. Near as I can figure, the person at the front must've left about when that deer did."

"There was another one?" Austin asked.

I blew out a breath and nodded. "No Dick or Jane prowler would care about a deer, even a glowing one. They'd just think their eyes were playing tricks. Only a magical person would know it was a shifter, and likely one using a potion or elixir. Them taking off means they were not happy to see one another." I put my hands on my hips and thought for a moment. "Keep Niamh watching the front. Tell her to call if the person at the front comes back. We'll check out the trail of the deer. I'm more concerned with whatever circumvented Ivy House's magic than a person in leather. Get Cedric but leave Ulric in the front, just in case. Let's go while the trail is still fresh. We'll circle back to the front after."

"Maybe they are working together and just pulled back at the same time?" Mr. Tom said.

"I don't know if that would be worse or better. Regardless, my parents will be caught in the crossfire. We have to find a way out of this, for their sakes."

CHAPTER 10

MARTHA GRABBED THE shoes from Jessie's floor. That girl had never learned to put her shoes away. If a body wasn't careful, there'd be a shoe garden in the living room, housing all of the discarded shoes that were never picked up. She placed them in the enormous closet only a quarter filled with clothes. Martha clucked her tongue. All of that time with no job and no child to look after, and she couldn't pick up a few things. Martha would never understand it. She loved shopping.

Speaking of which, she needed to take a tour of the downtown area. She'd seen the cutest little shops as she was passing through.

A pop caught her attention.

She straightened, bracing her hand against her lower back. These old bones were not what they used to be.

A crack had formed beside the dresser, from the floor nearly to the ceiling. More siding popping loose, no doubt. This house was falling apart!

A wave of worry washed over her. Poor Jessie. First Jimmy moved away, then Matt up and left her, and now she'd been taken for a ride by that Havercamp woman. This house might look okay on the outside, if a bit spooky, but it was clearly a fixer-upper. It would be an absolute money pit. Hopefully those nice young boys planned on sticking around for a while and paying rent. Jessie was going to need it.

Martha placed her palm on the wall and leaned into it, popping the siding back into place with a click. A few nails should do the trick. She'd let Pete know. He could hammer the problem spots back into place, easy.

Back in the room, she noticed a doll sitting on a pillow in the middle of Jessie's bed.

That was odd. She didn't remember seeing that doll when she'd come in. Then again, she hadn't been paying attention to the bed she'd made earlier, noticing instead the discarded shoes. Jessie must've set the doll up there, trying to make nice after putting them all away last night.

She left the room, and the butler fellow was out in the hall. The tuxedo was overkill and the cape just plain odd. She didn't dare mention it to Jessie so as not to upset her, but he was a weird man. Very eccentric.

"Good morning." Martha smiled at him. His coloring box might be shy of a few crayons, but manners were free and friendliness went a long way. Maybe he was just depressed and acting erratically. With a new house owner, he'd had some adjustments as well. He didn't seem dangerous and treated Jessie with the utmost respect, and Jessie did have good locks on her doors—Martha had tested them—so there didn't seem to be anything to worry about.

"Yes. Good morning. I trust you slept well," he said, the words polite but the tone stuffy. It was like he fashioned himself after the butlers in those black-and-white British movies. Someone should tell him he'd gotten the dress code wrong. She'd never known a butler to wear a cape, not even a British one. Although all the men in the house except Austin seemed to wear them. It must've been some sort of peer pressure situation, or fashion sense gone wrong.

She smiled brighter to break through those clouds. "I did, yes, thank you."

"Martha!" Pete's voice rang through the hall. "Martha! Come look at this."

"Will he be needing a bullhorn? I'm not sure the neighbors heard." Tom—or maybe Earl; everyone called him something different, perhaps contributing to the poor man's confusion—lifted his chin and walked on by.

"What is it now?" she grumbled to herself, startling

at the sight of a red-haired doll with a devilish smile standing at the end of the hallway, where the path turned right to another set of rooms and then some stairs leading to the back of the third floor. Standing, on its own. But a doll like that shouldn't have been able to stand; its feet were too small and body top-heavy. The thing had an enormous head. Maybe it was leaning?

She slowed, Pete momentarily forgotten. There was definitely a feeling of something being *off* in this house. Like a presence, or presence*s*, resided here. She'd seen two different doors move on their own—one opening, and another closing. Pete had said it was probably the wind, and that if she didn't watch it she was the one who'd get shipped off for losing her faculties. She had no idea what he was talking about, but she knew what she'd seen. No breeze in this house could've blown those doors open and shut that fast. He might not believe in ghosts, but she did, and this house was plenty old enough to have a whole bunch of them.

That didn't explain the doll, though…

She approached it slowly, half wondering if it would come alive, like in those scary movies.

"Don't go scaring yourself, Martha. Those are only make-believe," she murmured, getting within feet of it and peering over, trying to see if it was leaning.

"Martha!"

She jumped and squeaked, slapping her hand onto her mouth.

"I'm coming!" she hollered at Pete. "I don't have a jetpack on. Hold your horses."

A little closer and she could see over the doll's head. The back of its head touched the wall. It *was* leaning. Someone had clearly placed it there.

"Of course they did." She shook her head. "Of *course* someone placed it there. It couldn't have just walked there on its own."

She rolled her eyes at herself and took a deep breath. The house was getting to her.

Pete stood at the base of the stairs that led up to the third floor, this set reserved for the house staff of old, she bet. There was a larger and grander set nearer the front of the house. He held a big battle-axe positioned across his body, the edges gleaming. There wasn't a stich on him.

"Pete!" She jammed a fist onto her hip. "For the love of God, *put some clothes on!*"

"Why? Martha, the whole place runs around naked. It's like a damn nudist colony. If they can do it, I can do it. You don't have a set of begonias, you just don't understand."

"Would you stop saying—" She tried to will herself some patience. "Maybe not, but I have a set of garden shears and have done a lot of pruning in my day." She paused to let that sink in. "Pete, you are a guest in your daughter's house. She doesn't want to see you with your testicles out. *Put on some clothes.*"

He gave her a long-suffering sigh. "Fine. But look at this." He hefted the large axe.

"Where on God's earth did you get that? Go put it down before you slice off a thumb. Or something else."

"There's a whole attic of this kind of stuff. I found it when I was looking for some mousetraps. Come on, come look at it."

Curiosity getting the better of her, she said, "Oh, all right."

By the time they scaled the two sets of stairs, she was feeling it. The fatigue didn't last long as she surveyed the attic, the far wall absolutely covered with various weapons, polished to a high shine. Above each hung a small white square of paper with elegant scrawl in black. She squinted at them in surprise—each bore a fairly common person's name.

"And check this out." He placed the axe on its pegs below the name Jake and crossed the space with bare feet.

"Careful, you might step on a nail."

"Or a spike!"

"Yes, fine, or a spike. I don't know why you insist

on one-upping me all the time…"

He opened a drawer and extracted a large red stone. "She's got a whole drawer full of these things. Looks like a ruby, doesn't it?"

"Pete, now, I don't know about looking through her things."

"She said all this stuff came with the house. Maybe she doesn't even know they're here. Boy, wouldn't it be something if it was a real ruby?"

"Of course it isn't a real ruby." She peered at the costume gemstones. "This is probably for crafts or something."

"Or look at this one…" He pulled out a blue stone the size of the end of his thumb. "This could be worth more than our car."

"No one with precious gemstones like this would keep them in a drawer in the attic. Why are those weapons labeled with names, do you think? That is a bit odd."

"This whole place is a bit odd. They went looking for a deer last night, acting like it was some first-rate spy or something. They launched into some big talk about tracking and smelling and defenses—build a fence, you know? Deer can't climb fences. That's all the defense you need. I think that big guy is some sort of plant nut or something. He really seemed worried about that deer eating Jessie's flowers."

"He's caring. Don't you see the way he looks after her, pulling out her chair and guiding her through doorways? He's a real Prince Charming. I'd say she still has the chance to meet the love of her life. Matt wasn't it, we always knew that. What if Austin is the real Prince Charming?"

"Prince Charming had a castle, not a flower complex. Don't start, Martha. She doesn't need to be set up. The kid just got out of a marriage. She's bruised. Let her find her own way." He pushed the drawer closed. "Do you remember seeing a garage? I don't think chasing rats through a house with a battle-axe is the right way to play it, no matter how fun it sounds."

"Sometimes she just needs a little push, is all." Martha made her way down the stairs again, gripping the handrail tightly. Thinking about that red-headed doll down below. "Careful here, Pete, these are steep. I wonder if maybe I won't round up those dolls and put them away after all."

Click.

"Jiminy crickets," he said, "there's another bit of plaster coming loose down the hallway there. This place is going to fall down around us."

CHAPTER 11

"**H**ERE WE ARE." Mr. Tom stopped in front of what looked like a small house with a wraparound porch, heavily screened by two large maples. The noonday sun dappled the uneven sidewalk in front of the establishment, the tree roots pushing at the concrete. No sign announced a business and no cars waited in the parking lot to the right.

"This is Agnes's?" I asked, just to be sure, so tired that I barely knew my name.

We'd traveled through the entire wood last night, finding just one spot where Austin could pick up a scent. Just one. No scents, beyond the usual floral bombardment, trailed to or from the spot of munched flowers. Jasper had pinpointed the location perfectly, halfway from the flowers to the property line, the place where the deer had disappeared. If Jasper hadn't remembered the exact path he'd taken, Austin might never have found it.

The intruder was definitely a shifter—I didn't know

how Austin could tell, but he was sure—and shifters couldn't also be mages. Being a female gargoyle came with sorceress/mage perks, but whatever gene or magic turned a person into an animal shifter allowed only that one kind of magic. Which meant the deer shifter was using potions or elixirs—potions apparently being the stronger of the two—created by a master craftsman who may or may not be Elliot Graves.

The person at the front of the house hadn't been concealed. Their scent was all through the yards along the right side of the road. They were not a shifter, but beyond that, Austin couldn't tell.

The deer's late-night visit had opened up another question: if intruders had the ability to visit Ivy House unseen, were there others besides the deer that had walked around the property? Ones who didn't have a taste for flowers?

We still didn't know if those prowling the front were connected to those prowling the actual grounds. We didn't know much of anything, actually.

We'd gotten home just before dawn, and any sleep from then until midmorning had been fretful and plagued by dreams of fire-breathing deer sporting glowing red eyes. Some even had rocket launchers mounted on their backs. I kept waking up thinking the house was under attack.

Maybe it was, albeit silently. Stealthily.

"Yes. This is it." Edgar beamed, standing down the sidewalk a little with Niamh and Ulric.

"This is a lovely little spot," my mom said, she and my dad having tagged along with the group. She looked around the quiet street, somewhat removed from the downtown strip. "It is just so lovely here. So peaceful and green. Just gorgeous."

"Shall we?" Austin lightly touched the small of my back, the absence of pressure giving me a chance to linger on the sidewalk if I wanted.

"Do you guys want to check out the downtown shops and the tasting rooms?" I asked my mom. "This is just about gardening stuff, in here."

"Insects," Mr. Tom said.

I nodded and rubbed my eyes. "Right, yeah. Bugs." If my parents thought it was actual gardening, they might want to check it out. "We're just looking for something to take care of bugs."

"Flowers and capes," my dad said, shaking his head. "I think you're too wrapped up in flowers and capes."

"Oh, never mind." My mom waved him away. "Are there some little shops we can visit?"

"Yes. And tasting rooms, too." Mr. Tom gave them directions to the main drag, just three blocks over. There wasn't much to this small town, something I'd grown to like. If only a slower pace went with it. That was probably too much to ask for in my situation, though.

When my parents had turned the corner, I started forward as Ulric said, "They must think we are absolutely wackadoo. A bunch of guys wearing capes all the time?" Ulric laughed. "How can they rationalize that?"

"A cape is the very least of the things they have been rationalizing. The very least," I said, making it to the door. I lifted my hand to knock but the door swung open before I could, revealing a woman of indeterminate middle age with bright red-orange hair pulled up to the top of her head and strands of ringlets draping her face. Lipstick that matched her hair colored her plump, heart-shaped lips, and a wide nose adorned her thin face.

"Hello." Dual-colored eyes, one green and one blue, surveyed me for a moment before sticking to Austin's shoulders. "Alpha. What a pleasure."

She stepped back, allowing me to enter, her gaze staying put.

The building might've been the shell of a house, but the inside had been redone, a large space off to the left supported by beams with tables dotting the way and bookshelves lining the walls. A counter sat at the far corner, a cash register perched on the edge and the rest of the surface covered in bins stacked high. Crystals and colored rocks and candles covered every available space, organized in their bins or placed on their shelves, the whole place awash with color. Incense burned from the back, the smoke curling into the air before spreading out into a heinous-smelling fog.

The right side of the space was divided into two wooden stalls, the doorway covered with a curtain. I imagined tarot or fortunetelling went on in there.

"Please, come on back." Agnes's smile was hazy and her gaze didn't leave Austin's shoulders until she had to physically turn and lead the way to the back.

Through a hallway with more tables littered with crystals, we finally reached a small office with a desk covered in papers, two chairs facing it, and way too many plants. It was clear she used the same elixir that she sold to Edgar, and I wondered if she had a fear of basajaun eating all of her hard work as well.

"Jacinta, isn't it?" Agnes walked around the desk and took a seat before clasping her fingers together and resting them on the desk. Her gaze found Austin's shoulders again, roaming from one to the other and dipping toward his pecs in between. "I helped you with a forgetful elixir, I believe."

"Yes." I sat down in one of the chairs. Austin stood behind me, allowing Niamh to take the chair next to me. Mr. Tom stood behind her and the others waited in the hall. "Hello."

"Yes, hello. I hear you have the greatest crystals of all." Her gaze finally broke from Austin's shoulders. "Tell me about them."

"Is this…" I crinkled my nose within the predatory stare. "Is this part of the fee, or…"

"Agnes, we haven't time for that," Austin said. Her eyes zipped to his shoulders again. It was like she didn't know he had a head. "We need help with a potion."

"Hmm. I can't do many potions. I don't have the power; you know that."

"We're hoping you can possibly break down what this particular potion might be so that Jessie can create a counter-spell," Edgar said, leaning in the door. "Hello, by the way."

"Hi, Edgar. Lovely to see you, as always." Even though she continued to trace Austin's shoulders with her eyes, I could somehow tell she shifted her focus to me. "Edgar is my best customer, especially lately. Isn't that right, Edgar?"

"Ivy House is your best customer, actually," Edgar said. Mr. Tom sniffed as though annoyed. I wondered how much Edgar was actually spending, and if Mr. Tom had to pay for him, too.

"So then." Agnes smiled, and I didn't know how

Austin wasn't weirded out by the attention he was getting. In fairness to her, though, he did have a great set of shoulders. "What sort of potion are we thinking about?"

I described what'd I'd seen and then Austin described the lack of traceability.

"Hmmm," Agnes said, and looked at an old-school corded telephone at the corner of her desk. The styling might've come from the forties but quite a bit fancier, with cheaper-looking metal, a new product meant to look retro. "That is much too advanced for me. I bet my cousin's friend would know. Hold on."

She lifted the receiver from the cradle before slipping a pink nail into the hole and pulling the dial around, a system that took ages. The number finally in, she pushed a little button behind the leg that was definitely a modern addition. Ringing erupted from a speaker somewhere in the base of the phone.

"Yeah," a man answered in a gruff tone.

"Harlan, honey, it's Agnes."

"Hey," he responded. "How are you?"

"Good, love. I'm sitting here with the new alpha of my town and the mistress of Ivy House…"

"No sh—Are you serious? The mistress of Ivy House? What's she like? Have you seen her do any magic?"

"No, babe, though I'll mention that you're on speakerphone. Listen, I was wondering if you could help us out." She relayed what we had gone over.

"The house can sense people, huh? Wow. That's a trip." He blew out a breath. "Hiding someone's smell and tracks through an elixir is nothing. You know that."

"Yes," she replied, "but I can't weave in invisibility. The gargoyle in the sky said the deer just disappeared."

"You've got gargoyles, too? That town is starting to heat up. I might need to visit…"

"The new alpha is sitting right here," she said, and her tone suggested he better zip the lip in case he pissed Austin off somehow.

"Got it," the guy said. "How much do you trust the eyesight of that gargoyle? Because that is incredibly advanced potion making with a sh—sorry—buttload of power."

"So you can weave all that together?" I asked, leaning forward.

The line went quiet for a moment. "Oh God, is that her?" he whispered. "Did the mistress of Ivy House just speak to me?"

"Hi, I'm Jacinta," I said. "Jessie, if you want."

The guy's whispered voice increased in pitch. "*Did she just ask me to call her a nickname?*"

"How old is this lad?" Niamh asked exasperatedly.

"Mentally? Not very," Agnes said with a smile.

The guy cleared his throat. "Yeah, so a powerful enough mage can…weave all of that together. He or she can create a potion of invisibility, though it doesn't negate sound, usually. You won't be able to smell them, or see their tracks, or see them, but very few people in the world can also cut out the sound. It's one of those strange little magical phenomena."

"What about disappearing from the house itself?" Agnes asked. "Or glowing?"

"Uhhmm…" The man paused. "No, that has to be something different. You know what, my buddy's new girlfriend figures out spells. I bet she could help."

After I'd thanked him, we were given the number for his buddy Donald, who then gave us the number of his new girlfriend. Once we were connected to her, the story was told yet again. The quickness and ease with which she made sense of everything had me wishing we'd called her first.

"A simple elixir for masking tracks and smell can be layered over virtually any spell or potion if the elixir is made with enough power," the woman said, her voice quiet and reserved. "Given everything else you are saying, this mage has the power. I would guess that the elixir to disguise smell and tracks ran out at the point you were able to smell him, obviously, and he had to drink another. If you could see the...intruder at first, and then they disappeared when they drank another potion, I'd bet there are two potions and one elixir. There is the potion masking the person's signature from the house, which is layered with the elixir masking scent and footprints, and the potion for masking sight, scent, footprints and maybe smell, depending on the mage. Two potions and a high-powered elixir would be incredibly expensive to buy, and take a master at *least* a couple of days to make, though he or she could probably make a decent batch size with each. Maybe enough for four people."

"Do you think you can figure out how to make any of those?" Austin asked.

"The elixir and invisibility, yes. Easily. That's just a matter of looking it up. The first spell that made the deer glow... I'll do some research. I can't promise anything, but..."

Agnes beamed. "Fantastic! I have all the faith in you."

"Listen," the woman said. "A mage that can do all of this, or someone that can afford to buy these types of high-powered potions, is incredibly dangerous. *Incredibly* dangerous. You need to try to see your way out of their affairs as quickly as you can. You don't want to get mixed up with anyone of this caliber."

A tense beat of silence filled the room. Austin's hand rested on my shoulder.

I pushed the hair out of my face. "Too late now. I've accepted the magic. There is no going back."

CHAPTER 12

I NEARLY FELL through the door, I was so tired.

"She's gonna get it done, don't you worry, Jessie," Niamh said, following me into the house. The others trailed behind us, except my parents, who had, thankfully, stayed downtown to shop and taste wine. "Ye know what, I never realized just how little I knew about her until this afternoon."

"Just think, if you'd gotten better acquainted earlier, you could've had a friend all this time," Ulric said.

"Not a hope," she replied, the house almost sounding hollow without the noise from the TV spilling out of the sitting room. "She is much too chipper and sweet for me. All the smiles put me in a foul mood."

"Your very existence puts you in a foul mood," Mr. Tom said, straightening a painting in the hall.

"That is because I have to share that existence with ye, ya miserable old goat," she replied. "Now pull yer socks up, unless ye want to be fired from another butler gig."

He looked down at his feet. "I'll kindly ask you to leave my socks out of it." He paused. "You can't even see them!"

"It means get ta work. That auld mammy is running circles around ya, boy. She's handling the whole house with a smile, so she is. Jessie is probably rethinking having yer sad sack loafing around."

"Oh my God, please don't start at each other right now. I cannot handle it." I rubbed my temples and stopped outside the front sitting room, the one we usually used to discuss business or just hang out. We had a ton of stuff to work through. Agnes's contact was working on the potions, so that was out of our hands for the time being, but I had to work out guard schedules for the gargoyles within Ivy House, not to mention those staying in the hotel. Should we scatter them through the wood as lookouts? Edgar had been tasked with researching ways to circumvent Ivy House's magic, since the house admitted to me last night before I went to bed that she did know of this issue from the past, but didn't have a solution for me to fix it. She said she'd help Edgar in any way she could, but she didn't have a recipe for a counter-spell. Talking that out was probably necessary, since information had to exist somewhere, or how did Elliot Graves know?

But at this particular moment in time? I just

couldn't be bothered. I was too exhausted.

"Mr. Tom, can you make me a snack or something?" I asked. "I'm going into my private sitting room."

It hadn't started out as a private sitting room, but it was small, in a seldom-traversed back corner of the house, and everyone left me alone when I used it. Within the last couple months, I'd started calling it what it had become.

"Of course, miss. I'll be in directly. Would you like a snack for one, or…" He looked between Austin and me.

I wanted Austin's company, if only because he had some immensely broad shoulders to lean on, as Agnes had clearly noticed, but I did not feel like putting myself out there to ask. Fatigue and frustration had a way of bringing out my vulnerability. I didn't think leaders let their subordinates (the new gargoyles) see them cry on the cusp of battle, especially when it was over something as trivial as a guy not accepting an invite to join them for a sit and a think.

I shrugged and didn't comment, starting off down the hall, my mind spinning.

"For three," Austin said. "I'm hungry."

My eyes teared up in relief. I was a mess right now. I needed sleep.

When I stepped into the sitting room, the comforting smell of books greeted me, the small bookcase at my back holding my favorite volumes and a bunch of books on my to-be-read list. The actual house library was a great place to read, but it didn't offer the sense of comfort and seclusion this space did. I sighed as I sank into my favorite chair, the sun filtering in through the open window shades doing little to lighten my spirits.

Austin closed the door behind him before lowering into the chair opposite me. He propped his feet on the ottoman, crossed his ankles, and then entwined his fingers on his lap. His gaze drifted out the window to match mine, but he let the silence linger.

"Thanks," I said softly, watching the leaves wiggle on a large oak. "I wanted quiet, but didn't really want to be alone."

"Understandable. Dealing with this situation is a lot, especially with your parents already here.

I filled my lungs to bursting and then let the breath out slowly, feeling my muscles relax a little with the exhale. Not enough, though.

"I'm just…" My eyes teared up again. "I'm freaking tired, Austin." A tear escaped, and I wiped my cheek with the back of my hand. "I'm tired of this crap. If Elliot wants a piece of me, why doesn't he just show up and meet me face to face? Or attack the house or something? I hate all this stealth and secrecy. It's exhausting. I still don't even know how to work most of my magic. I am absolutely zero threat to someone like that, and whatever the proprietor of this house might've been to the magical world back in the day, it's not like that anymore. I'm a nobody with a weird, half-formed crew, no clue about politics, and no desire to do anything but hang out in this town and live in peace. Why doesn't he just go away? I can't help him. In fact, you know what? I'm going to write him a letter to tell him exactly that. Quit bothering me—I cannot help you."

More tears dripped down, and I batted them away furiously, annoyed that I was breaking down. Frustrated that I felt so helpless.

"The one thing I had going for me was Ivy House's protective magic," I continued, sobs threatening, "and now Graves—or someone—has found a way around it. And maybe I could work the defenses myself and do okay, but against two groups? Or even one spread-out group? I have to see the enemy to use the defenses, and if there are too many, I won't be able to. No matter how vigilant you and the others are, you can't be here all the time. I'm wide open. Now that he knows he can get someone onto my land without anyone noticing, what's to stop him from sending a mage? He won't send a weak one this time." I wiped away more tears, fear rolling through me. "I'm not strong enough for this,

Austin."

He rose from his chair, crossed the small space, lifted me into his arms, then returned to his spot and sat back down with me in his lap like I was a child. I didn't resist. Couldn't. The sobs bubbled up and overflowed, racking my body, pouring out all of my uncertainty and helplessness and exhaustion. He wrapped his strong arms around me and held me close, my face buried in his neck.

Finally, when the sobs died down and his neck was wet with my tears, he spoke.

"You are more than just this house." His voice vibrated through his chest in a low hum. "You are insightful, an incredibly fast learner, and already amazing with your magic after such a short period of time. What you've learned in months dwarfs what most magical people learn in years. Most importantly, you are courageous. When you were kidnapped a few months ago, you didn't sit down and wait to be rescued. You kept calm and made a friend of the basajaun, one of the most dangerous creatures in our world. *You* did that, not Ivy House. The mages figured out a way to cut you off from the house, yet you still triumphed. You are incredible all by yourself, Jess. Ivy House chose you because it knew it would be safe with you, not the other way around."

I shook my head, pushing away a little. "I wouldn't have been able to escape those mages without Ivy House, and I wouldn't have been able to escape that cage without you."

"Because you're still learning. Every student relies on their teachers. It's the way things should be. And that brings me to my second point. Ivy House isn't the only defense you have. You have me. Through me, you have this town. I'm still in the planning stages, but when I'm done, Ivy House will be your keep within my castle. I'll pack my territory with so much power that even Elliot Graves will think twice about going through me to get to you.

"Until then, you have a fearless crew, and we would all lay down our lives to see you safe. As soon as Agnes's uncle's drinking buddy's cousin's girlfriend or whoever"—he paused for my laugh—"lands on the type of spell the deer used, or even an idea of how it works, you and Edgar will figure out how to tear it down. I have every faith that this is in your wheelhouse. It's just another challenge to help you grow. We all need a spur in the side sometimes, and I think this is yours." He ran his fingers across my temple before tucking a strand of hair behind my ear. "When you *do* find a way to counter that potion, you can wait to use it until his people get good and close to Ivy House, assuming he sends more of them. Then you can tear away their protections and let Ivy House deal with them in the most gruesome ways she conjures up. You can let her have vengeance. Instead of a letter to Elliot, you can send a head."

I widened my eyes. "Wow. That devolved into un-speakable violence quickly."

His smile was slight and his eyes were full of warmth. "Welcome to the magical world, where there are penalties for bullying."

A soft rap came at the door. Mr. Tom was not usu-ally in the habit of knocking, but having guests in the house had apparently changed all his habits.

I made a move to climb off Austin's lap, but instead he stood and deposited me on my feet. He ran his hands down the outsides of my arms. "You good?"

I laid a hand on his chest, his heart beating against my palm. "Yeah. Thanks. You always know what to say."

"The truth. All I ever say is the truth. You're excep-tional, Jacinta, and not because of the magic. Not because of this house or your crew. Definitely not because of me. You are a shooting star in a dark sky."

My vision swam and my lip trembled. I nodded mutely.

When he stepped back, his movements were rigid,

like he was forcing himself to do it. He hated people in turmoil. The alpha in him clearly felt the need to soothe me.

I took a deep breath. It was time to pick myself up, dust myself off, and solve the problem—and the only way to do that was to act. I had all the tools; I just needed to use them.

"Come in," I called, returning to my chair as Austin sat down in his.

"Yes, miss. Here we go." Mr. Tom carried in a silver tray laden with sandwiches, cut veggies, chips, and fruit. "If you want anything else, just let me know." He placed the platter on a small round table in the corner. "To drink…" He ducked out into the hall and brought back a bottle of sparkling wine in a silver ice bucket, followed by a pitcher of sweet tea. "We also have a troubling amount of cheap American beer, should you want that. Or hard alcohol, if quickly numbing the pain is the order of the day."

"Thank you, Mr. Tom, you've outdone yourself."

He preened and shut the door behind him on his way out. After Austin and I made ourselves plates, I stared out the window in contemplation as I ate.

"No one thinks of danger when they see a deer," I said, thinking out loud. "Granted, this deer was glow-ing, which was disarming, but if the spell hadn't worked, we might have just thought a weirdly large deer was roaming around the woods. Either way, glowing or not, it's not the kind of creature that makes you think violent thoughts."

"It is certainly a benign creature. A deer wouldn't be used for much in the magical world. I doubt the shifter has battle experience or fighting prowess. It wouldn't have much status. From that we can assume, the shifter is considered expendable. It's being sent here to test the potions, and to get a good look at the goings-on of the house while it does so."

"The deer didn't come very close to the house. It stopped at the edge of the wood, and then kept its distance while it worked around to the side yard. It also didn't eat as many flowers as it wanted to, I could tell. If Edgar hadn't expanded the configuration of flowers to reach into the woods, I bet it wouldn't have been tempted into trying a couple. We wouldn't have known it was around."

"Edgar made a big deal about how addictive his flowers were." He shook his head, looking out the window again. "I hesitate to agree with him. If I do, it feels like I'm walking the very dangerous path that led him where he is now. Coo-coo."

I couldn't help but laugh. "I absolutely know what you mean. I've been there a few times."

Austin put his feet up and entwined his fingers again, leaning back on the headrest. "This room has a comfortable vibe. The view is nice, too, in a Monet sort of way, with the random splotches of color. Edgar is nuts, but he does know how to grow plants."

"He cheats."

"He's…dutiful and goes the extra mile."

"Cheat to win, in other words."

"Exactly so." A smile curled his lips. "Your father might have a point about the tracks. We're going to make sure the area's wet enough for them this evening, just so we know it's the potion working and not light feet on hard-packed dirt." His eyes came to rest on me. "I think you should move the tripwire to the grass so you'll only be alerted if the deer comes close enough to be a threat. You need to get some sleep tonight. There's nothing we can do right now but wait. We need to see what Agnes's network comes up with, or if we're lucky, Edgar will find answers first."

"All before Elliot decides the potion is a success and brings a host of his people through my property."

"You're positive that deer seemed spooked by the lurker in the front yard?" Austin asked.

I thought back, remembering how it had darted away. "Spooked for a deer. No idea for a shifter."

He thought for a moment. "There is a chance the

prowler was working with the deer shifter, wondering why he was taking so long, but it wouldn't make sense for the shifter to head off in a different direction. It doesn't seem likely that they're on the same team."

I rubbed my eyes. "Why would two people attack at once? Two prowlers on the same night? It doesn't make sense."

"It does in the magical world. I mostly stopped paying attention to the greater goings-on since I left my brother's pack, and I haven't had a chance to update my knowledge since I stepped up to alpha, but motives and politics never really change that much. Elliot Graves does not work with people because he is not the type to share. His suppliers are his suppliers alone. His contracted employees only work for him. So when he decided early on to go after you—coming even before you'd accepted the magic—he was declaring his intent to secure you for his interests. He will not suffer anyone else moving in and possibly getting lucky and grabbing you. He'll fight to get what he wants. Most magical people would. Hell, most Dicks and Janes would, too—they just don't jump to violence as quickly as people in the magical world do."

"I thought he was a big deal in the magical world. Why would someone else move into his proposed territory and risk facing his wrath?"

Austin smiled without humor. "There are many big deals in the magical world, and everyone is looking for an edge. If Elliot Graves wants a thing, and if that thing is still technically up for grabs, then others will try to get it, either for their own benefit or to barter with Elliot Graves. It sounds like the secret is out about you."

I blew out a breath. "Great."

"We have some time. My smell is all over that deer's trail, and all over the neighbor's yards. No one will want to tango with me. The two groups will stay cautious for a few days, the shifter probably making some shallow runs into the property to see if he can get away with it, and the front yard prowler inching closer to see if we notice. If I don't come after them, which I purposely won't, even though the thought of letting an intruder into this territory…" His jaw clenched, his gaze still fixed out the window. "If they get no opposition, they'll show near the house again for a test run. *That* is when the timer will start to count down."

"How can you be sure? What if the deer or prowler tells his or their bosses we're onto him and the boss rushes in?"

"A lesser boss might, but I don't think we're dealing with someone like that. If the person behind this isn't Elliot, it's a very wealthy mage. Those potions would be incredibly expensive, like Agnes's people said, and the shifter would need one of each per night, for however many nights. Someone with that kind of money is a major player in the magical world, and major players use strategy. They're smart. Which fits with what we're seeing. Last night granted us a few days. And until we have more information, we are dead in the water. You need to rest, take it easy, and conserve your energy until you have a way to act."

"That easy, huh?"

His gaze felt heavy on me. "I'll stay in Ivy House with you, if that's okay. I'll take the room next to yours. I won't let anything get to you, Jacinta. I will guard you when you sleep, so that you *can* sleep."

Tears welled in my eyes again and I looked away. Throat tight, I didn't trust myself to speak. All I could do was nod. Austin Steele, Sir Knight.

"What's your real last name?" I asked, my voice a whisper, not sure whether I was crossing some sort of boundary. I knew the town had chosen the last name Steele for him, but he'd never mentioned what it was instead of.

He was quiet for a beat. "Barraza. I left it behind when I left my pack, which is the custom for an alpha's siblings, who usually leave to head up a different pack or form a new one. Alphas earn their names, given to them by the pack they create or taken by force from an established pack leader. My brother took the name from my mother, who handled the pack before him."

"Your brother forcefully took the pack from your mom?"

"Yes, but the fight wasn't to the death. She was aging and he was ready. She made him work for it, but when it was clear he was dominant, she acquiesced. Normally old pack leaders are banished, but not always. My mother gracefully stepped aside, and my brother brought her onto his team of advisors. It was a seamless transition that exemplifies their strength in leadership. I'm the black sheep of the family."

"You just had a longer path. A harder path. You'll come out better for it. You'll do them proud, Austin, if you haven't already."

He looked at me for a long time before giving me a slight nod and looking away. I could tell he didn't really believe it, and my heart broke a little for him. He'd prove himself, though, of that I had no doubt. He might not trust himself because of his past, but I knew him as well as anyone, maybe better. I'd seen him lose control, I'd seen him do battle, and I'd watched him work with townspeople every day, with my people, showing them the patience of a saint. Giving them a helping hand and a place to belong. Protecting them. Protecting *me*. He'd walked a hard road, but he hadn't allowed it to turn him brittle. To break him. I hadn't seen the start of the journey, but I knew the end, and he was the best man I'd ever known.

I said as much.

He took a deep breath. "When you say things like that, I wonder what guy you're seeing."

"The one sitting in front of me."

"Hard to believe."

"Only if you're thick, like Niamh would say."

"I've been called worse."

"Yeah, but those were probably true."

His lips curled at the ends.

"So you really did leave everything behind when you left, including your name," I said.

"Well, not everything. I kept the money."

I spat out laughter, his comment surprising me. "Right."

"I wasn't totally desolate."

"Nothing wrong with a little nest egg. If you got stuck, you could just buy a winery." I wiped my mouth, feeling a lot lighter than when I'd come in earlier. "We're similar, in a way. I left everything behind, too. I'm not the girl who married Matt. He gave me a nametag when I signed into his life. It's a nametag for a different person. I'm not an Evans anymore. When I walked away from that life, I left parts of myself behind.

I shed my old skin. But I'm not a McMillian anymore either. I've developed—or maybe devolved—into a completely new person. Maybe I should come up with a new name, too."

"Or maybe just stick to one name, like Adele or Cher. Or, I know, create a title for yourself. Jacinta the Merciful, Decider of Fates, Ruiner of All Things Tedious."

I laughed. "That's a little long. What would the sign say in front of my placemat at weddings?"

"Oh…" He waved his finger around at the house at large. "No one you know around here is ever going to get married. They've missed that bus."

I frowned at him. "There is someone for everyone. Somewhere out there, there's a grumpy woman who is impossible to please, waiting for her knight in shining armor to sweep her off her feet." I tapped my chin. "I better give Mr. Tom some days off so he can go find her."

Austin shook with laughter. "You just described Niamh." He started to sing, his voice smooth and incredibly pleasing. "*Matchmaker, matchmaker, make me a dream…*"

I widened my eyes. "Wow. You have a really good voice. Like…really good."

His cheeks colored and he looked away, adorably

embarrassed.

"Do you dance, too?" I asked, leaning forward and bracing my elbow on my knee before resting my chin on my fist.

"Maybe."

"Oh my goodness, and the hot guy gets hotter." I sat back and fanned my face. "What other tricks do you have up your sleeve?"

"I have a horrible temper."

"Nah, no you don't. A rage problem when something sets you off, sure, but you're slow to anger. Do you play an instrument?"

"Guitar."

I rolled my eyes. "A *guitar*? Jesus, Austin, you're a cliché. What else? Fast car?"

"The Jeep isn't very fast."

"Yes, true. Strike against you."

"The Bugatti isn't so bad, though."

"That's a shame... Wait. A Bugatti?" I cocked my head. "Do you really have a Bugatti?"

He laughed and wiped his hand across his face. "I did. Left it behind. I came here on four paws. I got the Jeep here in town. I do miss going recklessly fast, though."

"Damarion bought a Lexus when he was here," I said. "He went recklessly fast. I didn't love it."

"First, recklessly fast in the right hands isn't scary, it is exhilarating. I would make you squeal in delight. Second, do not mention that man's name when it relates to you and dating or intimacy."

I froze, my mouth open to speak, but a rush of excitement flooded my body, and the words drifted away. He'd said the first in a playful, teasing way. His tone had changed at the end, shifting into something rough and intense and possessive, as though the aforementioned rage was bubbling to the surface, beyond his control.

Something dangerous kindled within his stare, trapping me to my seat, holding me there. I could barely breathe as fire moved through my veins, coiling within me, aching down low. My heart raced as the memory of his touch, of his lips whispering across my skin.

Someone who didn't belong walked into my woods.

I sat forward, responding to the trespasser. Or was I responding to Austin?

The heat in his eyes consumed me, made my thoughts hazy. Electricity crackled through the air around us. He pulled his feet down from the ottoman, slowly, purposefully, bracing them wide and leaning his elbows against his knees, a predatory look in his eyes.

My body would not move, caught in his stare, in his intense focus—nervous for reasons I didn't understand, excited for the same reasons. A crease formed between his brows, as though he was wrestling with his thoughts.

The stranger on the property came into sharper focus. The timing was terrible. I didn't want this moment interrupted.

I needed this moment interrupted.

CHAPTER 13

"**M**ISS!" MR. TOM pushed open the door. "Miss. Your parents are farting around the garden. Your dad found a used wine barrel on the side of the road with a 'free' sign and, after rolling it all the way home, is now trying to decorate the garden with it."

"Not now, Mr. Tom," I said, needing the lifeline he was offering but not wanting to take it. The fresh air would surely clear my head, but sitting in these close quarters with Austin, I wanted nothing more than to lock us in and throw away the key.

"Yes, miss, I can see you're winning a stare-off with Austin Steele, and let me tell you, that is an outstanding accomplishment, but I cannot get them to go back inside, and the basajaun is making haste toward the garden. His disguises aren't good. You need to get your parents into the house before he shows up, or your magical cover will surely be blown."

The crease between Austin's brows deepened. His eyes flicked toward Mr. Tom, as though he was just now starting to comprehend the words.

"You might need to slap me, Mr. Tom. My mind is rolling down the gutter," I said.

"Of course, miss—"

"If you lift a hand to her, Earl," Austin growled, "I will rip it off and beat you with it."

"Ah. You do make a compelling argument, Mr. Steele."

I shook myself out of my stupor, feeling a strange mix of regret and gratitude, wishing the moment could go on forever, and also that Mr. Tom had interrupted us ten minutes sooner.

The basajaun was moving fast, loping through the wood, straight for the backyard. If he got there and ate all of Edgar's flowers, I'd never hear the end of it. That outcome would be so much worse than my parents seeing Bigfoot.

"When it rains, it pours." I hurried out of the house and to the back door, finding my parents doing exactly what Mr. Tom had described, positioning an old, multicolored, stained, and badly weathered wine barrel next to the gorgeous cherry tree getting ready to bloom. The contrast of ugly and beautiful had never been so stark. Niamh stood off to the side, watching, looking bemused.

"What's... What'd you find?" I asked, out of breath

from my run and the situation I'd left behind in my private sitting room. I put my hands on my hips, trying to play it cool while monitoring the basajaun's progress through the trees.

"Your father found another free thing," my mom said, wrestling herself up under the tree. "He just can't leave them alone."

"Why would someone throw this away?" My dad hiked up his retreating pants, the belt not quite doing the trick. "Look at it. It's perfectly good. You'd have to pay fifty or a hundred dollars for this in a store."

"It's super weathered, dad," I said. "It's been sitting in someone else's yard, clearly, and they've realized it has outlived its glory days. It's a wreck."

"Well, if that isn't a commentary on this house, I don't know what is," Niamh murmured.

"Nah, it'll be fine." My dad tried to wipe away a dark stain that did not plan on going anywhere. "You can just sand it down, stain it, and there you go. It'll look really good. Too bad we didn't bring the truck, or I would take it home. Maybe if we go look around in the streets, we can find another one."

The basajaun was a hundred yards out. Time to make a move.

"Right. Fine." I motioned them toward the house. "Mom, Mr. Tom needs a little help with dinner. He doesn't know if he can handle cooking for this many people." Mr. Tom's lips tightened, but he didn't comment.

"Oh yes, of course," my mom said, lighting up. "I thought we could have Cornish game hens tonight. What do you think, Sir Tom?"

"Mr. Tom, madam, and that would be fine."

"Well, with the cape 'n' all, I thought maybe you'd like sir over mister. It really elevates the name, don't you think?" She led him to the back door. "There is always *Monsieur* Tom. Now *that* would be snazzy, wouldn't it?"

"Dad…what about those rats? Did you attack that problem?" I asked, bouncing from foot to foot, the basajaun really close now. He clearly had something on his mind. I hoped to hell it wasn't violence. I didn't want to fight a being that could literally spike a human's head.

"Huh?" Dad looked away from the nearly-gray-it-was-so-weather-beaten wine barrel. "Oh, I set some traps. I found some in your shed. Don't you worry, we'll get that taken care of. By the way, what's with moving that Chucky-looking doll into the TV room? Your mother said she didn't do it. Your dolls are nice and all, but some of them…aren't to my taste."

I gritted my teeth and ran my hands through my

hair. Ivy House was clearly messing with my parents. Was there a way to put a house on time-out?

"It's probably Ulric's idea of a joke," I said, glancing back toward the trees. Austin was already walking that way, his stride long and powerful and graceful, muscles playing across his back with the swing of his large shoulders. Butterflies filled my stomach, and I turned away. He'd at least head off the basajaun, hopefully leaving it in the trees.

Unless the basajaun *had* come for violence. Then there'd be a Bigfoot and a polar bear battling in the garden. When it rained, it poured, indeed.

"Here, Pete, I could use a beer, whaddya say?" Niamh said, motioning him toward the house. "When Edgar gets through with what he's doing, we'll get him sanding that barrel down. He's got the equipment somewhere, I think. Ye didn't finish telling me about yer ancestors and all the places they lived in Ireland…" She gave me a long-suffering look. She was taking one for the team on this one. My dad loved to go on and on about his family roots.

"Oh yeah, that's right." He turned away from the barrel. The basajaun slowed as he neared the tree line, not quite visible yet, but not far off. "Well…" He looked at the sky. "It's five o'clock somewhere."

"That's here. It's five o'clock here!" She motioned

him in again. "Near enough, anyway. Close enough that it doesn't matter."

The basajaun stepped through the trees, a bright red baseball cap perched backward on his much-too-large head, an orange construction vest barely clinging to his enormous shoulders, and a pair of cut-off sweats practically glued to his lower half. Everywhere else—hair. Dense hair covered his chest, partially obscured by his long and braided beard. It flowed over his head and down the side of his hairy face, his nose so prominent it was all one could look at. The hair draped down his arms and legs and puffed up on top of his bare feet.

"Good Lord," my dad said, having turned a little toward me. He'd spotted him.

I held my breath. Niamh's expression flattened. Austin tried to motion the basajaun back into the trees.

"That hairy guy is sure tall. What'd you think, seven feet, eight? He dwarfs that Steele guy, and he's a big guy."

I furrowed my brow, not realizing my dad had taken to calling Austin by his last name. That was odd. He also didn't seem to have a real grasp on height. The basajaun was more like nine feet tall.

"Yeah," I agreed. His assessment seemed like a better number for his mental health. "He's big, yeah. He's a local. Kind of a recluse. Lives in a cabin in the mountains."

"Well, he clearly lost his razor. People probably think there's a Bigfoot around here." Dad shook his head and headed for the door. "Strange group of characters hanging around this house," he muttered. "Almost as strange as the house itself. And the staff." He lifted his voice a little as he reached Niamh. "What's with the butler's cape? I can't figure it out. What's he dressed up as?"

"A gobshite, that's what." She led him through the back door.

With them gone, I jogged across the grass. The basajaun caught sight of me and stepped around Austin, walking to meet me, his stride so big that we were moving toward each other at the same speed.

"Hey…" I pointed at him. "I never did get your name."

"Yes. Sorry for the intrusion. Lovely garden you have. It is even nicer than the last time I was here. I dream of these flowers. There is such a beautiful taste to them…"

I dropped my hand. "Thanks, I'll be sure to let Edgar know—"

"They taste even better than they look, and that is a true marvel. When we traded, I had no idea it was such a one-sided bargain. I was the true victor in that dealing. Often a person will offer quantity when they don't have quality, but you offered both. I am humbled by your generosity."

"Oh no, I think the trade was equal. It—"

"I come today because of that, and also because of our mutual respect and granting of safe passage on each other's territories." He looked between Austin and me.

Austin had given him safe passage, but as far as I was concerned, I'd just agreed to let him eat some flowers and move along. I hadn't realized we'd struck a deal for safe travel.

But I pressed my lips together and lifted my eyebrows, listening. Basajaun had strangely specific rules regarding territory and trading and life in general, and I knew hardly any of them. Given the basajaun ruthlessly killed the people who broke those rules, I figured it best to see what was on his mind.

"I have found a few trespassers on my mountain," the basajaun said as Ulric and Jasper came out of the back door. Mr. Tom must've told them we had company. I wondered why he hadn't bothered with Cedric.

"Don't you get a lot of hikers this time of the year?" I asked.

"Trespassers meaning magical people who know the rules of established territories and don't follow them," Austin said.

"Yes. You are both correct. I get a lot of hikers, who are such fun to slowly sneak up on in the trees, stepping out at the right time so as to give them an incredible fright. Why, just the other day—"

"All due respect, Mr. Basajaun, but I've had a very long day." I pinched the bridge of my nose. "What about those trespassers?"

"Yes, of course. I apologize. My zeal for interacting with the public gets the better of me." The basajaun adjusted his strained construction vest, which was surely cutting off the blood flow to his armpits. "Shifters have been using my mountain as a highway of sorts. I came upon the trails a week or so ago. At first it was just a single line over the mountain. I didn't think much of it. It is a large mountain, and those not of this area do not realize it is my territory. But over the last couple days, they have come and gone freely. They have altered their course, and I can only assume it is because they have scented me. Instead of following my scent trail back to me and trading for passage, they are attempting to circumvent my authority. Yesterday, I scented what I think was a mage among them—"

"I've never deciphered mages to have a particular scent," Austin said.

"Mages themselves smell like typical humans, yes, but if you pay attention, you can smell the magic on them. They do magic so often that it leaves a lingering smell, faint in some, strong in those more powerful. It is a spicy sort of smell that snaps at your nose." He paused for a moment, studying Austin as Austin studied him. "I can lead you to the trail. Point out the flavor."

Austin nodded. "I'd be obliged. Name your terms."

I turned my lips downward, impressed. Austin clearly knew how to work with a basajaun.

"If you identify the trespassers who have been using my mountain," the basajaun said, "I would ask that you turn the information over."

"Done." Austin didn't reach out to shake hands, and the basajaun didn't seem to expect it.

I swallowed, worry rising through me. Austin had told me we had time, but if there were a few shifters and they were already bringing mages in…

"Was the mage powerful, or…" I asked, and my voice wavered.

The basajaun's light brown eyes held mine. He hadn't struck me as particularly intelligent in our previous dealings, but maybe he had a different kind of smarts. From the emotions flickering through his eyes—excitement, humor, compassion, protective-ness—I gathered that he sensed my fear and was deciding which way to lean with it. I hoped he didn't opt for a practical joke…

He turned just slightly, giving me his full attention. "I remember that you said you were new to Ivy House. You are just a cub. Cubs must be protected and nurtured. They must be taught the ways. It is forbidden to attack one so new." He nodded. "Yes, I will help. If you will allow me a daily flower break, I will help you with this threat."

"Ulric, go get Edgar," I said quickly. I was not about to pass up the chance of recruiting such a fearsome ally, but I had promised that Edgar could be present the next time I traded with his flowers.

"The magical worker who came over the mountain had a fair bit of power, yes," the basajaun said as Ulric took off running. "I do not know about the shifters. I cannot smell their power level."

"With shifters, it's usually determined by the animal—and they travel in accordance with their rank, the strongest usually at the back and the weakest in the middle," Austin said. "I can show you, if you'll return the favor and let me know if you find out anything about who's crossing your mountain in the direction of my growing territory."

"It is a trade." The basajaun nodded.

"This trading thing is tedious," I mumbled as Edgar loped behind Ulric, one running like a normal person, one looking like some sort of vaudeville act.

"So you were the creature that scared the deer away last night?" I asked, my tension easing. "You were following it?"

The basajaun frowned, the expression only evident by the changing configuration of his hair. "This is the first time I have been off my mountain in months. I have had plenty to interest me there."

Tension flowered inside of me again. Wishful thinking, clearly. There was still a Big Bad unaccounted for.

"Hello." Edgar licked his colorless lips as he stopped near the basajaun.

"Edgar, the basajaun has agreed to help us in exchange for a daily flower quota," I said, then held my breath, hoping he didn't make this difficult.

"Oh. Yes, we could use the help. For now, anyway." Edgar smiled, his canines elongated again. "Ivy House has delivered to me an additional book, and I am making some headway, but sadly, it doesn't contain anything in the way of a counter-spell. My research continues."

The basajaun shook his head slowly. Apparently he wasn't picking up what Edgar was putting down.

"Edgar, why don't you talk about the restrictions with the flowers," I said. "Didn't you say you were going to create some sort of meal plan for the basajaun?"

"Oh! Of course." Edgar turned to the basajaun.

"You must know that flower production takes time and love. I am better than most, but even I must wait for them to grow. For that reason, we'll need to limit how much you eat at a time. I have planted more, with you in mind, but we only have so much space. Come, follow me—I'll give you a sample of what I'm working on for you."

I watched them go, the basajaun stooping to catch every word.

Austin looked out over the wood. "I'll learn the way to smell magic. That will help me assess the prowler, if there is still a trail. If the magical presence in the street was of a higher caliber, we can assume he or she will be cautious. They'll try to figure out who they're competing with before pushing forward. Or they might just rush in, hoping to get there first. We need to bring in the other gargoyles."

I blew out a breath. "Ulric can work on a story to tell the parents."

Austin nodded and wrapped an arm around my shoulders, pulling me close. "That basajaun gives us a leg up. Not only is he incredibly vicious, but he's at home in the trees. He can move through the woods more stealthily than anyone our enemies have at their disposal. There is danger lurking, but we are equipped to handle it. After a full night's sleep, you'll see that."

I dropped my head to his shoulder. If it was Elliot Graves, he clearly had a team of people headed over the mountain, and who knew how many would come at us from the front. We'd be grossly understaffed, not to mention I had my parents holed up inside. Without Ivy House, Austin's confidence didn't ring true. It was a nice sentiment, and I appreciated the support, but it would take more than a night's sleep to see us out of this. I could send out a summons for help, but the previous times it had taken a while for anyone to show, and when they did, one of those groups had a problem with a competing alpha. That wouldn't help us now, with danger lurking just out of sight.

We'd need to go it alone. This might be the time I was successfully kidnapped.

CHAPTER 14

T HE NEXT AFTERNOON, I paused midway through sweeping on some makeup when I felt Austin step down on the property.

He'd delivered on all of the promises he'd made the previous night. He'd learned how to decipher the scent of a magical user, retraced the prowler's trail, deduced the unknown Big Bad out front was a middle-range magical worker at best—less than whoever was trekking over the Basajaun's mountain—and stayed the night so I could sleep soundly.

And I had. No nightmares had troubled me. Worry hadn't kept me tossing and turning. I'd woken up refreshed and ready to figure this thing out.

It was amazing how safe he made me feel.

Come morning, he hadn't shown any fatigue, but I'd tapped into our connection for long enough to feel it. I'd set to work on healing it without saying anything. After the breakfast forced on him by my mother, he'd given me a secret smile and whispered, "Thanks," before heading out to check in with the people he had watching the town. The guy never took a day off.

Not that I was complaining, given the situation.

He'd texted in the early afternoon telling me to get ready; he had somewhere to take me. He hadn't specified where.

Now he was here.

I was terrified he had bad news he didn't want to break to me over the phone.

Ever the optimist, though, I finished my makeup before checking to make sure I hadn't spilled any powder on my shirt. Could be bad news, or it could be a trip to the winery he planned to buy for barrel tasting, or something else less awful than people coming after me. Given nothing had triggered my magical tripwire last night, which I had put near the flowers even though he'd said to put it near the grass, and Edgar hadn't seen anyone at the front, Niamh and Austin reckoned the people interested in the house were taking a step back to size each other up.

But it could be bad news. Austin and Niamh had made their assessment this morning based on very little information. I was nervous, which was why I'd decided to put on nicer clothes and some makeup. When I felt bad on the inside, jazzing up my appearance helped distract me. In this particular situation, it was also an excuse to escape Mr. Tom and my parents for a second.

I reached the bottom of the stairs before Austin had made much progress at all, his slow pace making me more anxious. He was obviously reluctant to tell me whatever he'd found out.

Mr. Tom stepped forward and pointed to the front sitting room.

"In there, miss, while I greet Mr. Steele."

I frowned at him. Did Mr. Tom know what was going on? Oh God, they knew the attack was coming tonight and they didn't want to freak me out too soon.

My mother sat in a chair near the fireplace, book in hand. She smiled at me as I sat down, and then lowered the book, clearly seeing from my expression that something was wrong.

"What is it—"

I didn't hear her finish the question because I felt Austin's arrival. I could sense him stopping at the front door and Mr. Tom opening it. His words were but a hum, washed out by my mother repeating her question.

"Miss." Mr. Tom stood in the doorway, his expression grim. "Mr. Steele is here to see you."

"Oh, how nice!" My mother beamed. "And good choice on your clothes, dear. Sophisticated and pretty, but casual. It's inviting, but it doesn't make you look like a sure thing." She gave me an "okay" sign.

Stomach churning, I didn't comment as I left the room. Better for her to think Austin had come to whisk me away than to inform me that we'd shortly be attacked by two unknown forces with mages and shifters and who knew what else.

In the foyer, though, the first glimpse of Austin took my breath away. He stood just in front of the door wearing stylish ripped jeans that hugged his muscular thighs and a white dress shirt with cream-colored, somewhat metallic horizontal stripes—subtle, but just enough to showcase the girth of his muscular torso. A few buttons had been left open, showing the groove of his pec muscles without revealing too much. Man cleavage. The sleeves were rolled up to his forearms, displaying a shiny watch with diamonds around the face. His hair, long on top and short on the sides, was stylishly messy, swooshed just a little to the right in a way that enhanced his incredibly attractive face.

He held an orchid plant in a distressed wooden base. The middle of the flower was a bluish white that exploded into purples and deep blues toward the outer rim, colors unlike any I'd ever seen in that type of flower. The base was stylish and amazing and exactly my taste.

"What's…" I glanced behind him, not sure what I was looking for, then around, wondering if I'd fallen back asleep somewhere and was dreaming right now. "What's going on?"

"You need a break from this circus," Mr. Tom said. "You are wound up so tightly you're about to crack."

"Right, but…"

"Welcome to the perfect date," Austin said.

We stared at each other for a silent beat. Mr. Tom and I stared at each other for another silent beat.

"Oh, how wonderful," my mother exclaimed, listening at the door.

"Mother, stop listening at the door," I said. I lowered my voice. "Okay, but… There are people who can sneak onto the property. We don't know when they are going to attack. My parents are here. I'd love an outing, yes, but obviously that's not realistic. I can't possibly chill out for a freaking date."

"We have a window," Austin said, stepping closer and lowering his voice as well. "Just in case, I won't hide the fact that I'm taking you out of here. If anyone is watching, they will see that you are traveling with me. Leaving the house. They won't attack while you are gone—why would they? You're the prize, not the house. Your parents will be safe, and worst case, they can hide in the walls. Should anything happen, Niamh and Cedric will make sure they are out of harm's way."

"But…"

"Jasper, Ulric, and the hotel gargoyles will be following us overhead, close at hand. If anyone makes a move on you, we'll be ready. I'll hold the line while you take to the air. They've been staking you out at the house; they won't be ready for a moving target. I doubt they'd be able to regroup quickly enough to intercept us. Even still, I have an underground route they won't find. They might follow us for a ways, but they won't follow us forever. I can get you out of here in safety. This is doable."

"You need the break," Mr. Tom said. "You need your wits, and you need your rest. Let Mr. Steele take you for a reprieve."

I stared into Austin's cobalt eyes, at a loss. "Okay… But wow, you have your work cut out for you."

"One thing you must know about me, Jess. I always rise to the challenge." He smirked and held out the orchid. "I got you a living flower. It's something to remember me by when I'm not here." The smirk turned into a mouth-watering smile. "Or, if the date doesn't go well, you can take the garden shears to it. Vengeance."

I laughed despite my churning unease about the whole situation, moving forward to take the orchid. "Thanks. It's gorgeous."

Mr. Tom reached out for it, but I set it on the little table near the door. "The entranceway needed an orchid."

"Perfect start," Austin said softly.

"You do need this outing," Mr. Tom said, "but be mindful. He's had forty years of practice at these things."

Austin's eyes dulled and flicked to Mr. Tom. He leaned back just a little, his smile faltering.

"Oh now, don't listen to him." My mom bustled out of the room, where she'd clearly continued listening at the door. Hopefully she hadn't heard the whispered part of our conversation. "He wears a cape. His opinion is bound to be suspect." She smiled at Austin. "My, you sure do clean up nice. Well, shoo, you kids. Shoo, shoo." She gasped as she shoved me toward the door. "Look at that *gorgeous* orchid. And the base! Great taste. Did you pick that out all by yourself, Austin?"

"Yes, ma'am. Just struck me as something Jess might like."

"Well, yes, she does." My mom opened the front door and motioned Austin out of it. "You should have seen her old house. All the wood looked like she'd picked it up off the side of the street. Trendy, my big toe. Her father kept telling her that he could've found all that for free."

"Shabby *chic*," I muttered, pushed out after Austin.

"Stay safe. Don't worry about us. We won't wait

up." My mom waved and shut the door behind us.

"Send-off…" I made like I was writing on a tablet. "Less than ideal."

He paused by the passenger door of the Jeep, the tops and doors still on this early in the season. "Listen." His expression and tone were both dead serious. "I've never tried very hard on dates. I'm always respectful and try to show my date a good time, but I don't go out of my way. Not ever. For you—for this—I did. I care about you, Jess. I care about our friendship. This isn't an everyday kind of thing for me. I'm not pulling stuff out of some womanizer playbook to try to schmooze you." He paused, then added, "I just wanted you to know that. Whatever Earl and Niamh might say about me—those things might usually be true, but they're not when it comes you, okay? I will protect you in all things, including from myself if need be. I will not do you wrong."

My heart nearly exploded, and I put out my arms, wrapping them around his neck when he leaned down to hug me.

"Thank you. That's nice of you to say." I closed my eyes within the strength of his arms. "Send-off back to perfect."

"Back on track." He laughed and pulled back. "Before we head out…" He reached into his back pocket and pulled out a clump of crushed flowers. With his opposite finger, he spread them out along his palm. "Which do you fancy?"

A few wild daisies lay in a pile on the right side, small and delicate as though plucked out of a field. Buttercups lay next to that, the petals scattered across his hand from the rough treatment. The spread on the far left had a mixture of buttercups and a sort of blue-purple wildflower.

"Like…what do you mean?" I asked hesitantly.

"Group A…" He pointed at the delicate daisies before moving to the middle cluster. "B…and C. Which group would you rather have a bouquet of?"

Saying none would've been rude, but honestly, the orchid had been perfect. And plenty. He had something in mind, though, so I just went with it. "This." I pointed at group C. "The mix."

He nodded, tilted his hand, and let the flowers and loose petals flutter to the ground. Without another word, he helped me into the Jeep, moved around to the driver's side, and away we went.

I felt Jasper and Ulric take to the air when we were halfway down the road, quickly lost to me as soon as they crossed Ivy House's boundaries. I did know a sort of tracking magic that I could've applied to them, keeping tabs on them at all times until the magic wore off, but it would have required some sort of preparation. Having been blindsided by all this, I just had to trust Austin to make sure all was going according to plan. Easy to do.

"I feel like my luck has run out," I confided softly. "Like this time, I won't slip out of his grasp."

"I'd agree with you…if you'd previously slipped out of his grasp." Austin headed out of town, toward the foothills. "But you didn't. You broke out. You bested his people without apology, and you'll do it again."

"Sometimes it's annoying how much confidence you have in me. I feel like you don't see reality."

"It's not me who is missing the obvious. But you're scared, I get it."

"But do you? You don't seem like you're ever scared."

"I've never known greater fear in all my life than when I woke up in Edgar's cottage after you were taken. I promised myself it would never happen again. Then it did. It terrifies me to think he could grab you and I'd be helpless to save you. Fear is different than cowardice, though. Fear keeps us sharp. Fear is what creates courage. It's okay to be afraid. It's healthy. The danger is when you feel nothing at all."

I let my breath out slowly. "Okay, then. I'm afraid today, but I'll be courageous when the time comes."

"That's all we can hope for."

An hour later, the conversation having moved on to trivial nothings without ever faltering, he parked at the top of a little hill off the beaten track, grabbed some spare clothes out of a bag in the back, and walked us down to a wide stream with quickly moving water. Once there, he dropped the pile of clothes on the sandy bank, as though we'd gone frolicking as polar bear and gargoyle.

"This is going to take a bit of trust." He handed me a small vial filled with clear liquid. "I'm going to need you to drink that." He held up a similar vial. "I will, too. It's not a date rape drug, I promise. It'll mask our scent and tracks. It'll make us invisible to anyone trying to follow, just like what that deer shifter used. One of the things he used, anyway."

"Are you challenging me to a battle of wits?" I asked, holding up my vial and looking at his. "Do I take what I am given, or do I trade it for yours…"

The grin intensified. "Careful here. It is never wise to go against a Sicilian when death is on the line."

I laughed, delighted he'd caught the *Princess Bride* reference, and downed the contents of my vial. The liquid tasted fresh and sweet, not much more than a mouthful.

"Oops." Austin pulled out the little stopper on his

vial. "You chose wrong." He winked. "Been nice knowing ya."

"Meh." I batted the air. "You always say that. I'm still here, aren't I? Those dolls haven't gotten me yet."

Austin took my empty vial and pocketed them both. "Speaking of dolls." He held up his hand to keep me put for a moment. I felt the liquid fizzing down my body. "Is Ulric putting those around the house, or is it Ivy House? Your mother was not amused at dinner yesterday. Clearly she's not doing it."

"Ivy House," I said dryly. "I don't know how to reel her in. She is endlessly delighted by the ways my parents try to rationalize her magic. They apparently think the secret doors Ivy House keeps popping open are plaster siding or something that is about to fall off."

"Isn't plaster siding for the outside of a house?"

"I think so, but my mom doesn't know any better. They think the house is basically falling down around them. The dolls are a joke, the doors moving on their own are ghosts, the thumps are rats, and so on. I can tell the shifting mantelpiece carvings in the TV room are making my dad think he's losing his mind. He seems to ignore the carvings half the time and stare at them with a scowl the other half, as though daring it to move. What he thinks about you changing I have no idea. It's like he never saw it."

Austin shook his head, directing us right, looking back to check that we weren't leaving any tracks behind. "It's beyond me why it was so easy to convince you, yet they refuse to believe what's in front of their eyes."

"Yeah, right?"

"I hate to hurry you, but I need to hurry you. This stuff isn't that strong. I don't have access to impressive mages. Yet. This elixir won't last long."

"Strike one…"

He directed me to a mine shaft that was so well hidden that there was no way I would've found it without him, the bushes and trees creating a natural blind. We gingerly sank into it, Austin going first to watch out for bugs and spiders (I'd insisted, threatening him with a second strike). Once in, he asked again if I trusted him.

I stared down at the rickety old metal cart on the rusted set of tracks, leading down into the blackness.

"I mean…I do, but that doesn't exactly mean I want to get in this thing."

He crawled in, facing the black maw. Only a slight diffusion of light made it through the natural canopy blocking off the entrance. Once there, he put out his hands for me.

"I've taken this ride many times before," he said. "It's an escape hatch, so to speak. If someone is following you, they won't be able to follow us. Not quickly, anyway. Only a handful of people in the town know about it. I test it a couple of times a year to make sure it is still safe. It has not failed yet."

"Not *yet*, huh?" I closed the distance slowly. "I'm not going to lie, man, this is not shaping up to be a great date. I'm not so into this idea."

"Have faith." He stretched his arms out toward me and wiggled his fingers.

"Are there seatbelts? Helmets?"

"I can wrap my arms and legs around you, if you want?"

A spear of heat blasted through me. My breathing turned shallow, and against my better judgment, for a couple reasons, I climbed into the cart and nestled between his spread thighs.

"Your shirt is going to get dirty if you lean back," I said with a suddenly dry mouth.

"Too late." He pulled me back against his chest. His legs pushed into my sides and his arms came around me, wrapping me into his body. Into his smell, clean cotton and a delicious spicy sort of cologne. "Strike...three? I forgot what strike we're on now," he whispered, the heat from his body soaking into me, his breath enveloping my cheek. "You look absolutely beautiful tonight, Jess. I was waiting to tell you."

"Why?" I asked, turning my face, feeling his lips

brush against my jaw. I tightened my fingers on his knees. "Why wait?"

"Because if I told you right off the bat, I worried you'd think it was a line. Telling you now, right before I send you on a joyride that might kill you, seemed so much more fitting." His lips, against my temple now, curled up into a smile. "I'm biased, though. I thought you were the most beautiful woman I'd ever seen the second I met you."

His heart beat against my back, speeding up, matching mine. I turned, sliding my hand up his leg, my logic on hiatus, responding to his words, which I could tell were definitely not a line. He meant every syllable.

Still twisting, I lifted my lips toward his. Our breath mingled, heating up. He dipped his head, those full, lush lips skimming the corner of mine, nearly lining up. I closed my eyes, wanting this with everything I had.

He dropped his hand to my hip, pulling my body in tighter between his legs. He shifted his weight, leaning over me. I moved my hand from his leg toward his shoulder, uncomfortably twisted but not caring, needing to taste him. To feel his lips on mine.

As my hand moved, it hit something that knocked backward.

Clunk.

The metal box we were sitting in dropped a few

inches, startling me.

"Crap," he said, quickly grabbing my hips with both hands and wrenching me around so I was facing forward. He slapped his hands down on the sides of the box and pulled his legs up and over mine before leaning in, holding me to him. "Hold on. Here we go…"

CHAPTER 15

AUSTIN

A S THE MINE cart sped through the deserted hard-rock mine, Jess reached up around Austin's arms, squeezing his biceps for dear life. She wasn't screaming, though. With the first big drop, speeding up the cart to an exhilarating pace, loud, manic laughter flew back toward him.

He smiled at her delight, feeling the adrenaline himself. Truth be told, he took this ride more than a couple of times a year, loving the rush. Loving the adrenaline. Laughing at his fear. Just like she was.

If it wasn't for a turn coming up that would whip them to the side, clattering their heads together, he'd lean over her and kiss along her jaw.

Good thing he couldn't.

He had to stop this! He could not give in to this attraction. Not with her. The second she got a true glimpse of what it was like to be with an alpha like him, with his hang-ups, she'd go running for the hills. She'd cast him out of her circle and, if she grew powerful enough, out of her town. He wasn't like his brother. He couldn't temper his possessiveness. He couldn't balance his strong feelings. He'd be lost to her, and he would react in ways no Jane would tolerate. He would not be able to suffer another man touching her, for one, or even overtly flirting with her. It would eat at his soul until his animal exploded.

That wasn't a situation she needed to be in, especially so soon after getting divorced. It also wasn't the man he wanted to be. He'd chosen a mate once before, and it had brought out the very worst in him. His ambition. His greed. His anger. He'd made a vow to avoid getting that close to anyone ever again. He needed to remember that.

Not to mention that Jess wasn't looking for anything serious. Even if he would allow himself to lose control and give over to his incredible attraction for her, with a passion so fierce it felt like it was stretching his skin, she wasn't ready. She felt the electricity, she felt the pull, but she wasn't ready to handle what came next.

He had to be the brakes. He needed to be stronger than this!

After a few more turns, the cart slowed as they reached the first plateau, the tracks about to curve around a corner and plunge deeper into the ground. He eased the brake forward until the cart stopped. Sunlight filtered into the tunnel from a partially covered grate above, dappling Jess as she twisted to look back at him, her beautiful face flushed with excitement and wonder.

How the fuck was he supposed to be the brakes with a woman like her?

"That. Was. Ah-mazing," she said, beaming.

"Fun, right?" He smiled at her and unhooked his legs from hers.

"Tell the truth: you were planning that all along, weren't you? The potential spies watching the house were just an excuse."

"Can I lie and say yes?" He helped her get out before heading to a control panel on a pole sticking out of the rough-hewn ground. In no time the chains engaged under the cart and began pulling it back up to the top of the hill. He'd had that installed a handful of years ago, which was why he wasn't the only one who knew about the mine shaft. But the few people who'd done the work were trustworthy. "So." He helped her through a small exit in the side, over some wood and bricks and out of the natural canopy that concealed the opening. "Do you want to ride on me to our next destination, or would you prefer to fly? It's about ten miles from here."

"But…what about your car? Are we going to go

back and get it?"

"Jasper will take my Jeep back to Ivy House. It'll make it a little harder for your admirers to track you down. I can run us home afterward, or you can fly. Same choice."

He paused, waiting for her decision. Her eyes flicked down his body and red infused her cheeks.

Heat pulsed through him with the knowledge that she was thinking impure thoughts.

"I'll ride you—ride on you. If you don't mind." She put her hands to her hips and then slid them down, as though suddenly unsure what to do with them.

He pulled a plastic bag out of his back pocket and handed it to her. "Will you be the keeper of my clothes?"

"Sure, yeah."

She took his phone next, and he started stripping. There wasn't much he could do about the hard-on, especially since he got another shock of arousal when she glanced down at him and then released a slow breath while her eyes sparked fire.

She turned away.

"Sorry," she mumbled. "Didn't mean to look."

"I should've warned you." He laughed, not sure why. "I guess I don't have to ask you to keep my shirt clean. The back is all dirty."

"Why'd you wear white if you knew we were going in the dirty cart?"

He shrugged, handing his clothes over. "You always seem to notice and comment when I wear white shirts. I thought you might like this one."

"I do like this one. Definitely. You look really good in white. But I notice and comment on the T-shirts because they are tight and show off your physique, not strictly because they are white." She grinned mischievously. "If we're being honest."

"Ah."

"But I do like the white, as I said."

"Okay, ready?"

She nodded, and he shifted to his animal form, the discomfort short-lived and barely registering. He flattened onto his belly until she crawled onto his back, the only person he'd ever let ride him like a pony. Once he was up, he launched forward, reveling in her squeals of delight.

The ride was fast, faster than he might've expected, his focus less on his footfalls and more on her kneading hands, seeking out the soft inner fur in his coat and stroking it to distraction. The climb up the mountain was nothing, only worrisome when he basically crawled over a ledge to get to the rock shelf that was their destination. Finally there, seeing that Earl had set everything up as requested, Austin flattened to his belly again so she could get off.

Only she continued to sit there on his back, still kneading, utterly silent. Not able to ask her what was wrong, or to change—worried he'd burn her and her clothes with the release of energy—he just waited.

He'd never tried to give a woman her perfect date before. He hadn't ever thought it was in his wheelhouse. But he really wanted to please her. Maybe he'd totally screwed up.

CHAPTER 16

MOUTH OPEN, UTTERLY gob-smacked, I just stared. My fingers moved through Austin's soft inner coat, thick and luxurious, as I let my gaze travel from one side of the beautiful tableau to the other.

He'd set up my dream picnic.

I meant to pull my leg over his back and slide off, but instead I actually lay down for a moment, my chest on his back and my hands at his sides, seeking out his soft undercoat again.

We sat on a little shelf about midway up a mountain overlooking an absolutely gorgeous meadow awash with mostly blue flowers. It looked like a softly moving sea, the breeze rolling through and gently moving the flowers. The yellow buttercups were intermittently sprinkled amidst the blue, splashes of color only a true artist could render.

This was option C. He hadn't been asking me which flowers I liked best—he'd been asking which meadow.

A wide cream blanket had been set out on the shelf

of rock overlooking it, the back half covered in various pillows to lean against, and the front holding two TV trays, each set with a plate, utensils, a wine glass, and a water glass. A crystal carafe between the place settings contained what looked like sparkling water, and in front was a large array of cheeses, fresh fruits, nuts, and charcuterie items. A large box of wine bottles waited to the side, along with extra wine glasses, and behind that sat an additional tray with an array of chocolate items and a few cookies.

It was perfect. Utterly perfect.

I smiled, finally sitting up and throwing my leg over his back to get off. "The cookies are for you, I take it?"

The startling light and heat of his change radiated outward, and I turned my face away. The next thing I knew, Austin was standing next to me in human form with an adorable smile. "Yeah. I'm more of a cookie guy."

"This is…" I stared out at the scene as he got dressed. "You nailed it. All of it. Are you sure you didn't get this out of your 'woo a woman' playbook?"

After fastening his watch, he took my hand, his palm a little rough, which, thankfully, meant he wouldn't notice that I had yet to adopt a stringent hand lotion routine.

"I'm making a new playbook: 'Things that put Jess

in a good mood.' I'll use it for the many times I piss you off in the future."

I rolled my eyes as he paused before the blanket. "You haven't pissed me off once in all the time we've known each other."

"It'll happen, don't worry. One day, I will rub you the wrong way, and I'll need to pull out all the stops to get you to forgive me. Or even just tolerate me again."

"If I can handle Mr. Tom and Edgar, I can handle you."

"This is true. The bar is set awfully low." He bent and put his hand out for my foot. "Milady, may I have your foot? I must remove your glass slipper so that I can defile you while Prince Charming isn't looking."

I laughed, bracing my hand on his shoulder for balance. "I'd eat Prince Charming for breakfast."

"Not before you stole all his crap, you wouldn't. You're smarter than that."

I let him take off my boots, belatedly realizing he hadn't put on his shoes a moment ago when he was changing. He lowered me to sitting and took his place beside me.

"You knew I'd choose the blue and yellow flowers?" I asked, looking over the beautiful picture. It was like a fairytale.

"No. I texted Earl 'C' as I was getting into the Jeep.

He delivered everything and set it up. He is also loitering around the area, even though I told him you'd be safe with just me up here. I can smell him."

I chuckled. "He trusts no one."

"So." Austin pulled out a bottle of wine from the box. "Shall we taste?"

"Oh my God, *and* it's a winetasting? You really pay attention."

He grinned, opening the bottle and pouring a little for each of us. "I do have to rain on the parade a little bit." He corked the bottle and put it back in the box. "These are actually samples from various winemakers. I'm obviously going to need a new one for the winery."

I lifted my eyebrows, looking at the wine. "Oh, wow. How many samples did you bring?"

"Twelve. A case."

"I'm not sure I'll still taste the wine when we get to the twelfth bottle."

He shrugged and swirled the wine in his glass. "We can always do a part two with your mom while we're sitting in Ivy House, waiting to be attacked."

I blew out a breath as I picked up my plate. "Has Niamh heard anything from Agnes yet? She shooed me off her porch earlier when I asked, telling me I was getting on her nerves."

"They're all worried about you. They don't like to

see you this stressed. Obviously they're all handling their worry in different ways…" He popped a nut into his mouth. "Agnes and team are still working on it. She says they have some good ideas, but nowhere near enough power to re-create it."

"Sounds about right." I loaded my plate before sitting back against the pillows. "Edgar is muttering to himself all the time now, but I don't think he's any closer."

"Can he communicate with the house like you can?"

"No, but I think she can understand what people need. And he did say she gave him another book, but it clearly isn't enough."

Austin leaned toward me, his elbow on a pillow, his shoulder bumping my arm. "It's going to work out. Even if Ivy House can't help, I have shifters willing to step up and fight. We have the gargoyles. We have the house crew. We aren't defenseless. If we can't tear down the spell, we'll still be able to put up a good fight. You can unleash the dolls."

"I'd have to see the enemy to direct them, though. If they are all hiding in the trees or flitting in neighbor's yards, that won't be easy. Then again, if we all pull back to the house, I can…maybe…direct them from the air. Or the roof or something."

I bit my lip and let silence fall between us, mulling it

over.

He looked up at me, something I couldn't identify sparkling in his eyes. He nodded and turned his gaze back over the beautiful meadow below. "There. You see? When the worst comes knocking, you stand up and answer."

I sipped the wine, the flavors exploding on my tongue and easily making their way down my throat, no surprise squeezing from tannins. "Hmm, this is good."

"Listen, I wanted to ask you." He took a sip of his wine. "You know a lot about tasting rooms and wine and all that. I'm just a run-down bar owner."

"Good Lord. Don't sell yourself short or anything."

"Would you help me get this all set up? Would you help with the tasting room and everything?"

"Of course. I love giving my opinion. Usually that's when it *isn't* wanted, but I'll make an exception for you."

"How about…" He swallowed the last of his wine—his glass a lot fuller than mine, since he could handle a lot more alcohol—and grabbed the next bottle.

"Okay. Getting serious." I finished mine before biting into a strawberry.

With the next wine poured, he sat up, one hand resting on his knee and the other holding the glass. "Would you want to become business partners? I can handle a lot of the operations aspect, and you could focus more on customer interfacing. We could both play to our strengths." He put up his hand. "It's just a thought. No pressure. I just thought…" He shrugged again. "I don't know what I thought. I just…I want you in on it. If you're interested."

"Did you take a look into your rich-kid fund and realize the amount you thought was a lot back in the day isn't so much anymore?" I smiled to hide my nervousness, then took a sip. These new flavors demanded my attention, light and spicy with a hint of smoke. "Hmm, this one is good. Better than the other."

"I have plenty in my rich-kid fund. I'll be expanding the bar to new locations and buying up a few other properties and businesses. This is…" He sucked down the liquid in one gulp. "It's just an idea. You wouldn't have to put up any money. You could just—"

"She will put up the money, and she will be signed on as a fifty-percent owner." Mr. Tom's voice rained down on us.

I spun where I sat, the small wall of rock behind us leading to trees slanting up higher into the mountain. No shape stood behind those. Ripping away the block on our magical connection, I dragged my gaze upward to the top of a pine, finding a naked figure clinging to the branches halfway up.

"Good Lord," I whispered, turning back around.

"Also, your back is dirty, Austin Steele. I would've mentioned it earlier, but I was giving you your privacy."

"Hiding in a tree listening to our every word is not giving us privacy, Mr. Tom," I called out.

"Of course, miss. Semantics, as they say."

I opened my mouth and shook my head, really at a loss for words. That happened so often with Mr. Tom.

"Give us some space, Mr. Tom," I said in a more forceful tone.

"Yes, miss. I will climb a different tree a little farther away."

"Why does he have to climb a tree at all?" I mumbled. Even as I said it, I heard a branch crack behind me. Needles rained down, and Mr. Tom shouted, "Whoa, whoa, whoa!" as if he were trying to control a disobedient horse.

Thud.

Unable to hold in my laughter, I spun around as Austin hopped up. Mr. Tom picked himself up off the ground and dusted the pine needles out of his hair. His wings fluttered behind him.

"Well. Simple as that," he said, sniffed, and stiffly walked farther into the trees.

"Should I go make sure he's all right?" Austin asked. "I don't technically have to because he's not in my jurisdiction, but..."

"Nah. He'll be fine. You wouldn't want to hurt his pride."

Austin lowered back down and poured me the next taste, just a small amount in the bottom of the glass. Clearly he wanted me to taste all twelve before the alcohol started to affect me.

"Apparently that is a yes," I told him, leaning against his shoulder. "About us being partners."

"Don't let him push you into it. Only do it—"

"I want to." I smiled, something warm throbbing in my middle. "I mean, I've never run a business, and I haven't the first clue about—"

"I can teach you the business side. You'll pick it up, no problem. You can teach me about...nice atmospheres."

"Nice atmospheres?"

His grin was sheepish. "Niamh, in no uncertain terms, told me that winetasting is a civilized pastime, and people do not want to stick to the furniture. In other words, if I want to make the right impression, I need to try a little harder than I have with the bar. Which...let's be honest, probably also needs some improvements."

"Wow. You're going whole hog, huh?"

"I'm the alpha now. I have to rise to the title."

I nodded, still leaning against him, looking out over the flowers waving in the mild breeze.

"Can I have a half glass, please?" I held up my glass.

"Of course." He stretched so as not to disrupt the press of my shoulder, and did as I asked.

"I just want to sit and enjoy the moment." I swirled the next offering, delighted to discover it was the best yet. The tangerine sun lowered toward the horizon, sunset still a few hours off but the waning daylight adding a layer of color to the spray of flowers. "Thank you for doing this, Austin. This is easily the best date I've ever had. Good food, great wine, a beautiful view, excellent company, an adventure to get here, and a naked butler hiding in a tree. Can it get better?"

"Well, when you add all those elements together...yeah, probably. Maybe just one less ingredient in the pot, and you might have something."

"The food, right? That's the one thing you'd leave off?"

He laughed, leaning against me a little harder. Silence hung between us for a moment.

"I've been alone most of my life," he murmured, and I knew his low tone was to keep this conversation between us.

I lifted my hand and moved it around us, growing a spiral of magic in the shape of a cone.

"Now we're soundproofed. Mr. Tom can't hear," I whispered. While I wasn't worried about my volume—I knew for a fact the spell worked—this moment suddenly felt incredibly intimate.

He nodded. "Since Destiny, the ex who brought out my more dangerous side, I've sworn off letting anyone get too close. Even my brother. I've kept him and his family at a distance, never quite trusting myself with them. But since you walked into my life, forcing your friendship on me…"

"I don't regret it. I needed someone sane to talk to."

He inhaled deeply and let the breath out slowly, as though he were savoring the air of a crisp new morning. "I don't feel so solo anymore. I don't feel so disconnected, so isolated. Deciding to become an alpha has…given me a feeling of…worth. The outpouring of support has surprised and energized me. I'm still nervous, like I could misstep and let all my demons out, but with your friendship at my back, I feel more grounded than I ever have. Seeing you struggle with your awesome power— watching you charge at it with utter fearlessness— you've bolstered my courage. You've turned my life around, Jacinta." His use of my whole name spread goosebumps across my skin. "I want to thank you for that. You've made me a better man."

Without thinking, I slipped my hand down his forearm and entwined our fingers. I leaned my head against his shoulder.

"Yeah. I'm pretty great," I said.

He huffed out a laugh, pulling our joined hands across his lap and putting his other on top of them.

"You already know what you mean to me," I said seriously. "I wouldn't be where I am without you. I need you. The house needs you." I hesitated, trying to hold back what I knew I shouldn't say. What I knew I shouldn't even think. But the desire to get it out was too strong. "I *want* you."

He tensed, his shoulder bulging against my cheek, his hands putting pressure on mine. I lifted my face a little, remembering the sensation of leaning into him in that cart, our lips almost connecting as I twisted toward him.

He lowered his head a little, sweeping his lips across my forehead, then started to blaze a trail down my face, but he shook his head and pulled back. He gave my hand a last squeeze before dropping it gently to my knee.

"I want you too, please know that, but I will respect the boundaries we've set. It might sting now, but I have a feeling you'll thank me for it tomorrow, when the scene isn't so pretty and wine isn't flowing."

"Yeah," I said dismally, my body on fire, my core

pounding, even if deep down I knew he was right. "So annoying. I really need to break this dry spell."

He blew out a hard breath before pouring himself a full glass of wine and standing, walking out to the edge of the shelf. I thought about wrapping my arms around my knees and letting this sting me, but I wasn't twenty anymore. I was capable of thinking about more than just my own feelings.

I grabbed my half glass and went to him, moving the muffling spell as I did.

"We are still in the cone of silence," I said as I stopped by his side. "You okay? Did I say something wrong?"

"I want to help you with that, Jess. I really do. I want to remind you how fun sex can be. How amazing. I want to remind you what intense passion feels like." He paused. "Maybe I want you to remind me. But damn it, I can't. I can't for your sake and mine. I can't because of what it would mean for me, and how it would trap you. It's not a line I can cross."

I furrowed my brow, not sure how it could possibly trap me. I let it go, though. He seemed torn, on edge. I didn't want to make this any harder, because he was right. He had his reasons for wanting to stay solo, and I had my reasons for holding back, even if my convictions had become a little wobbly lately. We were a couple of adults. We could make this work.

"Totally," I said, my tone light and a little flippant, trying to ease the mood. "I'm not beat up about it, Austin. I understand. I'm thankful, actually. This is definitely for the best."

He looked away. "I'm here for whatever you need, at any time, but I don't think I can hear about your sexual exploits…when you start having them. Anything else is fair game, but…" He shook his head. "Probably not that."

"Mutual, because that's gross. Men talking about women like that."

"Double standard?" He glanced down at me with a sly smile.

"Yes. This *one time* the sexual double standard goes the opposite way. You have to let us have this one."

He chuckled. "Fair enough. It's probably better that we can't hook up. You'd tell everyone what a bad lay I was."

"Happened before, has it?" I wrapped my arm around his. "Can we go sit down to our G-rated picnic now? I have more tastings to do. Oh, and I need to ask your advice."

"I thought we just cleared the air about that," he teased, walking me back and lowering me to my place before taking his seat.

"Oh, you meant my solo sexual fun, too?"

His whole body stiffened. Fire lit his eyes. He leaned forward, braced his elbows on his knees, and rubbed his eyes with the heels of his palms. "God, Jess. Yes. I mean that, too. Yes. Please don't mention that to me, for entirely different reasons."

I laughed, this situation we found ourselves in beyond weird. Usually when a man and a woman were friends, one of them wanted to bang the other, and they didn't because they were friend-zoned. This was the first time I knew of that both parties were struggling to maintain a friendship despite both of them wanting more. Why did I always do things ass-backward?

"Actually, I've been wondering about my financial situation..." I checked the spell, making sure it was holding firm around us. This particular spell was sensitive, and an errant fingernail or piece of hair could render it useless. "Here's the thing. Ivy House is apparently worth a lot of money, and the heir can use that money as long as she is alive. She can't pass it on, but she can use it while she has it, basically. At the moment, Mr. Tom manages all of that. He insists on paying for everything. I have no idea how much I have, let alone if there's frivolous spending within the household. Like...how much is Edgar spending on flowers? I never thought that would be a concern, but..."

"Definitely a concern," Austin said.

"Yeah. It's like Mr. Tom is trying to keep it from me. It isn't really mine, and I have my own money, so I haven't been too pushy about it, but it's starting to feel...off. I don't know what to do. How do I broach the subject? I assume he'd never try to embezzle, but...well..."

Austin leaned back, like he was uncoiling, before lying down behind me. He pulled me back to lean against him, as though he hadn't just declared that we should keep our distance.

"You're thinking like a Jane," he said, "and he clearly hasn't explained how it works in the magical world for someone in your situation. Mistresses of great fortune, which is what you are now, are considered above handling their own daily affairs. You do not pay for things; you instruct your servant to pay for things. You do not carry your purchases; you do not drive yourself; you do not do anything that someone else could easily do for you. If you want to know more about the finances, ask him to bring the ledgers to your office or wherever. That's where he tallies the expenditures and totals and whatnot. You can make changes, and he'll see to it."

I digested that for a moment. "The ledgers... When you say ledgers, I'm thinking large volumes with handwritten computations."

"Probably, yeah. Earl is old. He probably does things the traditional way."

"So that's the first thing to go." I frowned, the light starting to dwindle, the wine starting to make my thoughts peacefully fuzzy. I thought back to the countless times Mr. Tom and I had passed the great old office together. What with its bulky furniture, the quills sticking out of inkpots on the desk, and strange abstract paintings on the wall, it had never appealed to me. He'd recommended that I head in there once in a while and "see to things." I'd thought he was referring to the outdated decorations. No thanks. Now, however…

"I wonder what other little things I've missed because he hasn't come right out and told me."

"Probably a lot. You should mention it to Niamh. She's a lot less hung up on formality. She'll figure out what's needed and let you know."

I ran my bottom lip through my teeth. "Good tip."

We stayed until sunset. I took over pouring the glasses and he continued to lie on his side, pulling me back against him when I wasn't grabbing food or drink. The day waned, the sun painting the landscape a dark amber before we finally packed it in and headed home, Mr. Tom taking the remains of the picnic and Austin carrying me as I twirled my fingers within his soft fur.

Once back at Ivy House, I did a quick mental check to see where everyone was within the house—my dad up in bed, my mom reading in the front room, Mr. Tom already back and in the kitchen, some of the gargoyles at windows, some stationed in rooms, and Edgar still down in the cavern below the house with the crystals, working day and night to get answers for me.

"I've always just assumed that vampires sleep, but...do they?" I asked Austin as he dressed within the trees. He met me on the grass, glancing at the nibbled patch of flowers as he passed. The ground was just a bit wet, probably not noticeable to anyone not looking for it. If the deer came, hopefully it wouldn't be looking.

"If they expend a lot of effort, they tend to binge-sleep." He stopped beside me. "Do you want to set the tripwire?" I nodded and got to it. "So they might sleep a week after a battle, but otherwise not so much. He doesn't do much around here, so I doubt he sleeps very often. All that time, and he still can't make a doily."

I laughed, tore down the spell, and started over. "Quiet for a moment. This still takes concentration."

I finished, and we continued on toward the house, Austin's pressure on my back directing me around to the front porch.

"Can't end a date at the back door," he said. Once there, he deposited me on the stoop before stepping back, his eyes deep and soft. "Thank you, Jacinta. I had a great time."

I felt antsy, like he might leave. "It was perfect, Austin. I would not change one thing, not even Mr. Tom falling from the tree." I picked at my nail. "Do you… You're coming in, right?"

"If this were a real date, no. I would bid you adieu and call you tomorrow. Since I'm sleeping here…I kinda have to."

"If this were a real date, you wouldn't come in?"

"No, because I wouldn't want the old guard to make assumptions. I wouldn't want them to think I had fallen into my old habits, or that my feelings for you were shallow."

"Since when do you care what other people think?"

"As it concerns you? Always."

I shook my head. "Stop always saying the right thing. It's annoying." I laughed, flicking my hair, a nervous movement. I didn't want to go back to normal life. I wanted this moment, this perfect date, to last forever. "What about a hug and kiss on the cheek? You'd give that to your granny."

"I wouldn't dare. She'd punch me in the balls if I tried. She's not a hugger."

He moved in slowly, his eyes holding mine, pulling me in. My stomach fluttered and expectant shivers coated me.

"But since you *are* a hugger," he said, barely a whisper, his voice deep and rough and sexy.

He slid his hands across my hips and around, pulling me to him firmly, our fronts pressing together. I couldn't help but moan, my eyes fluttering shut as he spread his hands on my back, his strength enveloping me. The squeeze felt so good, and I slid my palms down his chest to his pecs, feeling his muscle through his shirt.

As he released me, he touched his lips to my cheek, soft at first, then a little firmer. He dragged them a little, giving me another little kiss nearer my mouth, then dragged a little more, spreading a trail of fire across my skin. His lips skimmed the corner of mine, like they had in the mine before I threw a wrench in my own wicked plans. He paused for a moment, breathing faster, sharing the same heated air.

I couldn't take it anymore. I slid my hands back up his torso, the feeling beyond good, and turned my head just enough that our lips aligned, almost touching. Without another thought, he leaned in, pulling his hand around so his fingertips braced against my jaw. His taste exploded through me, wine and honey and cinnamon. He nibbled my bottom lip before deepening the kiss, almost like he couldn't help himself, stealing my breath.

My God, I'd forgotten how damn well he kissed. How consuming. I held on for dear life, lost to it, lost to him. Why weren't we supposed to do this, again? What was the big deal?

Too soon he pulled back, breathing heavily.

"Whoops," he said, his lips still so close, his fingers at my jaw, his other arm wrapped around me. "That got away from me. Did I just ruin the date?"

"Definitely. You had it locked down, and you just blew everything to hell."

He smiled, kissing me once more, light but languid, before backing off. "Can't happen again."

"I know."

"It was a friend kiss."

"Two for two on the friend kisses. Both after a winetasting."

"Right. No more winetasting." He stepped up onto the porch and reached for the door.

"Hey, Austin?"

He paused and turned back.

"Will you do me a huge favor?" I asked. "You don't have to. It won't be easy."

"Anything."

"Will you call Earl Mr. Tom? Just because I know he'd really appreciate it and it would be less confusing."

He stared at me for a long time. "Isn't there a song

about this? I'll do anything, but not that?"

I laughed, heading into the house. "It was worth a shot. Want to watch a little TV?"

"Only if I don't have to sit on the fart blanket. Your dad thunders the whole house. That blanket is under some serious stress. How it hasn't put up the white flag, I do not know."

I laughed harder, feeling my mom stir, and dragged Austin in behind me. I felt like a kid again. Like a teen sneaking a date into the house. The outcome wouldn't be the same, but I would take it while I had it, because I had a feeling that come tomorrow I'd be fighting for my house and my freedom once again.

CHAPTER 17

THE HEAD LOOMING over me in the dim lighting wasn't the one I was used to seeing upon first waking up. Before registering anything else about the figure, I screamed and threw up my hands, blasting the intruder up and away. He or she hit the door, across the room, which was closed, and crashed through it, tumbling through the hall in a rush of splintered wood.

I jumped up onto the bed like some sort of ninja, braced myself in the slinky little negligee I'd wanted to wear to bed after my date with Austin, and prepared for battle, all within the space of seconds. I'd really taken all the danger and training to heart. Muscle memory was a beautiful thing.

Austin rushed out of his room in his birthday suit, glancing my way first. When he saw I was ready for action, he shifted his attention to the trespasser, slowly getting up off the ground with a raised hand. More naked men filed into the hall—the other gargoyles had heard the commotion and come to help. Then my father showed up, his nude form standing out in a hallway full of them. He was also the only one who'd brought a weapon to a naked party.

"What's going on?" my dad hollered, holding Jake the battle-axe across his torso. "It's two in the morning, for Christ's sake."

It had unfortunately taken me that long to identify the person who'd invaded my slumber. The hunched figure slowly rising with the trembling, outstretched hand, silently asking for a truce, was poor Edgar.

"Dad, put some clothes on," I said, getting down off the bed.

"Why me?" Dad asked, gesturing around him.

"This is my house. I make the rules."

"You didn't adhere to my rules; I don't have to adhere to yours." He held the battle-axe a little tighter.

"And where did you get that battle-axe?" I demanded. "Put Jake back. You shouldn't have that."

"At least someone thought to bring a weapon," my dad said.

"He does have a point," Ulric said with a grin. "What's going on, Jessie?"

"Nothing." I surveyed my ruined door, one set of hinges still on and the other torn free. "Edgar surprised me, is all."

"Holy crap." Ulric widened his eyes. "If this is what

happens when someone surprises you, I count myself lucky to be on your side."

"We're good, everyone. Go back to your tasks," Austin said, helping Edgar up. The gargoyles peeled away slowly, heading off to sleep or keep watch out the windows.

"Miss." Mr. Tom turned the corner at the other end of the hall, appearing behind my dad, perfectly dressed like he was ready for the day. "Shall I get you some coffee?"

"Why weren't you here earlier?" Austin asked Mr. Tom, a growl riding his words. "She could've been in danger."

"I knew it was Edgar who had surprised her, and I've personally experienced what happens to anyone who surprises her out of her sleep. It's nice to know she has taken it easy on me in the past, and that she is comfortable with me now. Edgar, you have a bone popping out. That's not a good look."

"Yeah, my arm hurts a little." Edgar stuck out his right arm, his left still raised in surrender. A shard stuck out of his forearm, and I turned away and gagged. I never would've made it as a nurse, something I'd known for a long time, and this new life constantly reminded me of that fact.

"Oh my God, I am so sorry, Edgar." I immediately

sent a stream of magic to repair the damage.

"What's that?" My dad crept closer to Edgar. "Oh wow, yes, that doesn't look good. We need to get you to a hospital."

"Oh no, it'll be fine. I heal really quickly, Mr. Callium—"

"McMillian," I corrected him.

"Mr. McCallium," Edgar said. I let it go. "I've had worse. Once half my head was crushed in—"

"That explains some things," Mr. Tom murmured.

"So long as no one cuts off my head or stabs silver through my heart, I'll keep going, right as rain."

"Put your hand down, man, this is serious," my dad said, clearly at the end of his tether.

"Dad, head back to bed. We'll take Edgar to the hospital," I said even as my magic stitched up Edgar's arm. "It'll be fine by morning."

"How did he even—What happened?" my dad demanded, Jake still in a death grip, as though the ancient battle-axe was the only thing connecting him to sanity.

"He scared me and I threw him through the door."

My dad looked down the dim hall at me for a moment and blinked. "Huh." He nodded. "Atta girl." He shook his head, muttering to himself as he headed back to bed. By the time he left this house, nothing would faze him. Maybe nothing already did, given his non-reactions to everything he'd seen.

"Why did you want to see me, Edgar?" I asked, doing a sweep of the property, feeling the basajaun way out in the woods, moving slowly and probably silently, on patrol.

"I have something for you, Jessie. I found it! I think I found it, at any rate." He finally put his hand down, now cradling his injured arm to his body. "I've had a breakthrough regarding the intruders' ability to hide from Ivy House's magic."

Excitement rose through me, and I put out a finger. "Wait there. Let me get dressed."

"You might get dressed, too, Mr. Steele," Mr. Tom said.

Austin stood next to Edgar, his expression still hard but his focus now on me—or, more accurately, on my nighty.

Warmth infused my cheeks, and memories of last night filtered through my mind. I'd fallen asleep on the couch while watching TV with him, my legs across his thighs. I'd awoken in his arms while he gently transported me up to my room. I'd hugged him goodnight and then felt the need to sleep in something a little sexier than my normal T-shirt and undies.

Without a word, he turned and went back into his room. I returned to mine and changed in the closet so as not to give everyone another peep show. Austin and I met back in the hallway minutes later, both dressed. I could sense Edgar down in the kitchen with Mr. Tom, so I led the way, hurrying down the stairs as the house quieted down, everyone back in their rooms or their assigned spots for sentry duty.

"Coffee, miss?" Mr. Tom asked as I reached him. He held out a steaming white mug. "Mr. Steele?"

"Yeah, thanks," Austin said, in gray sweats that actually fit him. He'd clearly brought his own.

Edgar stood by the window, looking out. "That basajaun needs to stay near the house, not way out in the woods. This is where the enemy will end up."

"Basajaun rely on the woods for information," Austin said as he got his cup of coffee. "They listen to the trees and the birds and the wildlife. They feel sensations through the ground. If he's in the middle of the property, he can move in any direction at the first sign of a presence. Ivy House might not be able to sense the trespassers, but the intruders will brush against trees. They will be seen by the wildlife. Information of their presence will reach the basajaun. In the meantime, he isn't leaving his scent near the deer's usual hangout. No enemy wants to tango with a basajaun, no matter how fierce. Seeing it in action one time will tell you why."

"You could take him," I said. "You were bigger than

him on your hind legs."

"It's not about size, it's about ferocity, but yes, I could take him. I have my own unbridled ferocity. I cannot be tamed, despite how much I desperately wish I could."

His cobalt eyes beat into mine, that last sentence for me specifically, I knew. His demons had clearly been haunting him last night.

"No man can be tamed," I said, not trying to convince him or change the status quo, just speaking the truth as I knew it. "The only way a man can change is if he wants the change for himself. If it's not initiated by him, he can bend, he can pretend, but he'll go back to being exactly who he was at the get-go. And that's okay. None of us are perfect. None of us are fully comfortable with ourselves—there are always going to be things you don't like. Ghosts and insecurities, dark places. The trick is finding someone who is as comfortable with your dark side as you are with theirs. The trick is not to change someone to fit you, but to find someone with whom you don't have to change."

His nostrils flared as he breathed out, bracing his hands against the island. "Now look who's saying all the right things," he said softly.

"Well said, miss. Many a woman has tried to change me. But alas…" Mr. Tom held out his hands. "I am who

I am."

Sometimes I wished Niamh lived in Ivy House so she could always be on hand to laugh with me.

"Right. Fine. Edgar, showtime." I motioned for him to speak.

"Yes! Of course." Edgar spun around to face me, still cradling his arm. "What?"

I gave him a little numbing agent for the pain so he could focus.

"Why did you wake me up at two in the morning?" I asked.

"Oh yes." He gave a sheepish smile. "Follow me."

We entered the secret passageways near the back door, following the blue-lit halls until the path sloped downward, the wood of the walls turning to stone and then rough-hewn rock. I watched out for the jagged edges that in the past had left scratches across my arms.

After I ducked through the last bit of tunnel, directly behind Edgar, the ceiling curved up into an arch and the passageway opened into a vast chamber under the house. A wrought-iron light fixture hung from the bottom of a chain connected to the ceiling, the light within glowing the same pale blue that lit the secret hallways. Below that, rising on a pedestal, were large crystals in a plethora of colors.

A large volume lay open on a bookstand in front of

the crystals, something I hadn't seen before. The familiar text Edgar had been working on sat on the ground beside it, also open, with a piece of paper covered in Edgar's rough scribbles and a pen lying on top. A small round table had been brought in, covered in papers bearing various notes and pictures. A TV tray, badly leaning, sat off to the right, also covered in papers, strange symbols written on some of them in purple Sharpie. Pieces of colored construction paper, cut in strange shapes, were taped to the legs.

If that all wasn't weird enough, more papers— colorful and not so much—were taped to the rock walls, connected by lines of purple and orange yarn. A bunch of oddly shaped doilies sat in a leaning pile in the back.

"Wow." My mouth dropped open as I took it all in. "Edgar...this is an *A Beautiful Mind*-type situation."

"Why, thank you." He beamed, standing next to the volume on the bookstand.

"That wasn't a compliment. I think you might be crazy, buddy."

"Crazy amazing, right?" He chuckled to himself. "All jokes aside, I think I have it, Jessie. With Ivy House's help"—he laid his hand on the open volume— "I've looked through all the house's failures. Now, the information was not easy to find. She has a sense of humor, the ol' gal." He chuckled again.

"He might have to be put down after this," Mr. Tom whispered.

Edgar hovered his hand over the volume. "This book is much too advanced for you, Jessie. I dare not read much of it. But it seems our enemy doesn't have any consideration for the benefits of slow learning, and so we must speed a few things up. So, in the section entitled 'Life's Funny Little Jokes,' I found out about a whole host of the house's vulnerabilities. One of those is a certain spell that renders her sentry systems useless against trespassers. It's an obscure little note..." He walked around the pedestal with the crystals and approached a scrap of paper taped to the wall, cut through with orange string. "The volume also chronicles which of the house's various secrets have filtered into the world. Only one reference to this particular vulnerability has made it out of this book and into another. There's one copy, handwritten, unless it has been duplicated, but there is very little chance of that."

"Why?" I asked.

He turned back. "Because it is in Elliot Graves's private library, bought from Jessup and James's Fashionable Relics bookstore in London some decades ago. The bookstore keeps track of their items for authenticity, and Agnes knows some people who are very good with computers. She is being very helpful. We should have her over for dinner."

"We're paying her, right?" I asked Mr. Tom. "The deal was—"

"She's charging by the hour, yes, miss." Mr. Tom waved it away.

"The book he purchased was a complete history of this house and its various…interesting assets, complete with a great many of the house's little jokes, a.k.a. vulnerabilities. He purchased a different book from the store about the various heirs. That led me to question what else he might have snapped up about this house." He traced the orange string around the room. "From what Agnes's friend's people could find, most of the sources containing the house's secrets were acquired by Elliot Graves."

"He has a great fascination with this house," I murmured.

"A fascination he had before it even chose a new heir," Austin said.

"Yes." Edgar followed a different string, leading him back our way. "We can rest easy in the knowledge that he is not the kind of man to collaborate with other masterminds. He has never joined forces with anyone, neither during his climb to the top nor in the years he's spent fighting to stay there. He's also known for taking his time when he wants something. He studies. He plans. He moves in slowly, corralling his target, corner-ing them, and only then pounces. He's as meticulous as he is powerful, as organized as he is persistent. So... What's the good news?"

"You have the spell and a way to get around it?" I asked, holding my mug between both palms.

"No, but I do know the spell exists."

"Well, we all know it exists," I replied, frustrated. "The house knows it exists. We saw it with our own eyes."

"All this madness for hours on end"—Mr. Tom ges-tured around the room—"just to tell us what we saw in plain sight?"

"Why wouldn't the spell be in there?" I asked.

"The vulnerabilities are not spelled out," Edgar said, "probably because she doesn't know how it is done. If she did, she would be able to circumvent it. If a past heir figured it out, they never amended the book. I think that is something you should do—find the spell, find the counter-spell, and make note of them in the book. But that is for another day." He held up his finger. "There is good news. Elliot Graves has been moving slowly. Incredibly slowly, considering he started all of this before you were chosen. He's testing his theories on you. That's the best-case scenario, given the speed at which you're growing with Austin's help. You're ahead of the curve."

"Until this spell…" I reminded him.

He paused. "Well, yes. But that is okay. The spell itself is not in here, but there's information about the nature of it. This second book is a breeze to translate— only two languages, and one of those is English. It is meant to be consumed more than studied. I see now that the first book is the training wheels. We'll have plenty more work to do once you finish with it."

"Fine, so if Agnes doesn't come through with any-thing helpful, I'll at least know more about the spell Elliot's using. If I figure out how it's fooling Ivy House, maybe I can reverse engineer a way to dismantle it. I mean, that's just logic, right?" I scratched my head.

"The other good news is, as far as Ivy House knows," Edgar said, "it has not been leaked that the heir is capable of fully controlling the house's defenses. He might not know you're just as deadly without it."

Austin crossed his arms over his chest and rubbed the dark brown stubble on his chin. "That's smart."

"Who…" Edgar backed up a pace and put his fin-gers to his chest before looking around. "What is?"

"Even if Elliot knows or suspects you have the pow-er to control the house defenses," Austin went on, "he might not know you are able to yet." He held out a finger. "You are brand new to magic as a whole." A second finger. "You didn't know anything about this house before you moved here by other means." A third finger. "You just learned to fly a couple months ago…" He put his hand down again. "You should lean into that. Lean into your seeming inexperience when you're dealing with him. Make him think you're behind where you currently are. It'll give you an edge."

"What if they were around, watching me train?" I asked.

Austin shook his head. "I would've sensed the presence. Shifters have the sense that animals possess, to sense danger even though they might not have proof of it. Some of us are better at it than others, but I do possess that skill. I rarely have to use it, since I have keen scent and hearing, but it is a good backup. They would not have been close enough to see you train if they were on the property."

I nodded. My inexperience wouldn't be hard to sell. If those damn dolls were running wild, or the basajaun was celebrating victories, I'd probably look terrified or disgusted as a normal part of my day. I could whip up a little dumb blond schtick as the cherry on top. Men fell for that, regardless of hair color.

"We do still need to know how to tear down the spell, though," Mr. Tom said. "Edgar, I sure hope you didn't write your findings on one of these scraps of colorful paper. We have whole sheets in the craft box."

"We have a craft box?" I asked.

"Yes. It is in the office you never enter."

Did I hear a tone? Now that I knew a little more about the office, I was pretty sure I heard a tone…

"Oh, I…" Edgar lowered the half-formed, fuzzy-edged orange slip of paper he'd grabbed before putting it behind his back. "Let me just quickly go over it one last time, and I'll deliver it to you right away."

The blue-painted porcelain of the bottom of my coffee cup looked up at me accusatorially. I'd just drunk a whole cup of coffee, not to mention my mind was whirling from what I'd heard. No way could I got back to sleep.

"Just give me what you have." I held out my hand.

"*The power to combat the assault is within you,*" Ivy House whispered to me. "*The clues are there. You can piece them together. You must.*"

No pressure.

"I'll get working on this spell." I took the paper from Edgar.

"Well, then." Mr. Tom pulled at his lapels. "I'll make breakfast."

The sense of urgency settled onto my shoulders like a great weight, something in me knowing that my time was running out. I took off for my room, jogging all the way there, and then spread the page onto the table and sat down to study it.

"I'm going to head into town," Austin said, peeking his head in. "I don't have any sort of organized pack yet, but I have people there who can help. I'm going to put them on alert, if that's all right?"

He clearly felt the press of expectation, same as me.

"More the merrier," I answered, "as long as you can handle them."

He spared a moment to walk in behind me, laying his hands on my shoulders and kneading.

"You okay?" he asked quietly.

I closed my eyes for a moment. "Yeah. Just feeling the pressure."

"Have faith in yourself. You are an excellent problem solver. You can crack the code."

I wrapped my hand around one of his wrists, needing the contact. He stopped kneading with that hand and took mine, entwining our fingers. We stayed that way for a moment as the night peered in through the windows, all silent. The calm before the storm.

"Okay," Austin whispered, pulling his hand away. "I'm going to head out."

"Yup. And I need to work miracles."

"It's not a miracle—it's a challenge. You'll rise to it."

"Sometimes your supportiveness is just plain annoying," I groused.

"I concur." Mr. Tom came into the room with my coffee mug, steaming once again. "Much too support-ive. Who needs someone to believe blindly in us? What a bore."

I had a sneaking suspicion he was mocking me.

Austin slipped out of the room, leaving my line of sight, but I could feel him making his way to the side door—and then changing shape and darting into the trees in the side yard, hopefully slipping into the wood before anyone noticed. Speed was clearly on his mind, and he could move fastest in his polar bear form.

"I wish we had an idea of the numbers that might come at us," I said, looking down at Edgar's sloppy scrawl.

"Here." Mr. Tom sat in the empty chair and fished a sheet of paper and a pen out of his interior jacket pocket. He pulled the orange piece to him. "Let me make this legible. Austin Steele thinks the secret is out about you in the magical world. That people will start to take a greater interest. I happen to agree."

"This isn't the time to increase the pressure, Mr. Tom."

"My advice? End this coming battle hard and fast. Make a statement. Show both factions, if there are indeed two, that you will not be easy to cow, kidnap, or intimidate. If someone is coming for you, they'd better have their big-boy pants on, because you won't play nice when threatened."

"Make a statement, sure, sounds easy. Except I'm still brand new to magic, and I'm potentially up against a master and some other guy that isn't afraid of a master. How am I supposed to stand out when I'm the underdog?"

Mr. Tom chuckled. "I doubt even Elliot Graves can so easily blow someone up. Trust me, miss, you have more at your disposal than you think, including imagi-nation."

CHAPTER 18

BASED ON WHAT Edgar had found, Ivy House could sense living things through a sort of heat signature, and it identified the nature of those creatures based on the type of energy they put out. Just like with scent, animals had a different energy than people, shifters had a different energy in their animal form, and so on.

Somehow, Elliot was wrapping his people up in spell bubbles, containing their heat signatures and their energy.

My job was to pull those bubbles away. Something I was still in the process of figuring out in the underground cavern. I stood in front of the pulsing crystals at the core of the house, working magic in a spinning motion that sent sparkles tumbling through the air (a pretty effect that had a practical purpose—it helped me figure out if the magic was rolling in the right direction). My aim was to grab hold of the bubble spell and essentially unwind it. Once the person was exposed, even for a moment (I was working on the assumption that they could reapply the spell at will, aiming for our worst-case scenario), Ivy House could quickly capitalize on their vulnerability.

"*You need a way to dig into the spell,*" Ivy House said in our special communication. She had some good ideas on how to rip away the spell. Apparently this type of spell had been attempted many times in the past, but those other attempts had always been flawed. This was the first time someone had locked it down. Elliot was clearly very good at his craft.

I had to be better.

"*Otherwise your spell will just whoosh by. It won't catch.*"

I nodded, watching the sparkles tumble away before washing against the bare walls. I'd long since stripped the walls of the paper, my spells creating whirlwinds that the tape couldn't stand up to.

"What if ripping away the spell isn't the right way to play it?" I took up Mr. Tom's handwritten page for the millionth time, looking over the verbiage I'd all but memorized. "What if I should be counteracting it instead?"

"*You don't know what to counteract.*"

"Yes, exactly." I shook my head. "Maybe I'm spending all this time, going without sleep, for a spell that won't work."

"You have the power to rip that spell off. If he's using it on lesser-powered shifters, it can't be a volatile spell. You should be able to use might."

"I want to use brain, not brawn. I want to do this the right way."

"We all want something."

I glared at the crystals before stuffing the piece of paper into my pocket and leaving the room. Sure, it could very well work for most people, and the beauty of the spell we'd devised was that it would rip off other spells, too—ones that might be dangerous. But what if I came up against Elliot? He wouldn't succumb to such a simple tactic.

My gut told me I needed a counter-spell. A reveal spell. Maybe not for this battle, maybe not even for the next, but until I could properly counteract Elliot's masking spell, I'd always be vulnerable to it. For that, though, I'd some idea of the composition of the spell he was using. Agnes hadn't locked anything down.

"Oh, hello," my mom said when I made my way into the kitchen for more coffee, "you're up already." She beamed at me as she laid some bacon into a hot pan.

"Yeah, what time is it?" I looked around. "And where is Mr. Tom?"

"It's almost eight o'clock, and your caped crusader of a butler was scurrying about upstairs last I saw him, headed up to the third floor. He seemed a bit more animated today, and he hasn't once tried to shoo me out of the kitchen. What's up?"

I thought about just telling her and Dad to go home. To pack up and get out of here. But I knew they wouldn't go without a fight. Besides, the prowler had lurked from the front yard. If they were still out there somewhere, watching, I didn't want to deliver them hostages. Even though my parents would be in the middle of a battle zone, at this point, the house was probably the safest place for them.

"It's a pretty long story, but basically, we might have some trouble later on. When things heat up, we'll need to move you to a safe place within the house."

My mom's movements slowed and a crease formed between her brows. "What do you mean, some trouble?"

There was no easy way to say it, so I just went for the direct approach. "Long story short, this house is magical, and in accepting to live here, I became magical, too. Now some people want to use me for my power, I guess. They are here to take what is mine, and we'll be fighting them off. So we'll need to get you to safety."

My mom stared at me for a tense beat. Her flat expression lifted into a smile so broad that it scored her face. "Funny. You're as bad as that butler of yours. Do you want some breakfast?"

I sagged. "Yes, please. Let me just check in with Mr. Tom."

They'd need to be forced into safety, clearly, which was fine. Maybe we could just tell them we suspected a tornado or something. No, we didn't get tornados here, but they'd probably believe that a whole lot faster than they'd believe in magic.

CHAPTER 19

"HERE YOU GO, Jessie." Ulric bent over my position at the kitchen table and handed me a small brown box covered in glued-on stones. He bit into a sandwich as he watched me ease it to the table without breaking off any of the decor.

"Why?" I asked, and I wasn't sure if I was asking about the decor or why he was handing me the box.

"Edgar told me to give it to you. He checked in with Agnes earlier. They've been trying to re-create the potion. They managed to put together this elixir."

Heart in my throat, feeling a surge of newfound energy, I flipped the metal clasp and pulled open the light wooden lid. I took out a little vial resting on a purple pillow, the liquid inside iridescent magenta. "They're trying to re-create the potion? I thought she said she wouldn't have enough power?"

"Yeah, they didn't have enough to properly duplicate the spell, but this gives a low-level idea."

A folded-up piece of paper rested next to the pillow.

It had a list of ingredients, followed by instructions, like a recipe. I pulled up the pillow to find the plain brown wood beneath.

My mother bustled through with a pile of laundry just as I was lifting the vial to the light. For once Mr. Tom wasn't chasing behind her, demanding she hand over the laundry and go sit down.

"Ooh, pretty." She nodded at the vial. "Do you want a sandwich, hon? It's after twelve o'clock."

"No, I'm good—"

"Yes, she does, Mrs. McMillian, if you please," Ulric said. "Or we can get Mr. Tom to make it."

"Don't be silly. I'll be right back." My mom left the kitchen.

"You need to eat, and you need to sleep," Ulric said, sitting down at the table with me. "You're worn out. You won't come up with anything in this state. Give your brain a rest. They aren't attacking yet."

I sagged against the table. "I know, but they could come at any time and I'm not positive the spell I rigged up will work." I turned over the piece of paper, seeing more directions for the potion. "If they don't have enough power, how'd they get anything at all?"

"Reverse-engineering a spell is possible if you have the brains, ingenuity, analytics, and guts to pull it off. You don't necessarily need the power. These people can't make the full-fledged potion, but they can figure out how it was done and empower others to do what they can't." He held up the slip of paper. "Agnes has a good network of people, even though she's clearly…" He fingered the crystals glued to the side of the box. "She's not my speed, at any rate."

I blew out a breath. "So you're saying I can probably mostly trust this." I shook the vial.

"Yeah. They would have told us if it would kill you. You can think about the spell while you eat, and if you refuse to take a nap, I'll drink this vial—I also have guts—and you see if you can counteract it. Obviously this one will be easier to remove than the one Elliot's using on his people, but it'll give you an idea."

Ulric proved to be correct—he did have guts, and not just because he ingested a glowing pink elixir made by a stranger. He also stood in a small, never-used sitting room on the second floor, with the shades drawn and furniture cleared away, and allowed me to try out various renditions of counter-spells. When those didn't work, I started using the tear-away spell I'd been practicing earlier, attempting to pry it from his body.

"*Now that you have the recipe, you can fashion a spell from opposites,*" Ivy House practically yelled at me, her words vibrating through my body and echoing around in my cranium.

"I'm trying!" I paced the room as Ulric sat in a chair off to the side, waiting. "Nothing's *working*. The spell I practiced earlier doesn't seem to rip it away." I rubbed my puffy eyes, my brain mush right now. It felt like I was swimming through wet cement, I was so tired. I'd been healing the tired away most of the day, for myself as well as those who'd been awake with me, but I'd hit the wall. My energy level couldn't sustain the magic to continue healing, even with Ivy House's help. And just like that, the last of the pink glow surrounding Ulric wore off.

"What's going on?" Austin walked into the room, gray sweats adorning his bottom half and his bare torso glistening with sweat. He must've just gotten in.

I threw up my hands. "Nothing. Nothing is going on. I can't figure it out, and now the elixir has worn off."

"She's too tired," Ulric said calmly, somehow still upbeat despite the fact that his shirt had been torn to shreds with little patches of blood marring the rips. Toward the end, when desperation had started to set in, I'd gotten a little out of hand. Amazingly, he hadn't ever flinched or told me to calm down. He probably should have. "She needs sleep and a fresh perspective. I think she has it; she's just not putting it all together."

"How can you possibly think that?" I pointed at his

torso. "You look like you got caught in a briar patch."

"I could feel you ripping at the spell, but you hadn't dug in deeply enough. The next time you'd dig in deeply enough but forget to rip it away." He shrugged. "You're tired. Things slip when a person is tired."

"Nonsense." Mr. Tom walked into the room with a steaming mug. "She has a lot of mileage left in her. Here." He handed me the brew, and I took a seat to drink it, fatigue pulling at me.

"Austin doesn't need sleep," I said.

"I was about to take a nap. Why don't you join me?" Austin put out his hand to me.

I sighed. They were probably right—I was useless when I was too tired. I didn't see things clearly.

That clock was ticking down in the back of my head, though. I could feel danger coming, just on the horizon. Dare I take the time to sleep when I wasn't sure about a counter-spell?

"Do you know what would be best?" I said, then sipped the coffee. "If I could disintegrate the spell without them realizing it. You said you could feel that spell, Ulric?" I took another sip of the coffee, but it wasn't perking me up like it usually would. Now that I was sitting down, my eyelids were growing heavy.

"Yeah," Ulric replied. "It was kinda bubbly or fizzy. It felt like I was in a champagne bubble. I could see the glow around my limbs."

"Right, so I'd need to strip it away while applying a harmless, fizzy, glowing spell. They'd continue on like nothing was amiss while Ivy House was targeting her missiles." I took another sip and a wave of dizziness washed over me. I put my fingers to my temple. "I might need a cookie or something."

The mug was taken out of my hand, and I was thankful because I was incredibly woozy all of a sudden. My eyelids felt like they weighed a hundred pounds and my body had already started to relax, like sleep was inevitable.

"What was in that coffee, Mr. Tom?" I asked, sagging in the chair. A moment later, Austin's arms were around me, lifting me for the second time in twenty-four hours.

"A sleeping agent," Mr. Tom replied. "The coffee was decaf."

"Amazing. Not an ounce of guilt." My head lolled against Austin's shoulder.

"I am here to look after you, miss, even when you refuse to look after yourself," Mr. Tom said as Austin carried me from the room.

"We have unfinished business, you and I," I slurred at him. "Watch your back."

"I think the defenses might be more dangerous in

Jessie's hands than with Ivy House acting as a free agent," Ulric said, voice going dim as we moved away.

"Are you really going to take a nap?" I asked Austin as he climbed the stairs.

"Yes. You've stopped healing me. I'm tired." His voice was teasing. He dusted my forehead with a kiss. "No alpha in history has the benefits I do. The experience and intelligence of age, the strength and stamina of youth, and an incredibly generous powerhouse of a sorceress that makes sure I am always at my absolute best, even when it takes away from the healing efforts on herself. I'm the luckiest man alive."

"You only have to get blown up and magically knocked around to earn it."

"Anyone would trade places with me, even without seeing your beauty."

I rubbed my eyes and then buried my face in Austin's neck, my heart swelling.

He entered my room and closed the door behind him. "Do you mind if I sleep in here with you?" He laid me on the bed and moved around the room, closing the windows and drawing the shades.

"No, that's fine. I'm about to pass out, though. Whatever Mr. Tom gave me, it was strong. Two sips and I'm about done."

Austin kicked off his shoes. "My sweats are clean. I

put them on when I got here."

With great effort, I shimmied out of my jeans and slipped beneath the covers. There he met me, his arm out, welcoming me in. I scooted in until I could nestle my head in the hollow between his shoulder and his neck, curling up against his big body. Any other time and I'd probably feel the fire of his warmth, the deliciousness of proximity, but this time I just felt comfort.

"Don't let me sleep too long. I need to tackle that spell," I muttered, blinking. It felt like they were becoming stickier and stickier until they finally wouldn't open anymore.

"No sweat. Sweet dreams."

I didn't have sweet dreams, though. Images flashed through my mind of Edgar's crazy setup near the crystals, of random words floating off the orange paper, of Agnes's elixir, of Ulric standing there as I poked and prodded him with spells, of the gaping hole in my reasoning.

I sat up in a panic as the light dimmed within the cracks of the shades. Austin stirred beside me, reaching for me and dragging me back down to him. I curled up into his arms for one moment, his warmth soothing, my brain still firing. My subconscious had been working in overdrive the whole time my brain was powered down.

Facing the door, with Austin spooned around me, I

closed my eyes and envisioned the sort of spell Elliot had been using. Something to contain the heat and energy of a person. A bubble of sorts, fizzing because of all that heat and energy. Glowing from the contained power.

But a bubble didn't need to be torn away, per se—it needed to be popped. Perhaps my attempts at stripping Ulric of the spell hadn't worked because of the way I was tearing at it. A sharp, focused prick of power was the way to go.

I wondered if the potion would then dissolve away, or hang out on the body. The latter would be the best-case scenario for me, for sure. I wanted the trespassers to have a false sense of security and I doubted I'd have time to come up with a replacement fizzy spell. The beat of threat was pounding in my head, almost like a palpable thing. I couldn't feel anyone on my property, but my gut said they were out there, focused on this house. Focused on me and the prize of my magic.

Austin stirred again and rubbed his eyes. He nuzzled into my neck for a moment, as though breathing in my scent. He rolled away, standing.

"You feel the pressure too, huh?" I threw my legs over the edge of the bed.

He ran his fingers through his hair and opened his mouth to answer.

The feeling of movement stampeded through my chest. The basajaun was running. Toward the house.

Something was happening.

"Time to go." I stepped into my jeans as a lone howl drifted through the air, one beautiful note, wavering in the air. A wolf singing its song. One last placid moment before everything went to hell.

"That's Logan." Austin jogged to the door. "He's reliable and savage, and he has a good head on his shoulders. I put him in the woods along the entrance of the court to let us know if anyone was coming."

"The basajaun is running from the back. They're closing us in."

"Now we'll get to see if it is one faction or two."

I didn't see how it would really matter.

I felt Niamh set foot on Ivy House property, moving as though she wasn't in a hurry. Knowing her, that meant she felt pressure and was too stubborn to give in to it.

"Niamh is pulling in," I said. "They must be nearly at her house. I have to get that spell finished off."

"You better put on that muumuu, too. You might need to fly."

I breathed through the tremors of anticipation, adrenaline, and fear.

There was no reason to freak out. Even if we

couldn't get those potions off those bodies, I could trigger the house's defenses. We'd be fine. As long as we were on this property, we'd be good.

"Jessie, come quick," Ulric said through the newly fixed door.

Austin pulled it open, pausing for a beat to let me through first before following me out.

Ulric led the way without a word, bringing us to the closest bedroom with a view of the front yard. Four people, two men and two women, rolled a large device up the street toward us. Four tree-trunk posts at angles sat on a rolling platform, with a tree trunk at the top holding them all together. Swinging between the legs was a sixth trunk with a pointy end.

"Is that..." I leaned closer to the window. "Is that a battering ram?"

"Time to get your parents to safety," Austin said, his voice rough. "Time to fight."

CHAPTER 20

AUSTIN

AUSTIN WATCHED PANIC roll across Jess's face, something that happened right before every major skirmish. It was her sense of Jane reality taking the helm for one brief moment. In the past it had stressed him out. Now he just waited.

A moment later, he was rewarded with what he'd come to expect: the panic faded from her intelligent hazel eyes, and a look of stubborn determination took its place, that attitude also apparent in her clenched jaw and lowered brow. She leaned closer to the window again, her eyes surveying the front yard. Brilliant green grass shone in the late afternoon sun. Pink and blue tulips waved from beside the front path, moved by the light wind. Bushes and hedges stood tall. They were deep in the calm before the storm.

Teams of people emerged from the side yards of the houses up the street, forming what looked like a horde, a mass grouping of armed people in battle leathers. They marched toward Ivy House, sheets of soft, glittering air sliding down on either side of their group, masking their sound and maybe their appearance from the outside world, keeping this fight magical so Janes and Dicks would be none the wiser. Austin was sure there was a sheet behind them as well, pulling tighter and tighter and tighter as they moved toward the house. He also wondered if there was an attack spell woven in there, keeping anyone from slipping out of the mayhem and making a run for it through the spell. He wouldn't doubt it—they'd want to trap Jess in. They wouldn't want their prize escaping.

A wave of pure adrenaline washed through him, followed by a heavy dose of rage.

That spell would keep them trapped in as well. With *him*.

"Jacinta McMillian!" Her father appeared in the doorway. Jess didn't turn to look back. "Who are all these people in this house? More men with capes showed up. They're underfoot every time I turn around. And now your mother says there are a whole bunch of people walking this direction from down the street. Look at me when I speak to you."

"Kinda busy here, Dad."

"Doing what, looking out the window? This place is

like a bus station, Jacinta. If you need some money, your mother and I can lend you some. You don't need all of these people living here."

"Didn't Ulric fill you in about why they're here?" she asked in a faraway voice. She was likely planning which defenses she would enact to deal with the on-slaught from the front. She'd need to set them and run, because the people in the woods were almost certainly about to make their move. Austin didn't feel much on this property, not like the others, but he could feel that basajaun cutting through the wood, straight for the house, probably with news of an invading army that Ivy House couldn't feel.

"You can't house the whole forestry school, Jessie. Didn't I tell you that earlier? You're not a hotel."

Jess straightened up with a clenched jaw. She turned and walked quickly toward her dad, still filling the doorway.

"Dad, they aren't living here, they are auditioning to join my team. That team is in charge of protecting me and this house. Go look out the front window. That's what we're protecting it from. Soon there will be a host collecting out back as well. They're already hiding in the woods. Both of them want to take me for my magic. Surprise! The house is magical, and now so am I. Life has gotten a little more interesting for me since the divorce."

"Oh, horseshit. What are you saying, that you live in a place like Willy Wonka's?"

"Yes, only less fun and with much less chocolate. Come on, it's time for you and Mom to get to safety."

She tried to pass him, but his expression had turned stubborn. He clearly didn't plan on budging.

Before Austin could step in to help, he heard a small electrical sound, like a bug zapper. Her dad jolted, made a sound like "hahorr," and danced sideways as though on strings in the hands of a drunk puppeteer.

"See what I mean?" She walked through the door. "Things aren't as they seem."

"What was that?" her dad called after her.

Austin put his hand on her shoulder as she reached the downstairs landing, turning her to face him. "What do you need from me to help counteract the spell? A somewhat human guinea pig?"

Her eyes softened and she laid a palm on his chest, over his heart. The world paused for a moment as he stared into her beautiful honeycomb eyes. He'd never felt so helpless as he did with her, wanting to feel her touch, wanting to earn her smiles. He was in a bad way. He needed a break from her presence if he wanted to stay sane.

First he had to see her safe.

"You already helped," she said, her voice velvety smooth. "You and Mr. Tom. I know what I need to do." She blinked and looked down. "Though I'll have to figure out how. If you can keep these people off me for long enough, I can tear their spells down, and Ivy House can take up the slack."

"No sweat," he said, light as a feather. He was supposed to be the alpha in these parts, taking the command and leading his men and women, but with nothing more than a touch and a request, she'd just assumed the top dog role. His brother would be screaming with laughter right now.

Earl rushed up to Jessie in his purple house sweats. "I've gathered everyone on the backyard grass. We're waiting for you. The basajaun is almost there."

"I know. I feel him," she said. "Get my mom and dad into the walls. I'll ask Ivy House to lock them inside. Make sure they have snacks and a book or something."

"I am not going into any walls." Her father marched down the stairs, battle-axe in hand, his features hard.

Jess's mother followed. "Pete, watch out with that axe. You might fall and cleave your own head in. That thing is dangerous!"

"You got people coming to burn this place down?" Pete asked Jess. "Well, I've been in crime-riddled neighborhoods before. I've made it through riots. All you need to do is show you're not the weak one and they'll find somewhere else to be."

"Dad!" Jess pointed at the battle-axe. "Go put Jake back! You have no idea what you're doing with it."

"Oh, don't I?" He hefted it. "I can swing one of these as good as any bat. I was MVP of our softball club. I could—"

"That was years ago, Pete," Martha cut in.

"You guys!" Jess put up her hands. "I don't have time for this. Dad, you are staying in this house. You are not bringing a battle-axe to a magic fight."

Pete rolled his eyes. "What about a gun? You got a gun? The second they set foot on your property, they are fair game."

Jess hesitated. She glanced at Earl. "Do we have a rifle? He's actually a really good shot."

"I'm better than he is," Martha said indignantly.

"Jessie, what's the hold-up?" Niamh shouted as she walked up the hallway from the back. "They are setting up a battering ram, fer feck's sakes. What do they think, we have a drawbridge or something? Bunch o' maggots. They're all lining up just outside the property. They've clearly heard the stories."

"They'll have to cross the threshold to use that ram," Jess murmured, looking at Earl.

"We have a small arsenal, yes," Earl said. "I keep it locked in my room so the Paddy doesn't get it and terrorize the tourists with live ammo."

"Bollocks. I could get an unlicensed firearm without hassle," Niamh said. "Jessie, let him handle that. Let's go. Time's a-wastin'."

Jess pointed to Earl. "Either get them in the walls or get them armed. Preferably the former."

Jess jogged down the hall, Austin right behind her. She turned the corner, down another hall, and then they were pushing outside. The gargoyles stood in a line in their gargoyle forms, their wings tucked in to give everyone room. Beside them, with a large space between, stood the shifters in animal form, three wolves, a rat, a bobcat, and a snow leopard standing out front with a dozen others, ready for battle.

The basajaun broke through the trees. He didn't even pause to sniff the flowers, something incredibly rare for him, instead jumping over them in one awesome leap and landing on the grass. He slowed as he neared, no human disguises on his hairy body.

"They are amassing," he said, lifting his hands, fingers splayed, indicating both sides of what Austin could only assume was the woods. "They are moving slowly but in perfect synchronization. Their master is very organized. Can you feel them?"

A muscle pulsed in Jess's jaw. "No. They all have the potion, clearly. It's fine. We'll handle it."

Jess stopped in front of the gathered crew and Austin took his place slightly behind—this was her territory, her authority. Only when she gave him the floor would he step in.

"Hey, everyone, thanks for joining us." Jess walked in front of the waiting line, and Niamh—still in human form—filed in at the edge of the gargoyles with Edgar. The basajaun filled in the gap between the shifters and gargoyle, making Logan, on the end, jump. He held his position, though. Good sign.

"There are too many for me," the basajaun said. "Sixty or so. I came to ask for my orders."

Jess blew out a breath. "Sixty." She shook her head, about-facing and walking back down the line, thinking.

The shifters looked from her to Austin. They weren't used to lag time. Most alphas would have started barking orders by now, whether they were ready or not, to avoid showing any uncertainty in front of their underlings.

The gargoyles stared straight ahead, wings fluttering and arms at their sides, waiting patiently. They were familiar with Jess. They knew that she liked to have all her ducks in a row before settling on a plan of action.

Austin let the moment ride—the seconds ticked by,

turning into a minute, and the only thing that happened was that Jess paced back the other way, muttering to herself, and bent and looked at the ground. He wouldn't step in yet. They could spare a little more time. He needed to see if she would rise to the occasion on her own.

Metal clattering on wood stole his focus for a moment, coming from the front of the house. A rhythmic beat. *Thunk. Thunk. Thunk.*

"Edgar, go see what that is," Jess barked, not looking in that direction. Instead, she peered out into the wood. "Basajaun, what are the positions of the back army?" she asked.

"They are spreading out in a line. If I had not left my position, they would be herding me in toward the house. The image in my mind is like when someone goes lost in the wood and the townspeople go on the hunt. Sometimes they lock arms so that no area is missed. The enemy forces are not touching, but they're within sight of one another."

"They want to herd everyone to Ivy House." Jess turned to look off in the direction of the front of the house, her eyes distant.

"It's the enemy to the front," Edgar said, loping back. "They are in a haphazard sort of mob, banging swords and weapons against their shields. They have a couple of magical creatures on chains, but nothing to worry about. I've had a lot of experience. There was a portion of time when my clan tried to kill me off by sending me after fearsome creatures. All you need to do is scale them from behind, dangle down in front, and rip out their throats. Nothing to it once you get the hang of it."

Jess pointed at Edgar. "Obviously that is your job. Not because I want to kill you off, but because you can save the lives of others while doing something you excel at."

"Yes, of course, I didn't doubt that for a moment." Edgar nodded.

"You probably should've," Niamh murmured.

Jess pointed at her next. "Get into your horrible gremlin form. We have enough fliers. We need someone to skirt through the underbrush and start taking out the enemies in the back on the sly."

Niamh sighed, clearly not loving that form—one of two a puca could change into—but nevertheless she stepped away, shed her clothes, and changed.

"Two different organizational setups can only confirm that these are two factions," Austin said.

"Let's hope that means only one group has the potion. Regardless, end game is the same—we need to fight for our freedom." Jess pointed at the shifters.

"Austin, I don't know what they excel at. You'll work with them, obviously." She glanced back at him to make sure the command landed, like a natural, and he nodded once and stepped that way.

"Gargoyles," she said. Their wings fluttered harder in anticipation, but otherwise they didn't move. "I'll give you cover until nightfall. If you feel an updraft that doesn't make sense, that's me. Stay in the air, because I'm probably doing something with Ivy House. Otherwise, use the darkness to swoop in and grab whoever you can. We are hugely outnumbered, so we're looking for swift kills. If you hear random screaming, it's probably from my efforts with the defenses of this property. Just…pretend it doesn't send a shiver down your spine."

"They'll be good," Austin said.

She huffed out a laugh. "So you say. Basajaun, I'm going to need the people in the front to actually cross the threshold onto this property. Is that in your wheelhouse?"

He scratched his hairy chest, watching her watch him. "I think I could get them pushing that way."

"If you can't, head around to the back and work with Niamh to take out people on the sly, if you can."

"Why not both?" he asked.

"Indeed." She grinned, but anxiety edged into her

expression for a moment. "Okay, everyone, stay safe. If the tide turns against us, retreat into the house. I can combat the intruders from there if I need to. Thank you for showing up, thank you for helping me, and let's all get out of here in one piece, okay?" She snapped. "Oh, and if you see a bunch of dolls running around, don't mind them. They're on our side. Same goes for skeletons and dead bodies."

All eyes found her for one solid beat, most of them rounded.

"You'll see." She put her hands into the sky. "Say goodbye to the sun."

The mistress of Ivy House was about to unleash her magic.

CHAPTER 21

MARTHA

"PETE, THIS CAN'T be right. It feels like we're preparing for battle or something." Martha lifted the bolt handle of the rifle and slid it back, checking to make sure it was loaded. "I mean, look what we're doing. We are in second-story windows with deer rifles looking out on...derelicts, it looks like. That's a battering ram, Pete. Why haven't we called the police?"

"You've never lived in the slums during a riot. Things can get crazy, Martha. Police would take too long with all their gear and shields. We need to defend our home. That weird butler showed you how to access the secret tunnels if you can't handle it."

"See? That's the other thing. All this time I thought the house was coming apart, but the doors to the tunnels just weren't properly latched. That's kind of a cool feature, though, secret tunnels. But we aren't in a riot, Pete. And people don't walk down the street with battering rams during a riot."

"Some do. These guys are just a little more prepared than most, that's all." He hunted through his pocket. "I wish I had my chew. This calls for a little chew. Go ahead, honey, put your foot on this property. Go ahead. Make my day."

Martha rolled her eyes. Pete was getting a little too into this. It was like he'd lost hold of his faculties.

The muzzle of her rifle tapped the glass. "Oh, for heaven's sake." She put it down and opened the window, drawing the attention of a few people clad in black leather or dulled and scuffed metal mail, waiting for God knew what, tapping their swords against their battered shields like in some sort of gladiator movie. Back in her seat, she stuck the muzzle out of the window a little, and the people who'd noticed her shifted in place, probably nervous.

She hoped they were nervous. She really was a good shot, and the law was definitely on their side. Plus, that lovely older lady with the fantastic skin had joked about unmarked graves. That might come in handy if all these people surged at once.

What they were doing wasn't normal, though, and neither were the people waiting to rush the property, with their spiked weapons, swords, shields, and what on earth were those dog-looking creatures that were as big as elephants? She'd never seen anything like that in a zoo before. It felt like she was dreaming, which was probably why she was going along with it.

"Pete, Jessie said something about magic. Do you think it could be real? This would make more sense with magic. Anything makes sense if you just call it magic."

"Hogwash. Magic is about as real as flying pigs."

"Well, now, didn't you say you saw some sort of flying creature the other day? Maybe not a pig, but…"

"You'd like to think that, wouldn't you? It's all that"—he made bunny ears around his rifle—"'sleep aid' stuff you give me. You're just looking for an excuse to ship me away like your friend Denise did to her husband."

"Oh, don't be ridiculous. Her husband had… I can't think of the name. He needed medical help. He needed to be in a safe place for his condition."

"I know what the term is—tired of the ol' ball and chain. Well, I've still got all my faculties, thank you very much. Aside from that sleep stuff you give me, I'm right as rain. We've seen animals like that a million times in the magazines."

She affixed her glasses to the end of her nose, squinting down on the animal in question. It had what looked like a dog snout, front legs longer than the back, and enormous teeth. It was literally the size of an elephant, but it lacked a trunk, so it wasn't an uncommonly ugly elephant.

"No, Pete. My vision isn't great, but something is wrong with that animal. It looks like a drunk came up with it."

"That's just because you don't go to the circus."

"She didn't just mention magic once. She keeps mentioning it…" The pitter-patter of feet made her freeze up, turning to look out the open door and into the hall beyond. A doll stopped as it passed by, looking at her with a sad little smile on its cherubic face. It waved, of all things, and kept going, the first time she'd actually seen one of them moving. "I think this house might actually be magical, Pete. I'm not kidding. I don't think ghosts are this good at moving things."

Pete muttered something as the light suddenly dimmed, dark shadows unfurling from the sky.

Martha turned back and looked out the window, same as Pete, ducking a little to glance upward.

"What in the hell?" he said softly, a toothpick in his mouth and his gun at the ready. "Was there supposed to be an eclipse today?"

"I don't remember seeing anything like that in the paper." She tsked. "Jessie doesn't get the paper. It's magic, I tell you. If we can have UFOs, we can have magic." She let her words drift off for a moment.

"UFOs aren't real and neither is magic. There's no magic out there. Mother Nature can be savage. And all those people are clearly trying to get in here and get the goods. There's a lot of expensive stuff in this house. Even just those weapons in the attic. Those would go for a lotta money. Don't worry"—he pulled the bolt hammer back, checked inside, and slid it into place—"they won't get very far onto this property. They think they can take the goods, then they got another think comin'. You ready? They look like they're getting antsy."

"Well, I guess." Martha leaned forward. "I just think this is really outlandish. Magic is the only explanation."

Jessie had mentioned different rules for magic, like different laws, Martha guessed. This situation would make more sense if the magical rules were along the lines of barbarianism.

Nearly convinced, she squinted through the sudden low light and prepared for the onslaught.

CHAPTER 22

THE GARGOYLES TOOK to the sky, hiding in the darkness I'd magically created. Niamh scampered into the trees, immediately lost in the shadows. Austin changed, blessing the faux night with an enormous roar. A moment later, an answering roar sounded in the street behind the front enemy, the basajaun having run along the other side of the house, hopped a few fences, and worked his way behind them.

I ran around to the front, my heart thumping. I just needed to make sure this group of attackers didn't have the ability to conceal themselves from Ivy House, in which case, I'd leave this onslaught to the house and help with the more dangerous crew around back.

If they *could* hide themselves...

I'd cross that bridge when I came to it.

The non-glowing crowd at the front of the house shifted and shuffled around, bumping into one another. The basajaun roared, and I could see his head topping the crowd, his great arms lifted high and waving maniacally.

The crowd moved faster now, like a swarm of bees after a ball hit their nest. They turned toward him but back-pedaling, swords out, ramming into those standing too close to them. The people who'd been pushed staggered into the lines in front, finally making the first line edge onto the property. Their presences popped up in my mental radar. They hadn't taken the potion to hide from Ivy House.

A gunshot rang out and I ducked and covered my head, unable to help it. Wide-eyed, I spun to look at the shooter, only to see my mom and dad in a second-floor window, my dad sighting again through the barrel.

"Oh—" Another shot rang out, blasting through darkness. Someone screamed and grabbed their leg, sinking to the ground. "Crap." My word was like a wheeze of breath. I hadn't thought he'd actually shoot! He was also not aiming to kill, which wasn't ideal, given most magical people would heal quickly enough to head back into the fray.

Unless I could stop them from healing.

The basajaun grabbed someone and threw him at the crowd. He grabbed another man by the legs, bashed his head onto the ground, and then started pounding those around him with the body, gruesome as all hell.

The crowd surged, their courage faltering.

The basajaun pushed forward, manic, driving people toward the property. He flung the body, grabbed a wrist that held a sword, and ripped the whole thing clean off. He threw the arm at those backing away from him, crimson spraying, the sword flying free and stabbing someone in the back.

"Holy crap." I ignored my churning stomach.

To avoid focusing on the carnage, I fixed my attention on the two people my dad had shot—only for another blast to ring out, dropping a third. Healing meant stitching things back together. So if I just focused on reversing that magic, it should…

Screams of misery tore through the boiling, surging people—the non-fatal gunshot wounds had started expanding, skin unraveling like someone was pulling a thread in a knit sweater. That someone was me. Oops.

Like eddies of water, the crowd backed away from the growling, claw-swinging basajaun and around the miserable sods who were unraveling before their eyes.

More intruders than my dad could handle surged onto the property. Ivy House took up her mantle as protector.

Huge metal spears popped out of the grass and from under the cement walkway as spotlights pushed up near the base of the house and clicked on, flooding the scene with bright white light. The intruders ripped their arms up in front of their faces, shielding their eyes, and the large arrow points at the ends of the spears gleamed.

I heard my dad say, "Martha, look at that! Booby traps!"

A body flew up over the crowd as the spears launched forward, the metal rods collecting bodies two and three deep before the cables that tethered them went taut and yanked backward. The bodies slid off as the spears locked back in place, passing through two metal rods obviously for that purpose, ready for another release. Another body sailed overhead and gas released from the grass, so thick that the light almost couldn't penetrate it. Those caught in it began to cough, clutching their necks and chests.

"Basajaun," I yelled, making a *let's go* motion with my hand. Ivy House would alert me if anyone got past.

"*Make sure he is protected through the fog,*" she said to me, as though hearing my thoughts. "*Don't worry about your parents. Should the worst happen, I will force them away if necessary.*"

"Wait, what?" I threw a protective bubble around the basajaun as he charged through the crowd. Going around would've been easier, but whatever. "I've never done a bubble against gas!"

"*That'll do, pig.*"

I furrowed my brow at her antics as someone foolishly swiped at the basajaun with their sword. The sword dinged off the bubble I'd created, a force field on the outside, and the wall penetrable from within, ensuring he'd be safe from the gas unless he stuck his head out. He grabbed the woman's arm, wrenched it off, and smacked her across the face with it. Insult to injury.

He continued forward, waving his great arms, throwing people onto the grass. Their shouts of pain turned to wails of agony amid their coughs, whatever Ivy House had cooked up for them not for the faint-hearted.

The basajaun himself stopped just before the grass, eyeing the fog.

"You're safe." I motioned him closer. "Come through, you're safe!"

The battering ram hit the curb, these modern-day issues impeding the usefulness of old-school machines. Even if they got it over, or went across the driveway, they'd have to get around the fully functioning, enormous spears positioned on some sort of javelin machine that had ruined Edgar's perfectly tended grass. My front door wasn't going to feel the wrath of that machine today.

"You are protecting me from the poison fog," the basajaun said as he reached me.

"Yes, hurry. Ivy House can handle these people for

now. It's the people in the back who are going to be the problem."

"It is good to be on your side."

"Not really, since we're vastly outnumbered and the house can't help us with these guys. Not yet, anyway."

"This house is amazing."

I didn't feel like he was hearing anything I was saying, but I also didn't feel like there was any point in persisting, so I started to jog, finding Austin and the other shifters at the tree line, smushing the flowers as they peered into the darkness. The host of dolls waited off to the far right, standing because of Ivy House, but immobile since she didn't know where to direct them.

"Hey." I stopped beside Austin and put a hand on his furry shoulder, about level with my head, feeling him tense under the touch. I took my hand away. "Anything?" I whispered.

The basajaun leapt over the flowers, directing dirty looks at anyone standing on them, and pressed his large hand to the nearest tree trunk. He bent, crouching down, looking under the trees. "They're here," he whispered.

I crouched in my location, frustrated at their magic, and looked into the woods. Lines in the darkness, the trunks of trees standing sentinel. Bushes crawled across the ground, behind ferns. I couldn't see any movement.

Could they see me? Did they know we were waiting?

The cover of darkness was hurting us as much as it was helping us.

I reached up to tear the darkness away on this side of the house, then I spied it. Further back than I'd been looking, about fifty feet, I could see the soft blue glow of the spell keeping Ivy House and me from feeling the second group's presence. *Here* to a basajaun had a different interpretation than it did for me.

I bit my lip, watching as they slowly, ever so slowly, worked their way to us. Did they think the intruders up front had distracted us enough for us not to notice them? Probably. For any normal small group of people, that certainly would've been the case.

I gestured behind me, not really needing the hand movement to direct the dolls or my magic, but it gave my brain a set place to focus.

The dolls took off right, drifting into the tree line quietly, knives clutched in their little hands, one of them climbing a tree and tootling across a branch to the next tree. I knew from experience that more would do the same.

"Austin." I stood and put my hand to his shoulder again. "Send some people left to take out whoever they can and push the intruders into the middle. Our end goal is to get them to barrel toward the grass."

He nodded and looked to his side, and the wolves and snow leopard led the others in keeping with my orders, which basically left Austin. Fine by me.

"Okay. Time to see if I can break this spell." I jogged forward, the basajaun walking fast to keep pace, Austin behind us. A little ways in and Niamh skittered across a branch at about face height, nearly forcing a scream out of me. Mr. Tom sailed overhead, hidden by the darkness, directing the rest of the gargoyles to stay in line with me.

My heart rate increased as I wove through the trees, desperately trying to be quiet enough to sneak up on these people.

Something whistled. A paw hit my side, knocking me to the right. A spear shot through where I'd just been, smashing into a tree trunk.

Crap, they knew I was here.

I hit the deck, knees to dirt, catching sight of someone crouched twenty feet away. The person looked up, probably to tell her buddy where to aim the next spear.

My spell hit her center mass, exploding, shooting her and her buddy off their spots. Austin launched forward to the right and the basajaun took off left, both of them roaring, preparing to barrel into the crowd.

"No, no. I need to work at the spell. Damn it!" I hopped up and ran as well, straight ahead, Niamh keeping pace through the trees.

Mr. Tom dove in front of me, scooping someone up. His wings beat at the trees, a very tight fit. A jet of magic zipped right by his head, bright red light splitting the dark sky. Ulric dove, his wings tight to his body, snapping them open at the last second and slashing the mage who'd thrown the spell with the claws on his feet.

Niamh chittered beside me and yanked on my shirt. She hopped to the low branches, right where the dolls would be hunting. I blocked my connection to Mr. Tom, so he wouldn't keep breathing down my neck, and ran after her. A jet of light followed me, and I quickly erected a 360-degree shield that would soak in the energy of any spells that hit it, saving the power to be unleashed when I needed it. That was, if it worked. I hadn't tested this technique on anyone.

I plunged between two trees and turned right, nearly tripping on a doll. I grunted and jumped, kicking it a little before staggering to a stop. It lay on the ground, staring up at the dark sky with sightless eyes and a manic grin. I nudged it with a foot while trying to access it with my magic. Unresponsive.

What the hell? The one time I actually needed them to be scary, they'd suddenly become real dolls?

I felt Austin fighting, about as deep in the woods as I was now. Around me, though, there were no enemies covered in a blue glow. Maybe the dolls had already pushed them back.

I continued on, ducking to the right between a couple of trees and following a deer trail deeper in. It wasn't for another couple of steps that I realized the only sound I could hear was my feet stomping along the path. My connections to Austin and Niamh had been severed, and I hadn't done it.

I glanced down at my side, suddenly alone. Where had she gone?

Absolute quiet surrounded me, entirely unnatural right now, given two battles were underway in the vicinity. Confusion and fear stole my breath. I glanced back but didn't see anything. I turned to look. Nothing. I bent, checking the ground. Looked up into the trees. Nothing. If Niamh was chittering, I couldn't hear it.

"Hello."

I jolted, glancing up. Where a moment ago I'd been completely alone, suddenly I wasn't anymore.

A man stood between two trees in front of me wearing a white suit a little too tight in the stomach, with a white shirt underneath. His dark hair was parted on the right and slicked over, and his long mustache curled at the ends.

"Who are you?" I asked, noticing he had a glowing, ethereal quality.

His smile was faint, as though he were waiting for me to realize the punch line of a joke. "I work for Mr. Graves. You have been very elusive up until this point, Jacinta. He hoped I might reconcile that. Lovely to meet you. I do so enjoy your woods. I've made quite a home here, of late. You really should close the shades in your windows. I had to turn away a few times to preserve your modesty."

CHAPTER 23

MY HEART RUSHED in my ears, but I tried not to let myself feel vulnerable at the thought of this man peeping in my windows. Or angry that he'd somehow blocked me off from Ivy House's defenses and my crew. He was using a spell, and I needed to find my way around it.

Then I needed to rip him from limb to limb.

"You turn into a deer?" I asked, putting my hands behind my back. I preferred to use them while doing magic, but I couldn't clue him in.

"No, thankfully. My associate turns into a deer. He's not much use in a battle, I grant you. He's probably dead now. If not, he and his band of stupid critters will be soon. They are a mere distraction for the polar bear and...basajaun, correct? You somehow got a basajaun on your side? Did you bed one of his relatives or something? They usually only work with family."

"That's super gross, and you're not forgiven for it."

"You know, that deer shifter usually isn't noticed

when spying within a wood. It was the glow, wasn't it? I told Mr. Graves that the glow was sure to give us away. I am sure soon he will remedy that issue. He is exacting, as you can probably guess."

"A glowing deer is a little odd, yes," I said, looking this guy over.

Speaking of glow, his was minimal, nothing more than a pleasing effulgence of his skin and clothing. That was probably why he was wearing white, to disguise its presence. If he were wearing black, the glow would've stood out like a beacon. As it was, the glow wasn't nearly as bright as the deer's. Either it was a more powerful and efficient spell, or it was barely holding everything together.

I'd learn soon enough.

"Oooh." It struck me that I'd felt this way before—blocked off from my friends, from Ivy House—in the cave prison Elliot Graves's other lackeys had taken me to. "You're exploiting another of Ivy House's vulnerabilities, just like your buddies did a couple of months ago. Damn it. Elliot Graves is good."

The guy lifted his nose a little, snootily, and spoke, but I wasn't listening. What sort of spell could cut me off without creating a visual sign? There was no glow around me or the area, no veil draping down through the trees, like the one those mages had used to protect the cave. It was almost like he held one of those electrical things that cut off cell phone transmissions, only this was for Ivy House's magic.

"Hmm. I sure wish I knew more stuff," I said, walking toward him slowly, noticing his hands hung at his sides and a little red pocket square was nestled in his jacket pocket.

"That'll be fine. Just stay right there." He gave me a stop motion, his elbow pulled in tight to his side and his hand not venturing too far away from his chest. Even so, I could see the spell that engulfed him leave his chest like a sheet and stretch around his hand. How peculiar.

"Right, okay. Well?" I shrugged. "What's next?"

It dawned on me that I was at a disadvantage in my skin. My gargoyle form could withstand a magical attack much better than this human form. I needed to change. Hell, I needed to start fighting in my stronger form, full stop.

"You know what?" I said, grabbing the bottoms of my shirt and sweatshirt. "I'll trade you. My body for my freedom."

I gave him a sultry smile and pulled my shirt and sweatshirt over my head.

"No, that really won't be necessary."

"Why not?" I unclasped my bra and unhooked my pants, not the most glamorous of faux seductions, but probably the fastest.

His voice rose and his hands popped out of the glow. I still couldn't feel it, though. That stupid bubble!

"Stop now, or I will be forced to subdue you."

I rammed a spell into his body, the zip of it coming together right before it hit him. He shrieked, startled, flinging up his hands to cover his face. The spell hit his ribs as I slipped out of my pants. I changed form, feeling my spell scrabble around the slick potion covering him. It wasn't latching on. There went the puncture theory.

His eyes widened as he looked at my body. This form really stopped people up short. Catching him off guard could only help me, so I flapped my wings a couple times to get the rainbow effect going, light tracing through the dark patch of air, while I mentally regrouped.

He had a potion around him, and a bubble around us both. How was he doing that bubble?

It had been draped across one side of the cave, noticeably glittery. But maybe that had been because of the painful layer built into it.

I chanced a glance around us, ending at his feet. He'd barely moved since I'd shown up. He hadn't wanted me to walk toward him.

Mind racing, I remembered the spell at the bottom entrance to the cave where I'd been held captive, see-through one way, not the other. There were all types of draping spells. One could easily be around me right now, hanging from these trees, and I wouldn't be able see it because of the darkness.

Elliot clearly knew I liked to veil the place in darkness. How freaking annoying. He did his homework.

I ripped the darkness away, the last rays of the sun painting the sky a burnished orange. The light trickled in around us as the guy shot a jet of magic at me, blistering in its intensity. I threw up my hands, expecting the worst, but it was too late.

Surprisingly, it hit the defensive shield I'd erected before wandering in here, fizzing and searing as it spread across the surface and lost its power.

I'd forgotten about that little ditty. Good Lord had I been smart in erecting it.

Shimmering sheets of magic stretched across the canopy of trees and draped between branches, only noticeable because of the way the light shone across them when I moved my head just so.

"How incredibly tricky," I muttered.

He shot another blast of magic, walking toward me now, his curled mustache wiggling as he did so, his brow furrowed in anger.

"You really shouldn't keep doing that," I said lazily, power building across and within my defensive ring as the new spell relinquished its power to me. The defensive spell was working. Sweet hallelujah, the spell was working! "I'm stronger than you. This will come back and bite you on the ass. You should also know…" I sent a large wave of swirling magic through the trees, the spell I'd devised for possibly ripping away the glow potion. It would work for the spell draped within the trees. "I don't need the house to do magic. I'm better with her, but I'm plenty on my own."

"I have no idea what you are grunting, gargoyle," he shouted, and it occurred to me that what I'd meant to say had clearly come out a garbled mess because of my teeth. I hadn't been paying attention.

I released the pent-up ring of power around me, slashing out with it. It cut down the guy's side, opening up a red line across his chest and stomach and down his left leg. He cried out, bending, throwing out his hand to deliver a spell that went wide. The weird silence lifted, and I heard the chittering I'd been missing as Niamh emerged from between two trees and charged toward the mage at full speed. His protective spell, hiding him from Ivy House and me, fizzled away even as she reached him, chomping into his shoulder with her many rows of razor-sharp teeth.

That burst of energy turned into a slash had done the trick—it had punctured the spell *and* his body. I'd need to devise a more foolproof way to get the same result, but it would work for now.

The mage let out an agonized, high-pitched scream, certainly his last, as Niamh crawled onto his chest and went after his jugular.

I ran toward Austin, whose choking fear I'd felt as soon as the magical connections were restored. It had immediately faded into relief. Clearly he'd felt me get cut off and hadn't known why. I could feel him working his way toward me now.

Glowing shapes appeared in between the trees— some pushing against an invisible barrier that did not yield, others running my way in terror. Austin ran behind them, trying to catch those fleeing before him. They were not battle-hardened heroes, and it was obvious the mage hadn't planned on letting them escape alive.

I didn't know how I felt about that. They'd clearly been brought here as a sacrifice, a distraction for my forces, like that awful mustached mage had said. They didn't deserve death by polar bear. Maybe they just needed a refuge away from a tyrant.

"Noo, Aah-ston." I threw up a spell to block him from chomping down on a hare bounding away.

I stopped for a moment, summoning all of my power and energy, and pulling from Ivy House as well.

Instead of an explosive, I fashioned little needles for my attack, sharp enough to pierce spells and skin, but hopefully not deadly enough to kill a fast-healing shifter. This *had* to work on that blasted potion.

Running now, I covered Austin in a defensive layer, just in case my aim was terrible, and blasted the spell out, pelting all of the glowing blue creatures. Continuing on, I blasted it out again, and again, followed by Austin and Niamh and the gargoyles (overhead), reaching anyone with the potion and punching it away. At the other side of the wood I found the basajaun, hugging three glowing creatures in his great hairy arms. The creatures squeaked, probably the only air they could get out, before succumbing to the pressure. Lights out.

Further on, I found that the rest of the enemy had been trapped between the mage's magical wall and the shifters. No contest. The only experienced enemy had been up near the house, and we'd taken care of those early. These had clearly run at the first sign of assault. I hadn't saved all that many. Time had not been on my side.

I took to the sky with the rest of the gargoyles, soaring above my woods, real darkness descending now, but no more glowing creatures remaining. In the front I found Edgar in a swarm of insects, zipping after a leather-clad woman, who was chasing a large gray sort of humanoid. Was that the golem that one of the neighbors kept in their basement? It must've been.

I dove down next to Edgar. "Ah-tzz gooo-in ohh'n?"

He popped back into his vampire form but kept running, much slower this way. "Oh, hello, Jessie. The golem got out, which was very helpful for the battle, but he's about to get away, and I'm not sure this town needs any more nightmares. Can you scare him back the other way? He needs to be plunked back in his basement."

"Daaa ooo'man?" I asked, hoping he caught that I was asking about the woman.

"Oh, her? Well she's angry because the golem killed a bunch of her people and she's trying to kill him. But don't worry, I'll deal with her, if you could just get that golem turned back around…"

Honestly, I had better things to do.

I rose into the air and pointed at a couple of the gargoyles, Darid and Jim. Or was it Slith? I always mixed them up. I gestured toward the golem and made a circle in the air. *Round him up.*

They flew forward, lagging but managing. As I headed toward the front of the house, I noticed the magical shields set up by our extremely vanquished foes were still in effect, shimmering like I'd expected the magic in the woods to shimmer. The battle that had raged there, in a very tight vicinity, was evident in the many bodies piled up on the lawn. Those who'd survived the mounted spears had been done in by the poison fog. If they'd survived the fog or managed to skirt around it, as a few had, probably the mages, they'd succumbed to the grass giving way under their feet and dumping them down into a pit of spikes.

I hadn't even known those was there. Ivy House's defenses seemed endless, and I still hadn't needed to use any of the ones that would seriously deface the property.

The three people who'd made it through the front yard fun run had clearly found Edgar, who had to be plenty full and would no doubt sleep for a long time after this. He'd picked up the slack without having been told to. He might be weird as all hell, but he was a keeper.

Silence settled over the property, that strange absence of sound after the conclusion of the yelling, screaming, and clashing sounds of battle. We had a lot of work cut out for us tonight. There were a lot of unmarked graves that needed digging.

As I put my hands to my waist, gulping in the air and letting the stress of the evening die away, I heard, "Jacinta McMillian, you have some serious explaining to do!"

One battle down, one to go. I had to deal with my parents. There was no way they could ignore magic after this, but worse, they'd now know the danger that came with this new life. I just hoped it didn't cause any mental breakdowns.

Fortunately, it had to wait until after we got rid of the evidence. I had some time to stall before I faced the music.

CHAPTER 24

DIRT ON MY face, in my hair, and arms limp as spaghetti, I sighed as I looked over the front yard.

"I'll have this fixed up in no time, Jessie, don't you worry." Edgar wiped his forearm across his dirty face, leaning on a shovel beside me.

The bodies had been cleared away and given a resting place in the woods of Ivy House, to be called upon again when we had a need. The motorized magical spears had been shined up and then tucked back into the ground, covered over for now, although they'd left behind scores of dirt in thick lines through Edgar's lush grass. Little divots also dotted the greenery from where the nozzles had risen with the poisoned fog, perfectly visible, since the lights at the base of the house still shone.

I nodded at Edgar and made my way to the back of the grounds, mostly intact except for the patches of crushed flowers. Austin emerged from the trees, his chest bare and smeared with dirt, the gray sweats covering his lower half equally dirty. Logan, the barrel-chested guy from the bar who had once offered to help me kill and bury one of my internet dates, walked beside him. He'd been one of the wolves. On the other side walked a guy I didn't know, with a bald head, light blue eyes, and a strong but lithe body clad in purple house sweats except for his bare chest.

Austin spotted me and headed my way, his expression tight. "The basajaun is off to see to his mountain. He told me to tell you he'll be back to check in. It'll probably take him a week or so—they don't rush. He'll expect some flowers for his trouble. The enemy is all accounted for, either below the ground or let loose, as requested."

"They shouldn't have been here," I said. "They were forced in here, and kept here, for your distraction. It isn't right to punish them for basically being prey."

He shifted his weight between his feet, looking off to the side. "I know. You made the right call. I offered them sanctuary here if they need it. Most of the survivors will likely take me up on it."

I smiled up at him, relieved. His gaze zipped down to me and lingered for a moment, but he quickly looked away again.

"There was no way that mage could be revived after what Niamh did to him," Austin said. "We'll get no information there."

"What information do we need that he didn't directly tell me?" I turned and started walking toward the back door. The rest moved with me, Austin beside me and Edgar falling back with the shifters. "Except for how he knew I'd walk right into his trap."

Austin shook his head. "He had a few of those magical pockets set up. I walked into one, as did the basajaun, as did Layan." I saw the bald man nodding. "How the mage was able to follow your progress and get to the right setup while you were in it, I'm not sure."

"Magic," I said, only half joking.

"Yes. Magic. It would be nice if you could learn whatever magic that was."

"Yes, it would. We need a mage on staff. Someone experienced and resourceful."

"And patient," Edgar added.

I dragged my lip through my teeth. "Someone that could work with everyone in the house."

"A misfit, or they'd never get along with Mr. Tom and Niamh," Edgar said, which was somewhat rich, coming from him.

I stopped beside the back door, staring at my feet, thinking. Waiting. A moment later, it came, a shock wave of power pulling at my middle before rocketing out into the world, headed away to find someone with the attributes on my wish list. My third summons.

Austin stopped beside the back door. "And now we wait to see if we can handle whatever turns up."

I narrowed my eyes at him. "I thought you always came out on top."

He winked, and I laughed.

When I moved toward the house and he didn't follow, I turned back. "You're not going in?"

"No. I need to get home and change. Then I should check in at the bar."

"Oh." I pushed away the momentary feeling of disappointment. I'd gotten used to him hanging around, but I had to remember that the guy had a life. He didn't live here. "Right, well…thanks. For everything."

The shifters meandered away, and Edgar slipped into the house, shutting the door behind him to give Austin and me a moment. I licked my lips, suddenly nervous and not totally sure why, other than that Austin's serious expression, almost regretful, put me on edge.

"Of course," he said. "You did great this evening. You beat that mage at his own game. You're really coming along."

"Looks like I'll have to keep progressing fast, given the rate Elliot keeps turning up. He always seems to send a barely manageable challenge."

Austin nodded. "He probably sends people he thinks capable of easily besting you. No one in the history of magic learns this quickly and is this potent after less than a year. I bet you blindside him every time he goes up against you. That can't sit well with him."

I tucked a strand of hair behind my ear. "This one didn't totally make sense, though, did it? He attacked at the same time as someone else. We were all thinking it was so he could protect his interests, but Ivy House largely took care of the front yard attack. The two parties didn't have anything to do with each other at all. At least not here. Since no one was left alive from the front yard attack after Edgar caught the last, we can't very well research if there is some other connection. Regardless, it was more like Graves's guy was using the front yard attacks as a distraction to get me alone."

Austin turned just a bit, looking back into the woods. "He certainly wouldn't have been able to do much with the people at his disposal. They weren't fighters, as we've discussed. Maybe they thought we'd have to expend more resources on the other attack. It might have been another way to gauge Ivy House's strength—your strength."

I shrugged. "Hard to know." I took a deep breath. "It doesn't matter. What's done is done. At least I've identified two spells that make Ivy House vulnerable.

The others are listed in that book, and we know which ones Elliot is aware of so far. If I work with Edgar, I can set up some booby traps to find anyone sneaking around. We just have to figure out a way to target those particular spells. I don't want to accidentally blow up a hiker who's unintentionally trespassing. In the meantime, we'll work together to fortify the town and house." I paused, then added, "Oh, hey, I was thinking. I can't use those gargoyles at the hotel on my team here. Or Cedric. I only have a certain number of seats available in my council, and I don't want them all to go to the same magical species, but couldn't you use them? Some fliers in your pack wouldn't go amiss, as long as you have someone monitoring them closely. They are lazy as hell if you let them be."

His mouth turned downward as he thought. Finally, he said, "I could find a use for them if they stay. I'll get back to you." He reached out and gently squeezed my upper arm. "Time for me to go. I have a lot of work to get to, so I'll be away for a while. I'm getting things in place before I buy that winery, so…I'll talk to you about that at a later date. If you need me…" He paused, dropping his hand to his side, his robust muscles flexing, popping out all over his torso. "I'll see you around, okay? Call me if…you get into trouble."

I watched him leave with mixed emotions, wanting

desperately for him to stay. Although I knew he had to get back to his life, especially since he was still in the early stages of building his territory, it had been nice to have him around. Nice but also dangerous, because any longer and I would've forgotten why I was supposed to keep my hands off him. His comforting presence around the house calmed me in ways nothing else did. Pleased me, if I was being honest. Feeling him curl around my body, or his lips on mine…

I blew out a breath, tore my eyes away, and marched into the house. That guy was special, he was incredibly handsome, he was one of a kind, and he was not looking for a dame on his arm. I might be willing to peel back my regulations about work and pleasure, but he clearly wasn't planning on it, and that was just fine. He was too hot for the likes of me, anyway. Down with hot people—they made you feel like you had to try harder. I wanted to keep trying very little, thank you very much.

Back in the house, I found my mother in the kitchen, tidying the counters. Time to clear the air.

"Hey, Mom," I said, stopping at the counter. I felt Mr. Tom upstairs in the doll room, repairing those that had come back without arms, eyes, or a head. The intruders hadn't been as scared of the dolls as they were of the shifters and basajaun, and a few of the plastic and plaster horrors had been kicked or stomped to high heaven. "How's…everything?"

She placed a glass in the cabinet. "Jessie, you know that I'm pretty open-minded, but…" She shook her head. "What happened in the front yard… That was a little much. Magic or no, you can't go around wiping out leather-clad people like that. What if the cops find out? Visiting you in this house has been hard enough, I don't want to make arrangements to visit you in prison."

"I know. This whole thing has been an adjustment for me, too, but this is how the magical world works."

Her sigh was heavy and her body bowed. "Magic is real. All these years you think one thing, and then the wool is lifted from your eyes." She shook her head, suddenly looking older than her years. "It's going to take me a while to wrap my head around all this. We're going to leave tomorrow. We need a break."

"I get it. Sorry, about all of this. I know it's hard to process."

"Dolls walking around, strange animals—do the butler and those boys actually fly with those capes? Like Superman?"

I huffed out a laugh. "Those aren't capes, they are wings. They're gargoyles. When they turn into their other form, those turn into wings. Like a bat, kinda."

Her silent stare was a little manic.

"It took me a while to get used to it," I murmured. "But it isn't always so dangerous here, I promise. You just got unlucky." It was partially true.

She wiped down the already clean island. "I just don't know. I don't like the idea of all of this. Why not a peaceful life? Maybe throw your hat into the ring again for love. That Austin Steele is sure a lovely man. Quite the looker. I've seen the way you two look at each other. He dotes on you."

"He turns into a polar bear. He's not part of a peaceful life."

She groaned and put up her hand. "Let's not talk about that."

"He also has a rough past and isn't looking for a relationship."

"Well, that just sounds like fear, that's what that sounds like. He's gallant and a gentleman, but he's just as blind to love as the rest of them. He needs you to show him. Give him a nudge, Jessie—that's all he needs. Show him what you want, and he will serve you up the world, I can see it."

"I just want to get used to…this new life. I just got out of a divorce, Ma. I don't need a relationship either."

"Oh now, Jessie, you and Matt were emotionally divorced for years. It's about time you connected with someone again. Matt has. I hear he's happy with his new girlfriend. If he's moved on, why don't you? Why not choose someone like Austin?"

"I've moved on, trust me. It's just…" I threw up my hands. "Stop playing matchmaker, Mom. Gawd."

"I just want you to be happy," she called after me as I left the kitchen. "And don't mention the magic to your father. He is dead set against the idea. I told him this was a cult. That seemed to calm him down."

I stopped at the mouth of the kitchen and turned. "You what?"

"You know your father. He's stubborn. Just tell him it's a cult. Remember the neighbor across the street? Patricia? Her son got involved in a cult a while back, did I ever tell you? He was a follower and they took all his money. I told your father you were the leader. That's how you can afford the house. It's much better being a leader than a follower."

"How is that better than magic?" I asked.

She batted the air as though that was a ridiculous question.

I shook my head, suddenly exhausted. At least she was trying to get on board with the magic stuff. That was a relief. She'd need some time to process, but I had every belief she'd come around.

Her leaving me alone about the relationship stuff was another story.

My dad was in the TV room, as usual, staring up at the moving pictures and encased in a protective wall of noise. Niamh was in her new favorite chair beside him, a beer in hand, watching the TV with him.

"Hey, Dad." I walked in until he could easily see me and then leaned against the wall.

He muted the TV. "Jessie, quite the excitement earlier. Niamh says you got everything squared away." He touched the edge of his nose.

"Yeah, we took care of things. Hey, thanks again for helping. And keeping things quiet about the magic part of—"

"Don't start with that again." He gave Niamh a long-suffering look. "Always the theatrics with her."

"You don't have to tell me, sure ye don't. She's always on about the magical house, as though a few hidden doors leading into a secret tunnel makes it magical. I just go with it, though. She's had a hard breakup. She needs some time to ease into reality."

I frowned at her.

"Well, that's it. Too much change isn't good for a person. It can mess with their mind." My dad reached for his beer. "At least she has this cult or whatever Martha said it was. That'll keep her busy for a while. Police tend to give cults a wide berth until they get out of hand."

"I'll make sure that doesn't happen, o'course," Niamh said.

My dad nodded as though all of this made perfect sense—the pile of bodies, the creatures that Edgar had to take down, burying people out back… There were no limits to what this guy wouldn't rationalize to keep his current world-view. It was madness.

I let it go. It would just be easier. My mom was on board, and my dad had an explanation he could live with. If I couldn't call that a win, I could at least call it good enough.

"Anyway," I said, "Mom says you guys are leaving tomorrow?"

"Yeah, it's probably for the best. There is too much excitement around here for me." My dad patted his belly. "The plumber has our toilet patched up and they're working on fixing the water damage, so we're about ready, anyway."

"Well, it was nice having you," I said, aiming for an even tone. It was almost truthful. Next time would be much easier, if there was a next time.

"Yeah, thanks for having us. Oh, Jessie, where's that big fella you pal around with? Not the really hairy one, but the other one? What is he, six-two or three?"

"Austin. He had to head to his bar."

"Oh, too bad. He's a good guy. Well, you know, I

don't like to get involved in these types of things, but if shopping came to buying, I don't think you could go wrong with a guy like that. You know…" He adjusted in his seat, squinting at the ceiling. "Matt was always a fine choice—" He motioned to Niamh. "Matt was her ex. He was fine. Had a good job, good…" He paused. "He was all right. But that Austin fellow—well, he's a bit more capable, you know what I mean? He's a bit more solid regarding the important things in life."

"Like helping run the cult, ye mean," Niamh said. I glared at her again.

"Not… No, not the cult so much, but… Well, anyway. He seems capable, is all. He'd be one to protect you, not leave you out to dry. From what I've seen in the last week, you need it."

"Boy, doesn't she ever," Niamh agreed. "She's in up to her eyeballs most times."

"Would you stop?" I said through my teeth. She grinned at me.

"Anyway…" He squinted at me this time. "What is the story with all the people around here in capes? That's an awfully odd uniform choice for the cult. I think you should let them dress normally."

Niamh's face turned bright red and she shook in her seat, clearly holding back laughter. I didn't even know what to say.

Foreign footsteps traveled up the walkway. The humor dripped off Niamh's face, and I could feel Mr. Tom heading to the door.

"I'll be right back, Dad," I said, stepping out into the hall as someone knocked.

"Jessie, let Earl get it," Niamh called.

Mr. Tom was heading toward the stairs, but I closed the distance to the door anyway, feeling Niamh walking my way. I half expected to find Elliot Graves on my doorstep, tired of all these close calls and cat-and-mouse games, come to grab me himself. It would sure put a fast end to our drawn-out situation.

But when I opened the door, two boys in blue stood there, one I recognized from a previous house call, under similar circumstances, and one I did not.

"Ah, fer feck's sakes, Chuck, what are you at?" Niamh kept walking toward the door as Mr. Tom jogged down the stairs.

The younger guy with close-cropped brown hair, a large chin, and hands braced on his utility belt gave Niamh a bulldog-type stare. "I've had some complaints about the noise," he said to me.

"What noise?" Niamh looked around. "We're just enjoying an evening in, so we are."

"Yes, yes, we know the very idea of police officers doing their job is offensive to you, you crusty old woman." Mr. Tom stepped between Niamh and the officers with a wide, very fake smile. "My apologies. She isn't housebroken."

"They know who I am." Niamh stepped out of Mr. Tom's way. "I've been mindin' me manners, haven't I, boys? Haven't had to take me in in a dog's age, have ye? No. So why ye're comin' to pick on me now, I haven't—"

I walked out onto the porch and shut the door behind me, the officers moving back quickly so I wasn't in their space. "Don't mind her. She isn't great with authority. Which you know, I'm sure." I smiled nervously, then licked my lips, then wished I hadn't licked my lips because it probably made me look guilty.

A light clicked on overhead, and the door opened again, Mr. Tom stepping into the space.

The officers squinted at us, and I realized we hadn't cleaned off all the dirt.

"Looks like you had some issues with your yard." The older cop in the back clicked his flashlight on and painted light across the dirt lines running through the grass. Someone had, thankfully, turned the base lights off, so the damage wasn't quite as noticeable or glaring.

"Yes. Edgar is planning some improvements," I said quickly.

"Hello…"

The cops both flinched, dropping their hands to

their guns but not taking them out.

Edgar waved to them from the corner of the house. "It'll look worse before it looks better, but don't you worry, we'll be a shoo-in to win first place at the garden festival this year. This yard will really sing. I have big plans!"

"Yes, well…" The officer clicked off his light. "It seems there was some yelling from this area not too long ago."

Genuinely confused, if only because there'd been a noise block, I looked back at Mr. Tom. "Did you hear anything?"

"I most certainly did not. Edgar was howling much earlier than that—he gets in an awful state when he rips at the garden—but we've kept to ourselves as normal."

The younger one, Chuck, took his hand off his gun. "Well, Niamh has been downright placid since you came to live here, ma'am. We thank you for that."

"Oh." I put my hand to my chest. "I don't know that that's necessarily my doing…"

"It certainly doesn't seem like it has hurt." He nodded at me, eyed the front yard, and stepped back. "If there isn't any trouble…?"

"No." I shrugged, also looking around the front yard. "No trouble."

Chuck nodded. "Just try to keep it down."

"Thank you, officers." Mr. Tom pushed back into the house, gesturing for me to follow. "We'll try to keep a leash on her."

Edgar waved awkwardly when they glanced back at him. They wisely pretended not to notice.

I stayed outside for a moment, checking the dark, silent street, wondering if a man with a goatee would appear out of nowhere and whisper on the wind. Nothing happened, though. I waved as the police car pulled out of the circular end of the street, and then closed the door on the crazy aftermath of the day. If Elliot Graves had called the cops this time, he hadn't done it so he could make an appearance.

I wondered if he would.

I wondered if I would actually meet him soon, like he'd promised those many months ago.

I wondered if I'd escape his next attempt to capture me.

CHAPTER 25

"**R**EADY?" I ASKED Ulric and Jasper, the only two gargoyles I'd offered a place on my team. A permanent place, with an assigned seat and Ivy House magic. They were the only two who'd really jibed with the house crew, and who also did great work with very little prompting. They followed me loyally and gave their all when helping me train and in battle. I could do far worse than these two.

It had been only two days since the battle, but I hadn't wanted to keep stringing them along. Everyone needed an answer, including the gargoyles I wouldn't be using. They'd agreed to stay, anyway, and would be joining Austin's pack once he got around to officially forming one.

Jasper nodded, as silent and resolute as always, but Ulric shifted in place, a sheen of sweat covering his forehead and his mouth a thin line.

We stood just outside the council room. The house crew was already seated, waiting for Ivy House to assign roles to these two.

"You okay?" I asked Ulric quietly.

He wiped his hands on his crisp black dress shirt—his palms were apparently sweating, and he was too distracted to realize how gross that was. "Yeah. It's just…" He licked his lips and his eyes turned glassy. "If my mom could see me now. No one ever thought I'd amount to anything. They looked down on me, looked down on her because of me—she's the only one who believed I'd make something of myself. And here I am, about to join the most elite force my kind could hope for. I get to help protect a female gargoyle, one of only three gargoyles chosen for that task. All my hard work, all the brick walls standing in my way in life, and now…" He wiped away a tear. "This is a dream come true. Beyond a dream come true. Thank you for choosing me, Miss Jessie. It is an absolute honor."

I pulled him into a hug. "You earned it." I didn't have the heart to tell him that if he wanted an elite force, this wasn't the place. If he hadn't figured that out already, he had blinders on as thick as my father's.

"Okay, when you get in there, you just let the house steer you, okay? I choose the people; she chooses the seats."

They nodded, and I turned, walking slowly into the room in a pantsuit that somewhat matched the color of my gargoyle skin. Mr. Tom had tried to sew rainbow-colored sparkly streamers to the back, signifying the eddies of light, but I'd refused. There had to be lines drawn against the weird in this house or it would run amok.

A tray of champagne sat on the little table by the window. I passed it and made my way into the center of the circle, smiling at Austin in his number one seat, and glancing at the others—Edgar in the twelfth seat, Mr. Tom in the ninth, and Niamh in the third.

I put my hand out toward the door.

"Please welcome our newest members to the circle."

Ulric and Jasper walked in slowly, their path leading them around the outside of the seats until they reached the little flag behind Austin's chair, a space separating him and Edgar, allowing the two gargoyles to enter the circle, one at a time.

Ulric went first, pausing three steps in, as though he were listening. Then he kept walking until he about-faced in front of the sixth seat, wiped another tear, and sat.

"*He is your balance,*" Ivy House whispered to me. "*When the team is fraying, look to him to pull you back together. He has kept his head through much strife in his life, and he will continue to keep his head for this cause.*"

I nodded even as he wiped away another tear.

Jasper entered next, pausing where Ulric did. He turned before walking to the seventh seat.

"*He's strong and stoic, he is loyal to a fault, but he needs to be near his kind or he will lose his way. For that reason, I am placing him near Ulric, who will keep as close to him as a brother. Who will pull the gargoyles together much like he will pull the team as a whole together when they fray. You have one or two gargoyles yet to come. Most heirs chose a solid gargoyle team, but this approach you're taking is wise. Land and sky, many different strengths and weaknesses—I approve of it.*"

"*What about Austin? You never gave commentary when he joined.*"

"*You must find your own way with him.*"

I put my hands out in an *are you serious* kind of way. That made literally no sense, given she'd just provided me with a rundown of the other two.

The silence of the room jogged me out of my annoyance.

"Welcome," I said again, smiling at Ulric and Jasper. "Champagne?"

The celebratory drinks were short-lived before Austin approached me, face stern and chest pointed at the door.

"I better get going," he said.

The energy between us heated up the air. "Sounds

good. It was nice seeing you."

He looked like he was about to say something, but instead walked past me, out of the door. He didn't get far before I felt a stranger on the walkway.

"Man, what happened to a quiet life?" I muttered.

"Wicked, you can feel where people are in the house," Ulric said. "And where Jessie—"

"Wait, Austin." I caught up to him in the hallway.

"Listen, Jess, I really feel like we need to give each other some space at the moment," he said in a gush of words. "We're getting a little too close in the wrong ways. We just need to take a step back and regroup, I think. We work together, and I know you didn't want to cross that line. And I'm... I live a solo life. For good reason. For an important reason. I don't want to cross that line."

The words were a machine-gun-fire affirmation of what I'd suspected he had been thinking. They were completely true, and more, they were responsible. I couldn't help that they still hurt.

I tried my best to brush it off.

"Awesome, yeah, that sounds good, but wait before going out the door. I've got a visitor." I pushed past him.

A man started when I pulled open the door, his brown delivery service uniform wrinkled and his truck crookedly parked by the curb. He eyed the scarred lawn for a moment before holding out a letter. "I'll need a signature."

"Allow me." Mr. Tom stepped around me, took the letter, and held out his hand for the tablet to sign.

"Uhmm…no." The man read his tablet. "Jacinta Evans. I need a signature from her."

"Give the thing over to him," Niamh said, passing by the door. "Since when do people like you care about your work?"

"Ignore that insufferable old woman." Mr. Tom smiled kindly at the deliveryman. "Though she does have a point. I sign for the letters and packages at this house. It is my role. I am protected against those sorts of curses." He took the tablet. "I'm sure you understand."

"There is no way he understands," I said, standing off to the side while Mr. Tom took care of it. I knew better than to fight him about it.

The delivery guy glanced at me from under his eyelashes, his eyes so pale blue they almost didn't register as a color. He shrugged. "Whatever."

Once the letter was signed for, Mr. Tom worked at the top, trying to open it.

"Would you…" I grabbed it. "I can open it myself, thanks."

He scowled at me, sniffed, and re-entered the house. "Who would like some snacks? Caviar, anyone? The parents are gone and we have two new additions, so I think that calls for a little something extra."

The delivery guy glanced at the tablet before making his way back to his truck.

Austin joined me on the front porch, pausing for a moment. "Sorry about that," he said softly.

"What's that?" I opened the envelope as the delivery truck started up.

"About what I said in there. Or…actually, the way that I said it. I came off as obtuse. I just have a lot of things going on right now. I don't have a lot of time."

"Austin, it's fine. Don't worry about it." I pulled a second envelope out of the delivery envelope, this one square and a matte black. "You were absolutely right." I met his eyes, tucking the delivery envelope under my arm so I could get at the other one. "We've been getting close in the wrong ways. You have your lone cowboy thing, and I want to keep things professional. We both know this."

"It's just…"

I peeled back the flap on the black envelope, looking up as the delivery truck started forward. The driver waved as I pulled out the card inside.

I waved back with the card before glancing down at

it. My world went white and hazy for a moment.

"What is it?" Austin asked.

I pulled the delivery envelope from under my arm. It didn't have an address on it. Not a return address or one for delivery.

"It's from Elliot Graves." I handed off the card as I ran forward. "Stop!" I sent a jet of magic, a wall, to drop in front of the truck. A hand lazily drifted out of the truck window, flicking. My spell vanished and, a moment later, so did the truck. Vanished like it had never been there.

"Oh crap." Breathing heavily, I stopped on the sidewalk, looking down the street. "Was that Elliot Graves himself? He looked twenty! The guy I remember from before seemed like he was in his forties. With a goatee. That guy looked like someone completely different."

Austin crouched beside me, then straightened up and shook his head. "No smell." He brought the card to his nose, then the envelope that he'd taken from me. "No smells on anything. The best mages can alter their appearance."

Austin looked down at the card before handing it over.

I took it.

Roses are red,

Violets are blue,

Your growth is startling,

I thought I had you.

-Elliot Graves

P.S. Protect yourself. It's a madhouse out there.

All I could do was stare. He'd been on my property. He'd hand-delivered me mail!

"He's playing games with me," I said, something in my middle clenching. "This is all a game to him."

"For now." Austin's voice was rough. "Nothing changes. We still need to prepare. Given his schedule so far, it seems like we've got a couple months before his next move. That's enough time." He put a hand on my shoulder. "I'll be well underway with a pack by then, Jess, and you'll have grown leaps and bounds again. In two months, we'll be ready."

I hoped he was right. Even if he wasn't, Elliot Graves was clearly much too invested to walk away. He would come for me eventually, and when he did, I had no choice but to be ready.

"Best get some champagne," I said, heading into the house. "It'll dull the anxiety."

Austin didn't follow me inside, and I paused to say

goodbye. He stared down the street for a beat, his body tense, as though indecisive. When I opened my mouth to speak, he sagged, as though defeated. He turned toward me.

"I'll tell Mr. Tom to pour me a glass, too," he said.

I started in surprise. "Oh. Are you sure—Wait." I smiled, suddenly warm and fuzzy. "You're using his made-up name!"

A grin worked at his lips. "A good friend asked me to. It's hard to say no to her."

I beamed at him. "He'll be so happy. After the stress with my parents, he'll really appreciate it."

"Jess, listen." He clasped my arm. "I don't want to mess anything up with you. You are incredibly important to me. That's all I meant earlier. I want to be the man you need me to be, not the mess that I am. A little bit of space will get my head back on straight, that's all."

My mother's words echoed in my ear.

Well, that just sounds like fear, that's what that sounds like.

I hugged him. "I know. And you're right, a little space will go a long way. It's good timing, too. I still need to make a show of sitting in the office so I can look over the house finances."

A wave of tingles washed over me.

I'd asked Niamh about it like Austin had advised.

When I sat at that desk, my first order of business would be to officially transfer the house to me. This wasn't done by a deed, though. The transfer happened with a blood oath. The fate of Ivy House and my council would be magically tied to my life, and be my ultimate responsibility. If I failed in doing right by the house, I would die.

At least, that was what Niamh had said. I hadn't asked any more about it. That had scared me right down to the ground. I'd need another moment to build up some courage to face that.

Clearly Austin wasn't the only one afraid. Maybe we both just had to get over it.

Eventually.

I patted his chest as I pushed away. "Now let's go welcome in the new people and hope the normal people of this house crew finally outweigh the strange."

"That won't ever happen."

"One can dream."

I barely heard him murmur, as though a thought to himself, "A guy certainly can."

THE END

About the Author

K.F. Breene is a Wall Street Journal, USA Today, Washington Post, Amazon Most Sold Charts and #1 Kindle Store bestselling author of paranormal romance, urban fantasy and fantasy novels. With over three million books sold, when she's not penning stories about magic and what goes bump in the night, she's sipping wine and planning shenanigans. She lives in Northern California with her husband, two children, and out of work treadmill.

Sign up for her newsletter to hear about the latest news and receive free bonus content.

www.kfbreene.com

Made in the USA
Monee, IL
03 August 2024

63205900R00215